The River's Bend

Beth Larson Sherk

Copyright © 2011 by Beth Larson Sherk.

Library of Congress Control Number: 2010915502
ISBN: Hardcover   978-1-4535-9756-9
         Softcover   978-1-4535-9755-2

All rights reserved. No part of this book may be reproduced or transmitted in any form or by any means, electronic or mechanical, including photocopying, recording, or by any information storage and retrieval system, without permission in writing from the copyright owner.

This is a work of fiction. Names, characters, places and incidents either are the product of the author's imagination or are used fictitiously, and any resemblance to any actual persons, living or dead, events, or locales is entirely coincidental.

This book was printed in the United States of America.

To order additional copies of this book, contact:
Xlibris Corporation
1-888-795-4274
www.Xlibris.com
Orders@Xlibris.com
67100

The River's Bend

I would like to dedicate this book to my mother

ACKNOWLEDGEMENT

I would like to extend my sincere thanks to Susan Harper for her great suggestions as well as for caring about this story enough to fall in love with Calvin and for demanding more to the story! Also, thanks goes to Kaileen Sherk for her careful and incisive reading, tough minded feedback and support without which I could never have made it to the finish line.

CHAPTER 1

The New City Lady Discovers More than Trees

The Toyota ploughed recklessly down the dirt lane, winding through an untamed pasture and on past a crumbling tobacco barn, where it ended at a rustic old farmhouse. Here, tall oaks stood guard like sentinels and cedars mingled in the meadow like guests at a cocktail party.

Without bothering to shut the car door, Leslie rushed into the house to pee and then came back out at a more leisurely pace, pausing to stretch her aching back and to gaze at the beauty all around her. From the rotted steps of a porch draped in wisteria and honeysuckle, there was a clear view of the sky arcing over distant rolling hills nestled against misty blue Virginia Mountains. Though she could not see it from here, it was a comfort to know that beyond a rambling tangle of forest there lay the cozy meandering river that had given this place its name.

According to her mother, this was nothing but a run-down shack; however, as usual, the very things that horrified her were what made it all so irresistible to her wayward daughter. How could someone *not* want to live where birds nested above the front door and friendly vines crowded in at the unscreened windows as if seeking conversation? Every corner was ripe with the spirits of lives lived in simple honest labor; a house constructed of hand-hewn lumber set squarely on stone foundations, a house of simple, direct beauty and proportion. Here was where she needed to be. She'd known it at first sight. On a whim, she pulled the cord of an old ship's bell mounted beside the front door, and it broke open the stillness with a loud clang. She closed her eyes and listened until the reverberations melted back into the silence. Here, she thought with a deep sigh, was a place where she could heal.

A breeze lifted, carrying a whiff of tobacco smoke through the heavy heat, and for a moment she thought she heard the sound of whistling, but looking around, there was no one to be seen.

The three men left standing at the row of rusty mailboxes, hands raised in a country greeting, had gotten only a mouthful of dust for their trouble, for the new woman in the gray Toyota hadn't given them so much as a glance as she'd barreled on past. Instead, she'd bumped on up the dirt lane to River's Bend as if her life depended on it. This kind of behavior did not surprise them, however, as city people were often a little rough around the edges.

This would be their first close-up look at the city woman moving into the old Carver home place down in the crook of the river. Likewise, that was her first intimation that there were more than just trees in the neighborhood, for as often as she had dreamed about living in the country, it had never occurred to her that there would actually be people there as well. Yet as she would soon discover, they were very much there and as aware of her as she was unaware of them. They'd be watching all week as her car ferried back and forth from Richmond, loaded with cargo, adding fuel to the theories already flying about this solitary city woman moving into a house that had stood empty for years.

The city lady knew nothing of this one way or another. She had come as a caretaker for a woman she'd met through the artist's co-op. However, it wasn't just the free rent that had drawn Leslie Hillerman to River's Bend but the isolation. That was what she craved right now—isolation and trees.

"That must be her," remarked Frank Hawkins, a jovial, big-bellied joker, adding with a judicious squint of the eye that she'd certainly taken that turn a little fast.

"Liable to bust a tie rod," agreed his neighbor Pendleton Caughey, an intense little white-haired banty rooster of a man from New Jersey standing no more than five foot three on a good day. "I still don't get why anybody would want to live there after all these years!"

"Wonder if she even knows!" The two exchanged a dark little snicker. They were talking about the ghost, of course; the one that haunted River's Bend. Over the years, conflicting rumors had circulated among the youth in the area. One had it that he'd shot his wife and her lover and then hung himself in the attic; another that he'd lost his hand in a corn picker and had been looking for it ever since. They were too young to know that the simple truth was he'd fallen down the cellar stairs and broken his neck—a far less interesting tale.

Calvin, the tallest, hairiest, and youngest of the three, said nothing to all this. He was too busy pretending not to have noticed that she was dark haired and, beneath her crazy-looking sunglasses, pretty enough and about the right age. But it could not be denied that he'd seen something else that pricked his interest, perhaps even more—a painting clearly visible through the rear window, a large painting of a weird angular face, green with three red eyes and what appeared to be snakes for hair. So she was an artist, he thought, and along with this came a strange and unaccountable pang of apprehension.

Calvin's sudden moodiness had not escaped the sharp eyes of Frank Hawkins. "The new neighbor lady's pretty good lookin', Cal!" He gave a sly grin. "You better get over there before somebody snaps her up!" Frank Hawkins had a knack for pushing buttons, and his reclusive neighbor's ineptitude with women was well-known to be a sore point.

Calvin, a great rumpled Viking of a man, standing six foot six with a voluminous red beard and untamed sandy blond hair, had just turned thirty-eight. Never married and never good with a comeback, he retreated into a glowering murkiness, pulling the brim of his dusty brown fedora low over eyes that shifted remarkably from blue to green, depending on his mood.

"You ain't chicken, are ya?" piped up Pendleton "Penny" Caughey with gleeful anticipation of a thorough ribbing. He'd always considered Calvin a mama's boy, who needed a good shove, and if anyone was qualified to deliver it, it was Pendleton J. Caughey. Despite his short stature, he was the self-appointed expert on women, being currently married to not only his fifth wife but a woman half his age.

"Well, I hear she's married—okay? So shut up about it!" muttered the giant irritably.

"I ain't seen a man's name on any of her mail," persisted Frank. He was the local mail carrier, and not much happened in the county that he didn't know about. He plucked a wild daisy and waved it under Calvin's nose. "When you go, don't forget the flowers!"

With a snarl, Calvin waved the flower aside.

Meanwhile, the mention of flowers reminded Pendleton Caughey of how Calvin's pet son-of-a-bitch goat, Gulliver, had ripped up his flower bed earlier that afternoon, setting off another tirade on the subject of staking versus fencing. He was a firm believer in staking a goat to a chain especially when the fences were built by anyone by the name of Calvin Creed.

With his usual benign indifference, Calvin flatly stated that as far as staking went, he wouldn't do that to a dog.

The aggressor, standing barely as high as Calvin's elbow, unconsciously puffed out his chest as if to increase his volume on the matter. "Yeah, well, one of these days, you're gonna have a dead goat on your hands, Creed." This would have been an onerous threat had it not been given so many times before. Confrontation was his middle name, and even at age seventy, Penny was still convinced that he was in good enough shape to take on any comers.

"Just tell me what I owe, Caughey!" Beneath his outward calm, Cal's eyes had shifted from a cloudy green to a searing blue. As usual, Penny Caughey took his adversary's imperturbability as a direct insult.

"You can't pay me the value of a garden!" cried Penny Caughey, glaring up at his neighbor, his trim white mustache furiously twitching. Though his florid complexion gave him an outdoorsy glow, it was really just the sign of a man with a quick temper and overheated kidneys. "The time and labor that went into it—why, you can't pay me the value!"

At this point, Ace, a small black terrier tucked under Calvin's arm, started a low rumble in his throat. In response, Penny's hound dog, Peanut, looked up in his saggy way with a note of concern as if to say, "What now?"

From out of the distant woods, a pack of dogs was clearly coming their way. Man and dog braced themselves as a herd of unruly mongrels burst out of the trees and onto the road, barking and snarling, snapping and growling. These were Frank's dogs, the mongrel horde as Cal had dubbed them. Actually, they were all strays Frank's wife had collected. She had a weakness for strays, and there were easily fifteen more howling in chorus from a small chain-link pen up behind Frank's double-wide trailer.

The mere sight of this mangy crew made Penny's blood boil. "Come and get me, you sons of bitches," he roared, heaving a rock from an arsenal he kept piled up for just such an occasion. The most aggressive male yelped off into the bushes as the rear guard splintered and melted away. Meanwhile, two stalwart young lieutenants made a few half-hearted threats, but it was all a bluff, just a few parting shots before they joined their leader in retreat.

"Yeah, go on, ya cowards!" crowed Penny, in full glory now, hefting another heavy stone. "That black one is the ring leader! He's taken the yellow one's place, and so help me, I'll kill the son of bitch if he takes one step on my property! I'll blast him to kingdom come!" Nothing got him going like Frank's dogs.

The yellow dog, Sue, happened to be a sore point between him and Frank, as Penny had run him over several weeks before. Frank was convinced that Penny had done it deliberately, and even if he hadn't exactly *intended* to hit him, no doubt he'd deliberately intended not to *miss* him!

Sue, a sneaky, evil-tempered, and ugly mutt, had been Frank's favorite . . . a real guard dog, an assassin by nature. Now Shadow, a surly black dog who was all snarls, had moved into Sue's position as leader of the pack.

"You ain't afraid of old Shadow, are ya?" taunted Frank Hawkins, his small sharp eyes glittering with amusement. "You know he's all mouth."

"Well, he ain't gonna have such a big mouth after I'm through him!"

Calvin had often thought that this was really just the latest installment of the Civil War. Frank Hawkins, a Southern good ol' boy raised in the mountains of the Blue Ridge versus Penny Caughey, a tough northeastern shipyard kid. To Penny, Frank's slow Southern drawl sounded less intelligent than the village half-wit while in Frank's ears, Penny's thick New Jersey accent was like fingernails on a chalkboard.

"Come on, Caughey . . . Shadow ain't interested in you. It's that fierce man-eating dog of yours he wants to fight!"

All eyes turned toward Peanut, who, at the moment, was squeezing himself between his master's legs. Nobody but Frank would have had the nerve to insult Peanut's manhood.

"In his day, Peanut could make mincemeat out of any one of your dogs, Hawkins!" declared Pendleton J. Caughey, summoning all the powers of intimidation his five feet three inches (with shoes on) could muster.

"Mincemeat!" hooted Franked. "Look at 'im! Looky there! Hiding under the mother hen!"

Caughey withdrew in dignified retreat. "Yeah, well—he'd be suicidal to take on that pack of flea-bitten dog meat, and you know it! Get him out in fair fight one-on-one, and we'll see who's the better dog!"

"Aw come on, old man. That bag of bones can barely make it to his supper bowl."

The words "old man" rendered the sting intended. "Come on, Peanut. Let's go home." Injured but never one to admit failure, Penny gave Peanut's collar a yank, and with a yelp, Peanut lurched to his feet. "You ain't gonna be laughing so hard when I call the animal warden and report you for dog neglect, Hawkins!" Penny stalked off, his back straight as a ramrod. With his parting shot, he'd made up for Peanut's humiliation.

With Frank Hawkins's good humor suddenly gone flat, Cal knew to make his getaway or he'd have to listen to another tirade against northerners. Mumbling something about manure, he departed, leaving Frank in the midst of a swirling uproar of whining, snarling, snapping, nipping, stinking canines.

"Shut the hell up!" he growled and kicked his way back to the double-wide.

At his approach, half a dozen puppies swarmed cheerfully out from under the front stoop. He had to boot the most persistent ones aside so he could even open the door, keeping them at bay with his foot so he could close it again without all of them tumbling in after him. "Shut up all that racket, y'all . . ." But the din did not abate.

Grumbling to himself, he headed to the kitchen for a snack. A gray cat with yellow eyes was sitting at her station on top of the refrigerator. This had been Clarice's favorite cat. She'd named her Eloise, but Frank called her Freaky.

"Come on, Freaky! Cut me some slack here. I'm tired and I just wanna nice cold beer." It was a familiar standoff. Predictably, as he eased his hand slowly toward the refrigerator door, she arched her back and hissed. Having felt the sting of her claws more than once, he knew to be cautious. "You know," he said, easing the broom out of the closet, "without me you'd be eating grasshoppers right about now! But if this is the way you want to play it—" He knocked her yowling to the floor. She pounced on the broom with all fours. "Go on, get the broom, crazy lady. Go on, get it!" He proceeded to sweep her into the broom closet and slammed the door, where she would continue to howl for a good while. "Welcome to your very own padded cell, you ol' psycho!"

By now three more cats had assembled on the countertop. "What are y'all looking at? Get down! Get down off of there! Now!" Oh, how he hated cats. He'd always hated cats. Cats never obeyed. They didn't know the meaning of the word. He flailed his arms threateningly and they scattered.

"Yeah, you better get out of my way! And spread the word! The man ain't in a good mood today!" He grabbed the cheese and a box of crackers and his beer and went out to the living room. The couch was covered in cats. "And get the hell off my couch before I decide to make me a fur coat!" He roared like a lion, the way he used to do while playing monster with his daughter so many years before. The cats evaporated.

He got his newspaper and was just settling in when the phone rang. "Now where the *hell* is the phone! Just when I'm finally gonna get to relax!" Since Clarice had walked out on him, a year had gone by, and the place had really gone downhill. Now he had cause to survey his dominion with a critical eye, for nowhere in the clutter of newspapers, clothes, and food wrappers was there a cordless phone to be seen. A few rings later, he knew the sound was coming from somewhere directly beneath him.

"Damnation and hellfire!" With some difficulty, he launched his great weight off the couch and down onto his knees, peering into the murky depths below, spotting it just out of reach. Red faced and cursing his luck, he lowered himself down onto his prodigious belly meanwhile fending off a battalion of calico kittens batting at him through a hole in the lining.

Once he got to the phone, it was already giving the recorded message. It was Clarice. Her tone was all business, which meant she wouldn't be talking long. "I called to tell you that my lawyer—"

"What is it!" interrupted Frank, irritably.

"My lawyer has drawn up the papers."

Frank's lips pulled back into a snarl. "Aren't you even going to ask how I am first?"

There was a huge sigh on the other end. "How *are* you, Frank?"

"If you really want to know, I am going out of my ever lovin' mind with all these gol' durned cats and dogs you left me with . . . in case you want to know."

"Frank, I told you that as soon as I get a bigger place with a yard—"

"And when is that going to be, Clarice? Next week? Next month? Next year? Because I can't take it. I'm telling you right now, I'm getting real close to getting my shotgun and—"

"Don't you dare!"

"And what are you gonna do to stop me?"

"I'll take you to court for animal cruelty, that's what I'll do!"

"Well, I'll sue *you* for animal *and* husband desertion!"

"Frank . . ." Her voice was soft and pleading now. "Ple-e-ase promise me you won't do anything rash. I swear I'll come get 'em soon. Just as soon as I can."

"You've been saying that for a year, Clarice!"

Clarice was a small, slender blonde woman with a sweet faded loveliness, gentle as her husband was brash. Her passion was for animals. She'd never turned away a stray in her life, and it seemed every cast-off animal within a twenty-mile radius was magnetically drawn into her loving care. A year ago to Frank's utter surprise, she'd suddenly up and left. She'd been saving money on the side, rented an apartment in Richmond, and wanted a divorce.

Despite his anger, his voice got tight. "Clarice—" For a minute, it appeared he might get emotional. Meanwhile, she started talking to someone in the background. A male voice answered. All semblance of tears instantly vanished. "Who's that you're talking to?"

"It's the man here to fix the copy machine."

"The copy machine, huh? Put him on the line."

"Frank, don't be that way."

"What way? I'm your husband."

"I'm free now, and I don't need to answer to you anymore."

"Well, maybe you're *not* free 'til I sign those papers, sugah. And maybe I just *won't* sign 'em 'til you vacate these animals from my premises!"

"Damn it, Frank—can't you be reasonable for once in your life?"

Suddenly he felt his sense of humor returning to him. It was a rare event to get a rise out of her. For a finishing touch, he hung up on her. Always end with the ball in your court. That was his philosophy.

Frank and his wife, Clarice, had moved into this double-wide a few years back. Actually, Frank had bought the land without her consent. Forty acres of rolling wooded river front bought over Clarice's dead body. Over and over again, she had pointed out how impractical it was for her to have to live forty miles from the city, where she worked. If he did want some land, why not get it closer to Richmond so she wouldn't have to drive an hour in and an hour back five days a week? However, it was no use. Frank was completely impervious to reason and had gone ahead and bought the land anyway.

So after a year, Clarice left and went to live in an apartment in Richmond—but an apartment that did not allow pets of any kind, not even a bird. Consequently, Frank had inherited this mangy crew, half of whom were pregnant—a population time bomb ready to go off. He figured he had lots of reasons to be depressed. He had no wife, nobody to cook for him, nobody to clean for him, nobody to sleep with him. He had quickly deteriorated, kept strange hours, drank too much, and would soon completely disappear under a pile of dirty laundry and unwashed dishes. He would never admit to anyone that he was depressed—leastwise to himself. He just concentrated on his rage. It was justified. He'd been cheated. His wife had made a deal to be there through thick and thin, and now she was gone.

The sound of a car horn tooting insistently drew him to the front window. It was the gray Toyota coming back from River's Bend. She'd made the mistake of slowing down at the turn and gotten surrounded by a barking, howling melee of canine flesh. Like starving children in the streets of Bombay, they'd brought her almost to a standstill. Frank Hawkins shook his head and then went back and turned on the TV set. It was nothing but static. Cursing softly, he started the delicate process of adjusting the antennae.

Pendleton "Penny" Caughey lived in an old white-frame farmhouse sheltered by a cluster of enormous trees across the road and up a ways from Frank Hawkins. He shared a property line with Frank Hawkins to the east and Calvin to the south. He counted himself fortunate that he was far enough from Frank's menageries of howling mutts to see them and deaf enough that he didn't have to hear them howling deep in the night. It was amazing what turning down a hearing aid could do for a man's peace of mind.

Originally from New Jersey, Penny was handsome, well built, and short. Between that and an overbearing father and the Great Depression, he'd been sufficiently toughened up to live the rest of his life in smoldering resentment of one thing or another. Married five times and the father of nine, he'd spent the better part of his life moving—from one state to another, one job to another, one wife to another. Penny was never satisfied. Even now at the age of seventy-three, as a retired "wallpaperer," roofer, and one-time navy seaman, he was just as miserable as he had ever been.

All he'd ever really wanted was to be a veterinarian. A good dog was the only peace and contentment he had ever really known. And now, seeing Peanut fading with age hurt his heart. As Peanut snored gently at his feet, Penny sat on the front porch glider, stroking his thin white mustache and contemplating the day he would have to lay old Peanut in his grave. He wouldn't let him suffer, he was sure of that. He'd shoot the dog first before he let him suffer.

He'd made that mistake once before. A spaniel named Lady. The most beautiful, intelligent dog he'd ever known. She'd gotten cancer. Penny had fought desperately to keep her alive—medications, operations—but nothing worked. Finally, when she couldn't walk anymore and her bladder had given out, he'd taken her out to a freshly dug hole and shot her right between the eyes. It had pretty much ripped him apart. In fact, he'd felt more loss over that dog than he'd ever felt over a woman—and of women, he'd had his share. That thought made him smile. He may be short, but his virility could never be questioned. Libby, his present wife, was thirty-five years younger than he, and he'd never had a problem keeping her happy in bed.

In other areas, however, it was a different story. He was the first to admit he was difficult—sometimes damned difficult—to get along with. Fortunately, Libby was easygoing. As long as she had something good to eat, she was happy. Well, maybe that wasn't exactly true. As long as she had something in her mouth, she wasn't complaining. Libby was naturally curvaceous, and this is what he had found so pleasing about her when they'd first met. Now she was plump but quickly leaving the "pleasing" category behind. Things had not been good between them lately. He told her to go see a damned doctor about her PMS. The woman had it bad—all month long. Nothing satisfied her. If it wasn't one thing, it was another, but mostly it was about him. She said he was too negative! Too negative, bull!

His thoughts rumbled down that well-worn corridor. It was dark down there and hard to breathe. A blue bunting perched on the railing right in front of him, but he didn't even see it until Peanut roused himself with a pitiful whine. This snapped Penny out of his reverie just in time to see the tiny blue bird fly away. "An Indigo Bunting! Well, I'll be damned!" A look of childlike enchantment transformed his face as he hurried out into the yard to catch another glimpse of it flying into the highest branches of the chestnut tree.

Just then, Libby came driving up the gravel driveway in her new red Escort. She was singing with the radio turned up full blast. She kept the radio on after she'd turned off the motor and sat in the car until the song ended.

"Turn that down! What are you tryin' to do? Make me go deaf?" shouted Penny, shoving his heavy black-framed glasses back up his nose. It was a stupid bubble gum song from the sixties. He hated that music and he'd always hated it. When his own kids had used to try to play that stuff, he'd ripped the plugs out of the walls; he hated it so much.

Libby's mouth flattened into a grim line. "You're already deaf, so what's the difference?" She turned the music up even louder.

"I'll rip that damn radio right out of that crap car of yours, see if I don't!" His blood pressure was squirting up the charts, turning him beet red.

"This is my car, Penny, and you will not touch it!" A look of alarm appeared on her pretty round face because she knew he was fully capable of acting out his threats.

"Provoke me, woman, and see if I don't do it!" He headed for the car, whereupon she quickly rolled up the windows and locked the doors. But her triumph quickly turned to horror as he calmly went into the garage and brought out a pair of pliers and a screwdriver.

"What are you doing with those?" she demanded. Her New Jersey accent was as thick as his. They'd come down together, but she'd taken to the Southerners, where he had not.

"What do you think? I'm gonna disconnect the battery! Open the hood!"

"No!"

Again, he disappeared into the garage, this time returning with a sledge hammer. "Open up or I'll smash the hood in!"

"Are you out of your freaking mind?" She was screaming now as he pretended he was going to take a swing. "You are a freakin' mental case! You know that? You should be locked up!" She turned off the radio and got out of the car, slamming the door behind her, her eyes bulging with pure hatred. She stomped into the house and slammed the door so hard the windowpanes rattled—but the music was off. He'd won. He wasn't about to let a woman run him around.

Whistling a merry tune, he went into the garage, where he puttered around for a half an hour, at which point the front door opened and out came Libby carrying two suitcases.

"Where are *you* goin'?"

"Over to Mary Alice's." She struggled with the suitcases over to the car and proceeded to open the trunk.

"What the hell for?" It seemed as if he really didn't know.

She rolled her eyes in disbelief. "What are you? Blind, deaf, and stupid? I've had it with you! That's why!"

"What have I done?"

"What have you done? You almost broke my car with a sledge hammer!"

"Besides that!"

"You're impossible!"

"I'm impossible! I cook for you every night! I clean the damned house stem to stern. Don't that mean nothin' to you?"

"You're absolutely impossible! I can't talk to you anymore, Penny. You won't listen, so why should I even try?"

"It's that time of the month again, isn't it! I should have known. Did you go to the doctor like I told you? You need some pills or something."

"No pill is going to make this marriage work, Penny! And I *don't* have PMS! We have serious issues in our relationship!"

"What was it with all this garbage about issues? Politics has issues. Not relationships!" Libby was the first wife he'd ever had who insisted on analyzing every dammed thing. It wasn't healthy as far as he was concerned, and it just made everything seem worse than it was, but today she looked madder than usual. "Okay, okay! Put the suitcase down and we'll talk it out!" (The good old-fashioned way, he thought, in bed, where all good wives belonged). He took off his glasses and put them in his pocket. He was better looking without them.

"No, the time for talk is over, Penny. I've tried over and over to get through to you, but nothing ever changes!"

"Okay—so what is the issue? Tell me." A feeling of unreality suddenly crept upon him, as if he were standing outside of himself, watching someone else.

"If you had the sense God gave a grapefruit, you'd already know, but you don't, so fine! To be brief you're self-centered, vicious, angry, narrow-minded, and a real drag to be around, and the bottom line is

I'm not gonna take it anymore! Good-bye!" She was struggling to lift the suitcases. In a fog, he took them from her and placed them in the trunk, slamming the hatchback shut. Turning, he looked deeply into her eyes. This would be the moment to apologize, but apologies always had a way of sticking in his throat. There was a breathless pause, and her mascara-smudged eyes filled with tears. For a moment, he thought she might walk into his arms like she always had before. *Give in*, he said to her in his mind, *give in*.

But the moment passed. Her face hardened. "Good-bye, Penny." She got into the car, turned the key, and nothing happened. She squeezed her eyes shut and set her jaw, lest she become homicidal.

Penny ventured a cheerful expression. "Guess you can't go after all!"

"Fix it," she growled.

He already knew it wasn't starting because she still had it in gear, but he fiddled around under the hood first, stalling for time. However, when her icy expression showed no signs of melting, he obediently moved the gear stick to "park." "There's your problem."

She turned the key. It started right up. "Thank you," she said and drove out of his life. Watching her disappear into a cloud of dust, he remembered the lasagna he'd made for dinner, her favorite. She'd always raved about his cooking. A stab of pain made its way to his heart, and he knew it would be a while before it went away again. He turned and went into the house. Suddenly, he did not feel much like eating.

Just then he heard a car, and Peanut let out a wail. "What is it, boy?" Thinking it was Libby coming back, Penny put on his glasses and hurried to the window, but it was only the gray Toyota on the other side of the boxwoods, barreling back down the dirt lane. "Oh," he said, his heart sinking down to his ankles. "It's just that new woman." He laid down on the couch and stared at the ceiling.

CHAPTER 2

The Creeds Come to Call

Calvin Creed lived with his mother, Ruby, on the Willow Oaks Farm that ran about 450 acres along the river. She'd grown up next door, so to speak, at River's Bend during the Depression, and it had always been a foregone conclusion that she and Stephen Creed would marry, so they did. Stephen, being the oldest son, was naturally to inherit Willow Oaks, which is how the young couple came to live there with his aging parents until they passed. Ruby and Stephen went on to farm there for the next forty-two years, growing tomatoes for the local cannery, tobacco to be shipped by train to Richmond, corn and hay for the livestock. They raised hogs, chickens, cattle, sheep, milk cows, and horses. Ruby was a prolific canner and always kept a big garden with butter beans, collards, squash and green beans, okra, kale, spinach, onions, peppers, broccoli, and carrots. That's the way they'd made it, raising nine children, all girls except the one.

When she was in her midforties, she'd gotten pregnant one last time, and that's when Calvin was born. Calvin had always been "pewly," as Ruby had always put it. His milk didn't agree with him, and for the first few months, he cried all the time though he grew to be a "right pretty" child, Ruby would always say, with great blue eyes and curly blond hair. His older sisters begged to keep it long so they could brush it, but when he was three, his father had hauled him into the yard under the mulberry tree and whacked it all off. The sisters wept because now Calvin looked like a convict in the penitentiary, but Stephen Creed had just laughed. He had always loved to make the girls cry. It was part of being a man, and that's just what Calvin was going to be—a man!

That's the way his father was—direct and forceful. When he wanted something, he made sure he got it. However, in town and at church socials, they called him a charmer, a real ladies' man. Unlike his father, Calvin had always shrunk from the limelight and only acted sulky and slow when his father tried to get him to speak out in public. He wasn't a good worker either, and that nettled his father to no end. Being a hard worker was something Stephen Creed prided himself on. He had more energy and strength and could work twice as fast, twice as hard, and twice as long as anybody he knew. He was also a perfectionist, who kept his helpers standing around like doorstops, afraid to make an independent move for fear that it would be all wrong. All in all, this made Cal hate work.

Calvin had a fisherman's temperament, like his mother's daddy, and would rather sit long hours idling on the riverbank, with a pole propped against his knee. As a boy he had been loath to get started on any chore he was made to do and quick to sneak off to read a book in one of his forest hiding places. Only later when he was older did he learn to appreciate physical labor. For example, chopping wood, which had been a dreaded chore as a kid, had become a source of pleasure, and now there were cords and cords of firewood stacked all around the place. He had discovered that so long as nobody was telling him to do something, he didn't much mind doing it.

When Cal was a senior in high school, his father died. He was seventy years old. By then, he had fairly washed his hands of his son, and their relationship ended marred in mutual contempt. All the girls had married and settled elsewhere, leaving only Calvin to keep the farm and his mother in one piece. Stricken with grief and fits of listless moodiness, she'd clung to Calvin, and together they'd drifted into isolation. Though outwardly, she lamented Calvin's failure to push out into the world; it suited her that he was the shy type, and knowingly or not, she encouraged it by planting seeds of doubt and by making him feel guilty for any thoughts of leaving her behind all by herself. All in all, it wasn't difficult, given his natural inclination to dread social situations.

Calvin had never had that social grease his father had had and was, by and large, awkward around the opposite sex. Over the years, he'd had a few short-lived relationships with women, but nothing had ever stuck. Ruby said that some people just weren't made for marriage, and she was just as glad because she needed him to run the farm, but there had been the one girl he'd been crazy over in high school. Though he never spoke of it, everyone in the family knew she'd broken his heart. Ruby claimed she couldn't remember the name, but that wasn't so. She remembered, all right, and for reasons she had kept to herself these many long years.

Under Calvin's care, the farm had fallen into disrepair. He only grew hay now and had sold off the dairy cows and the other animals. Beef cattle were easier to take care of. His mother was nearly eighty-four now and finally grown feeble enough to need a cane to help steady her over the mole-ridden ground. Her hearing was pretty much gone, so it was all but useless to say anything very complicated to her. Their communications were more like interrogations. "Did you wipe your feet, Calvin?" she'd call out in her sharp crow's voice. She would say things like, "You know I don't want you tracking in any cow pies!" or "Are you going to take a bath today, Calvin. You smell like that old billy goat," and so forth. Calvin, without looking up from his magazine, would either shout "Yes, Ma!" or "No, Ma!" and when she was satisfied, she'd nod off in her chair in front of the television.

Calvin's closest companion was Ace, a little black dog that liked to curl up on the back of Calvin's easy chair. Ace was very protective of his master, and if anyone dared to come too close, they would likely get a nip for their trouble. Cal usually made himself scarce when visitors came, especially Thelma, his older sister, who was liable to criticize. He preferred the solitude of his workshop, where he kept his typewriter and his notebooks. Ruby said he was writing a book, but nobody had ever read a solitary word of what he'd written. Once, Thelma and Ruby had tried to find his novel so they could read it, and when he found out, he'd flown into such a fury they never dared try it again.

After that, they knew not to disturb him or try to read over his shoulder or he would lash out at them. At times, his sister Thelma grumbled about his wasting time with all that kind of nonsense, but Ruby felt a creeping sadness about it. Deep inside, she felt bad for what she'd done, destroying that high school girl's letters to ensure that Calvin never left home, but she'd never spoken a word of that to anyone, leastwise Calvin.

As for Calvin, as much as he craved to be alone and as much as his mother could drive him crazy sometimes, he didn't care to think about the day that she'd be passing on. The month before last, there'd been an episode in the middle of the night in which he'd had to take her to the emergency room. It had been only a mild heart attack, but ever since, a faint depression had been hovering close, tugging on him at weak moments. Soon, he really would be all alone.

Today as he came into the kitchen, he was surprised to find his mother standing at the sink in her blue silk church dress. "What're y'all dressed up for, Ma? Going to church?" Cal gave her a peck on the cheek and then opened the refrigerator and pulled out the milk and the orange juice, looking for the last can of soda hidden in the back.

"Put that back. Thelma's made a cake, and we're going to take it to the new neighbor. So go on now and get y'self cleaned up." She wanted to tell him to go shave off that god-awful beard but didn't dare. As it was, he already had that stubborn look on his face.

Diplomacy had never been Ruby's strong suit, but in later years, she learned that on the subject of Calvin's beard, it was best to bite her tongue. She had a single-minded abhorrence for facial hair of any kind because it reminded her of all those smelly old farmers she'd grown up around as a child. Sometimes it was a terrible trial when she had to look at that wild, curly, hairy thing growing off his face. Sometimes things better left unsaid had a way of jumping out of her mouth like ugly frogs.

For Calvin, however, a beard represented freedom and efficiency. Why shave when it will just grow back again? Besides, he was never one for style. Simplicity was his ideal and he prided himself on being that way. There was a time he'd felt hopelessly behind the styles, but he was beyond all that now. "Style" was merely a money-making machine cooked up by the fashion industry to keep the sheep enslaved. Though she knew her opinions meant slightly less than a hill of beans, Ruby was quick to point out that Calvin's contempt for modernity had become a sort of style unto itself! Why he'd even refused to type on an electric typewriter and insisted on using the old manual for heaven's sake! She blamed her son's peculiar notions on the fact that he read way too many books and liked to remind him (and often) that just because somebody writes something in a book didn't make it true. But beyond that, it was a matter of temperament, and for that she faulted his father's blood—Mennonites going way back and the oddest people she'd ever known.

Calvin's typical response tended to be a little too long and windy for her taste. He called it more of a philosophy than a style—"style" signifying something shallow and pretentious. No, his philosophy of living came of a deeply held reverence for simplicity. Nature did not contrive to be; it just was. Ruby's answer to that was that her son did way too much thinking.

At the moment, looking at that hairy mess on his face, she could feel those impatient frogs lining up to jump out of her mouth, but she had to remind herself that there wasn't time for World War III. A car was pulling up in the yard and it was Thelma.

"Come on now, Cal—do as I say for once. Put on a clean shirt before Thelma gets in here."

"Why? I'm not goin'!" He nabbed the root beer. He had to make his escape now or never because one didn't easily say no to his older sister. He headed swiftly out through the living room, thinking that while Thelma was coming in the kitchen way, he'd be long gone—but too late. She was there to greet him at the front door, measuring tape in hand.

"Hello there, little brother! Thought I'd quick get the measurements so I can get that replacement glass when I go to Charlottesville tomorrow." She withered him with a look that said she was finally doing something he should have done six months ago.

Back in the fall, the wind had blown the door shut and shattered the decorative glass pane. It had been covered by cardboard and plastic ever since. Thelma was a workaholic—just like their daddy had been—and a walking reminder of Calvin's inadequacy. Cal muttered something about how he was going to do it but just hadn't gotten around to it yet.

"Well, I sure hope you weren't planning on going to Hank's. He is way too overpriced." Thelma was a large woman, square jawed and vigorous with a resounding voice, more like their daddy than Ruby. She'd practically raised Calvin and still treated him like a little boy, which rankled his last nerve. He disliked confrontation, however, so kept a low profile when she was around. She had a way of digging around and nosing things out into the light of day that should have been kept secret like the time she took it upon herself to spring clean his room up in the attic and found all his girlie magazines under the bed. He'd come home to find her making a bonfire in the burning barrel, holding them up like somebody's dirty underwear. Even Ruby agreed that she'd gotten pious since marrying into a family of preachers.

Their own family had never been more than nominally religious. Ruby's faith was tentative, something she kept hidden from prying eyes like a guilty secret. Even so, she was steadfast on one point: a *good* person went to church whether they believed or not. Calvin, however, had dispensed with that obligation years ago. Thelma moaned and groaned that his morals were going straight to hell in a handbasket while Ruby could only throw up her hands. She never *had* been able to do a thing with that boy.

Thelma was now looking him over critically. "I hope you're not planning to wear those dirty old overalls, and it wouldn't kill you to shave!" She deemed it sheer laziness, a man not shaving.

"There's some fence to fix and I can't go." He made one final effort to push past her.

"You're gonna have to go sooner or later, and it might as well be now."

"And like I'm telling you, I don't have time!"

"Calvin Theodore Creed! We are going to be civilized and go welcome her to the county! Now go! Besides, I hear she's single. Aren't you a little curious about her?"

"No," he said but turned anyway and headed on up to his attic room, like an old bull driven into the pen. Inside, he was cursing, but underneath, he was nervous as hell.

Seeing as Thelma wouldn't think of taking her nice new car down the rutted dirt road that led to River's Bend, they all squeezed into the cab of Calvin's battered truck. It was a tight fit for the three of them on the cracked vinyl seat, as Thelma and Ruby were wide in the hips. Thelma's compressed bulk exuded the overpowering aroma of thick sweet perfume with strong overtones of Ban roll-on deodorant. Cal leaned as far out the window as he could to get away from the smell and Thelma's commentary.

"When are you going to get yourself a decent truck, Cal? I said, when are . . ."

"I heard you the first time."

"Well, then are you going to answer me?"

Calvin sighed. Thelma was not one to be ignored. "There's nothing wrong with the truck. The engine runs perfectly fine."

"It's an eyesore. Don't you have any pride at all? Why, I'm embarrassed to be seen in this junk heap!"

"You're welcome to walk, Thelma," replied Calvin pleasantly.

Thelma scowled. "And I hope you're not wearing that god-awful hat!"

"There's nothin' wrong my hat!"

Both women rolled their eyes with cries of exasperation. This was a longstanding struggle. They'd tried many times to get him to change to a new one, but soon that grungy old hat would find its way back on his head. For Cal it was like an old friend and, by now, had seen its way through many a season of rain and snow and blistering sun. It even had a hole in the crown, where a sharp branch had caught hold of it.

Calvin had found it in an attic trunk the year his father dropped dead of the heart attack and worn it ever since. Cal liked it because it wasn't the typical farmer's hat but the kind Humphrey Bogart wore in old movies, besides the fact that it had been his grandfather's hat. Calvin liked to think that wearing Pap's hat had given him powers—word powers. Pap, the consummate storyteller, never wrote a word down on paper in his life but could keep a crowd mesmerized for hours. There were good memories in that hat, like sitting up on the riverbank, fishing pole in hand, listening to Pap ramble about the past.

"Oh, you're impossible. Isn't he impossible?" Thelma started rummaging through a pocketbook the size of a small suitcase. "Mama, you want a breath mint?" Ruby, who had been wincing with every jolt in the road, meekly accepted the mint her daughter popped into her mouth. "Here, Cal. Take a breath mint."

"I don't want a breath mint."

"Well, believe me, you need one. Take it! You don't want to knock the poor woman senseless when she opens the door, do you?"

Calvin felt a familiar stab of shame. Thelma hadn't the slightest notion how deep and dark his feelings ran.

The lady painter's rutted dirt lane snaked along the weedy edge of Calvin's north hay field and continued on for half a mile or so to the picturesque hill where, in 1728, the original settler, Calvin's maternal great-great-great-grandfather, Ogden Clayton Carver, had set his frame house on its stone foundation and called it River's Bend. Years ago, it had been sold to a wealthy woman in Richmond. She'd bought it for her son, an old hippy and a writer of historical fiction obsessed with the Civil War period. Now he was in prison. A helicopter had spotted his marijuana patch one day down on the flood plain. It had been quite the local scandal.

Calvin had really liked the old hippy Sonny Hay and had spent many long hours on his front porch talking about anything and everything. He had such a different view of life and the world. He'd traveled all over the globe and had the most amazing stories to tell. Cal missed him still. Coming around the curve, Cal realized he hadn't been here since the day Sonny had been taken away. That had been five years ago, and River's Bend had stood empty and neglected ever since.

Aside from a dangling gutter and a missing piece of roof slate, the house hadn't changed much—still resplendent in its deterioration, nestled in amongst the overgrowth of honeysuckle and wisteria vines like an enchanted cottage in a fairy tale. At present, a desolate push mower choked in the high grass was the only sign of human occupation.

"Why anybody would want to live here is beyond me," muttered Thelma.

As was the custom, Calvin lightly beeped the horn, and they waited politely in the truck until a slender woman with dark hair hanging down her back in one thick braid appeared from around the side of the house. She carried orange hedge clippers and wore an uncertain smile. After an awkward moment, she waved. They waved back. It was still awkward.

"Don't just sit there like a log! Get out and open our door, Calvin!" hissed Thelma. She was getting red in the face from having to reach across her mother's lap to open the door handle. "Perfect condition, huh! Can't even open the doggone door!"

"Thelma, your blood pressure!" reminded Ruby. "I don't want you havin' a stroke on me like your daddy!"

"I wouldn't have to have a stroke," snapped Thelma, "if Calvin would just get a decent truck with door handles that worked!"

In the midst of this calamity, Leslie Hillerman walked up to Ruby's window to introduce herself. Though dying of embarrassment on in the inside, Thelma and Ruby switched on bright smiles. Calvin sat, stone-faced. "Open the door, Calvin," hissed Ruby through a frozen smile, "so *maybe* we can get out sometime before the next century?"

He obeyed but woodenly, without directly acknowledging Leslie in any way.

"That's my brother. For goodness sake, Calvin, introduce yourself!" ordered Thelma in her cheerful booming way, meanwhile wiggling her heft out of the truck. "I'm Thelma Turner. *His* sister." She made a face as if to say that that was a fate worse than death. "And this is my mother, Ruby Creed."

Leslie stuck out her hand and pretended not to notice Calvin's mask of stony indifference and reddening face. "Good to meet you at last," she said with an impish smile that lit her whole face.

"He's awful shy," said Ruby. She and Thelma were in the habit of doing the talking for Calvin in social situations.

"Mama and Calvin live in the white house on the right as you come in your road," said Thelma, meanwhile pulling her skirt from out between her legs and hoisting her waistline back into place.

Leslie's look of uncertainty melted, her face brightening with recognition. "Oh, the one with the red shed!"

"Oh, the red shed. Yes, that's it," said Thelma with a pained look directed at Calvin, who was responsible for the color scheme.

"Oh—that awful red shed," echoed Ruby dolefully.

"And—and you have a goat too, right?" said the lady painter brightly.

"Oh, that goat—," moaned Ruby, "ate my nightgown right off the clothesline."

"That's Calvin's goat," explained Thelma darkly, lips pressed thin.

Leslie laughed but then stopped when nobody else joined in.

"He sure loves that goat," echoed Ruby mournfully.

"He likes animals better than people, don't ya, Cal!"

Calvin glowered. Thelma had never lost the knack of saying exactly the most wrong thing possible.

Leslie beamed up into the bearded wilderness of his face with a cautious and friendly eye. "Another St. Francis," she suggested.

Not beautiful but pleasing, he thought, looking into her face with its upturned elfin nose, smooth rosy skin, and warm brown eyes. They crinkled up when she smiled. He asked if that was her push mower in the weeds.

She shook her head with an air of resignation. "Yes, and I'm afraid it's losing the battle." Her fingers were stained, he noted, with purple and green. They were clever-looking hands that talked into the air.

"Calvin's got a bush hog," volunteered Ruby.

"Oh! I wouldn't want to impose—"

"He'd be *glad* to do it," interceded Thelma as if someone might disagree.

Leslie hesitated. Meanwhile, they all seemed to be anxiously waiting for Calvin to speak, but he just looked off in the other direction. Finally, he said he guessed he would.

"Calvin!" Thelma gave him a sharp elbow.

"I said I'd do it, didn't I?" Calvin eyed the roofline moodily.

Thelma rolled her eyes at her mother as if to say, "What did I tell you?" and Ruby shook her head, disgusted.

There was a rift in the conversation, and as nobody had made a move to leave, Leslie felt compelled to invite them in for iced tea.

Ruby took this as her cue to begin rambling about how this had been the house where she'd been born and how she hadn't been here in years and how bad it looked and had she mentioned that she was born here?

"Mama," Thelma shouted in Ruby's ear.

"Cal, when was the last time you reckon we was over here?" continued Ruby, unabated.

"Mama! She *said* why don't we come in for some *iced tea*!"

Ruby blinked. "For me?"

"Tea! Iced tea! To drink!"

"Oh, tea! Well sure. Get the cake, Thelma."

"I only hope it ain't ruined, bumping around back there," muttered Thelma resentfully. "It's coconut. You like coconut, don't you, Miz Hillerman?"

Leslie tried to appear sufficiently delighted though Thelma barely seemed to notice, as she was fussing at Calvin, who was getting the cake out of the back of the truck.

"My prize-winning coconut cake. County Fair three-time winner," was Ruby's side note. "Sour cream is my secret."

Leslie sprang to Ruby's side to guide her. "The yard is really bumpy, I'm afraid. Take my arm."

"It's those dang moles. Ain't it the moles, Calvin?" Ruby paused in front of the overgrown porch. "And don't them wisteria vines just take over the place!"

"I've been chopping away all morning, and I'm afraid it still looks like Sleeping Beauty's castle!" sighed Leslie.

Ruby chuckled. "Once, Stephen wanted to plant them on our porch, but I wouldn't let him because they'd run wild over everything and you pay heck getting them out again."

"Mama!" snapped Thelma. "Can we please get a move on here!"

"Watch your step, Mrs. Creed."

"Stephen was my husband." continued Ruby serenely. "As stubborn and ornery a man as ever walked but I loved him 'til the day he died, I reckon." Ruby clutched Leslie's arm with an iron grip as they ascended the broken steps of the overgrown front porch. The old woman paused at the front doorsill to ring the ship's bell. "Daddy was in the navy back in the First World War," she said and then gazed wistfully down the wide airy front hall leading straight to the back door opening to yet another vine-laden back porch. "Mama raised nine of us in this house."

There was an impatient sigh from Thelma. "Mama! My arms are ready to give out holding this cake!"

Meanwhile, Leslie was looking around in amazement. Nine children! There weren't but four rooms in the entire house, excluding the narrow kitchen. "But where on earth did you fit all those people?"

Ruby indicated the steep narrow staircase to the right. "Oh, the children slept upstairs. Boys in one room, girls in another, and Mama and Papa slept down here in this room." She poked her head into the large room on the right. It was empty except for a small table and chair in front of an enormous stone hearth and an easel with a large canvas covered in funereal splotches of paint. Out of the mélange, like forms emerging from a fog, the figure of a woman, broken, a mournful face, an empty hand reaching out. It was a dark, grim picture. For a moment, Ruby stood silent, as if digesting it. "I heard you was an artist." Her eyes trailed to the sink splashed with paint in the small kitchen beyond and the stick of burning incense stuck in a crevice of the fireplace. Her nose crinkled suspiciously. "What *is* that smell I'm smelling?"

"Sandalwood. It's incense."

"Oh! Are you a Catholic?" Ruby said this in an undertone as if it were some kind of dirty secret.

"Mama! You don't have to be a Catholic to burn incense!"

Ruby waved Thelma's outburst aside. "Well anyways, it smells good in here. I reckon it must have smelled pretty dank being empty so long. When I was growing up, it always smelled of fresh bread. Mama made it every day. Daddy built that kitchen the year the summer kitchen burned down. If you look out in the yard, you'll see four big ol' stones where it used to sit on. And look here—this is where my brother Teddy carved 'I love Polly' on the door jam. Daddy gave him a whuppin' he would never forget." Ruby stood and laughed about this until tears stood out in the corners of her eyes. "Oh, me—that Teddy was a character! He's dead now though. They all are except for me. I'm the very last one."

"That must be hard for you," murmured Leslie sympathetically.

Ruby tossed her head. "Naw! Everybody's gotta go sometime. I reckon I'll have my turn soon enough. And while I'm on the subject, if you see Daddy roaming around, don't worry. Just tell him 'hi' from me. He fell down the cellar stairs one day and broke his neck, poor soul, and I guess he never left. But he won't hurt you none!"

Thelma rolled her eyes. "Come on, Mama! You'll talk all day long if we aren't careful." Thelma took a firm hold of Ruby's arm and steered her into the living room. As Leslie took the cake into the kitchen, she overheard Ruby tell her daughter that in her day, they tried to paint *pretty* pictures a person would want to look at.

The room opposite was another large square room with an identical stone hearth, a baby grand piano, a large flowery sofa, two overstuffed chairs, and a wall of built-in bookshelves full of books. It wasn't a fussy room but comfortable, with a careless sort of grace. Thelma and Ruby sat on the couch while Calvin stood in the corner behind the piano, apparently absorbed in examining the large painting that hung on the wall. When it dawned on him that he was staring at a picture of naked bodies in fragmented cubes, he quickly started looking at the bookshelf instead. He arbitrarily pulled one out and opened it up as if reading, but the words were all a blur. His mind had frozen shut, the tactless comments of his relations still revolving in his brain.

Leslie was now at his elbow, looking at the books with him. "Feel free to borrow anything you like." She had a clean flowery smell that awakened in him a sad longing, which he would not unravel until later, when he'd realized it was White Shoulders, the perfume Annie Clay had always worn. But for the time being, he merely nodded stiffly and cleared his throat, saying that that would be fine. He was bound to take the book now, though he hadn't even read the title.

"Calvin's always reading and writing poetry and stories," muttered Ruby with a touch of woe because reading and writing meant work not done.

Calvin delivered her the severest look he could muster.

"You're a writer?" Leslie's eyes lit with a new interest.

"It's just—stuff," he replied gruffly, as if he resented having the subject even come up. He pretended to go on reading. The word to describe her eyes would definitely have to be chocolate, warm chocolaty brown.

"Oh, hush! You should see all the stories and poems stacked up all over Daddy's workshop. Only he never lets anybody read them!"

"So—is your husband coming home soon?" interrupted Thelma in a pleasant tone, hoping to aim the conversation in a more interesting direction. From the moment she'd stepped foot across the threshold, Thelma had searched in vain for telltale signs of a male inhabitant, as this was a question of great interest among the locals. There were few single women in the area unless they were widowed or divorced with children, in which case, they mostly remarried or moved to the city.

Leslie Hillerman promptly flushed a bright pink. "We're—getting divorced, actually—and I've always wanted to live in the country so—" She looked at the floor, mortified. She devoutly disliked revealing personal details. However, their eyebrows had not yet gone down, as if expecting more.

"What did she say, Thelma?" shouted Ruby deafly.

"She's getting a divorce!" bellowed Thelma.

"A horse?"

"No, Mama! Dee-vorce—divorce! And she wants to live in the country for a while!"

Ruby looked perplexed. "Without her husband?" Thelma rolled her eyes.

"Excuse me . . . I'll be right back with your tea." Leslie promptly evacuated to the kitchen. Ruby's mouth was still open in consternation.

"Don't put yourself out now!" bellowed Thelma, giving her mother a severe look.

Ruby blinked and whispered with some urgency, "But what about her *husband*?"

"Shush, Mama!" Thelma glared, bug eyed.

"What'd I say?" whined Ruby, indignant now.

After that, Thelma did most of the talking, which was as per usual. The newcomer listened patiently, murmuring sounds of polite interest while keeping a concerned eye out for Calvin, who drifted like a ghost on the periphery. Periodically, she would ask if he wanted to sit down, and he would shake his great hairy head and mumble. When he eventually did sit, however, he unwittingly chose the chair with the broken springs and was nearly swallowed whole, his great long legs folded up somewhere near his chin.

"Oh dear, Mr. Creed! That is the world's worst chair! Let me help you," cried Leslie, trying desperately not to laugh.

Meanwhile, Thelma and Ruby cackled with unabashed glee. "Cal! You look like a big ol' ox stuck in a bog! Don't he, Mama?"

Ruby giggled so hard, she had to press her side to keep from getting a cramp. "Just a-wallowing like a big ox!"

Cal, however, remained solemn as Leslie hoisted him out.

Calvin would not take his first complete breath until the excruciating visit was over and they were making dust on the way out.

"Isn't it a shame how some people can't seem to stay married?" observed Thelma smugly. "People don't have no stayin' power these days."

Ruby nodded. "The first rainy day and they're gone!"

Thelma's elbow dug into Calvin's ribs one more time as she foraged in her purse. "Chewing gum, Mama?" She tore off half a stick, peeled the wrapper, and popped it into her mother's open mouth.

Ruby made a sour face. "Juicy Fruit!" She preferred Doublemint. "Calvin? Want some?"

Calvin mumbled something unintelligible. At the moment, he had more important things to think about—like how he'd made a fool of himself back there in front of the new neighbor.

CHAPTER 3

Looking Back

As Calvin's battered old truck disappeared in a cloud of red dust, Leslie was left fervently hoping she wouldn't have to see much of these neighbors of hers. She hadn't come to the country for social interaction. It was trees and silence she craved.

As she turned into the house to gather the cake plates, she was stunned by the fleeting glimpse of a child reflected in the hall mirror, a blond, curly-headed, blue-eyed boy barely able to stand. In a moment it was gone, but somehow she had always known it was a boy, for she'd seen this vision before. A twinge of sadness caught in her throat along with a senseless kind of hope, and she went to find the solace of her rocking chair on the porch in the comfort of the low-handing wisteria vines.

She'd found this chair in an old flea market in Richmond years ago. At the time, it had been a deep forest green. Over the years, it had served time as indigo blue, magenta, and now a bright sunflower yellow. The wicker seat, however, had finally given out and just a plain piece of pine board lay across the frame. Even so, for thinking, real thinking, it was still her favorite place to sit. She stared at the overgrown lawn, feeling the weight of everything yet undone, but now there was no energy to do it. Seeing the child again had brought up a clash of unwanted feelings that she thought had been safely locked away.

"Well then," she said, standing up with a zest she did not feel. "We can't sit around all day like a zombie now, can we?" Since moving to the country alone, she'd adopted the habit of talking to herself. This particular voice had an English accent, brisk but kind, and somewhat on the order of a Mary Poppins.

"Is it crazy if no one sees?" she asked herself, giving her reflection in the hall mirror a wry look. That's when she noticed, with a little shock, that the door to the cellar was standing mysteriously ajar. Not since she'd been here had she made the first move toward going down into that dismal place, so who had opened it? She looked down into the receding inky darkness below. She flipped on the switch, and with a delayed reaction, a sickly yellow light flickered on, illuminating dirty whitewashed walls and a bare earthen floor. Involuntarily, a vision of the old man, thin and wiry, lying dead at the foot of the steps flashed before her eyes.

"Don't stand there like a ninny," interrupted the nanny firmly. "It's off to the river with you! Chop, chop!" Leslie shut the door with a determined click. She was here now living alone in the country and did not have the luxury of worrying about ghosts.

The river was no more than a ten-minute walk through the forest along an old logging road, a gentle sunlit river with a clear sandy bottom shaded by ancient trees with great intricate roots clutching the banks like gnarled fingers. It was a magical place, but she'd been here a week and still hadn't managed to find the time to get down there. With an upsurge of determination, she threw her sketchbook and a bottle of water into a bag.

It was time to make some art again. She gazed sadly at her very first painting—the green-faced, red-eyed Medusa leaning against the wall in the front hall. Though it was crude, it was bold and alive and a reminder of simpler times. Where had it gone, that reckless spirit? She tried to remember how it was back before the *Mystic Horse* series had become such a production line, back before Stuart had gotten dollar signs in his eyes. ("If people want Mystic Horses then for god's sake paint more Mystic Horses!") But somehow, making art for money had never meant anything to her.

The painting she was working on now was something so completely different from anything she'd done before, very dark and introspective—a self-portrait of pain, she called it. "Forget it," Stuart would say if he saw it. "It won't sell."

It was humid. By the time she got to the edge of the forest, she had already broken a sweat. She forged ahead into the shade of the welcoming trees, down the rutted path, glancing neither right nor left, pausing only to untangle herself from spiderwebs. She did not hear the singing birds in the tree above however and at the bend in the road, she was startled out of the gray rumble of her thoughts by a small herd of young deer grazing on the woody plants. They were gone in an instant, all but one big eyed faun staring frozen in fascination her white fluffy tail waving uncertainly. They stared at each other for a long breathless moment before the faun vanished like smoke.

Just ahead, the glimmering river beckoned through the trees as she picked her way down the steep riverbank toward the cool rushing water. All thoughts of making art cast aside, she threw off her clothes, dug her toes into the soft muddy banks, and descended naked into the clear golden brown water. It was deliciously cool against her bare skin and shallow enough that she could sit on the soft sandy bottom or wade upstream and then float back down, giving her body entirely to the current, allowing it to turn and slowly drift like a twig.

Gazing up at the white clouds in a perfect blue sky, the dark clot of sadness inside started to loosen its grip. When was the last time she had simply gazed at the sky? When had life gotten to be such a grim chore? A heron cruised low over the water like a fighter pilot on the lookout for shadowy fish moving below, but suddenly, all she could see was the house of glass and mirrors at Brandon Mills, the house that had swallowed her alive.

Just that morning, Stuart had left a long "I know you must be feeling hurt" speech on her answering machine, but what he'd really meant to talk about was the house. Until now, there had been no mention of selling it, but suddenly, he seemed in a hurry. He'd chastised her for not answering her phone and then added that he hoped they could be businesslike about this because he didn't have "time to play games."

Strange that it should upset her like this, she thought. That house had never felt right. Maybe it was because everything in it had been chosen to please her mother-in-law or maybe because no matter if it was winter or summer, it was always so cold. Still, selling it suddenly seemed like such a final thing to do.

She thought back to their first house on Park Street, the Pink House, they'd called it, a one-hundred-year-old shotgun house in the Fan District, with a charming front porch and old-fashioned oak door with leaded glass panes. There was a sweeping staircase and a wide front hall that ran the length of the house, opening into spacious rooms with high ceilings, ornate woodwork, and fireplaces in every room. The entire place was pink as bubble gum, Pepto-Bismol pink, and it had been love at first sight.

She and Stuart had spent weeks scraping off old paint, but it had been a labor of love. She remembered the backyard as a jungle of boxwoods and lilacs growing in the shade of three ancient oak trees. There was an old ivy-covered carriage house that sat facing an alley, and inside the rusty wrought iron fence all manner of day lilies and daffodils, tulips and crocus grew up in luxuriant tufts at their appointed hour. There was even a mildewed statue of Venus beside a quaint old cement fish pond full of muddy stagnant water choked with weeds.

The neighbors were a mix of old-timers and student artists and eccentrics. A gay couple lived on one side, and an eighty-year-old woman painter lived on the other. It was a tree-lined street, quiet and leafy, with birds and squirrels, bicycles chained up to signposts, and pedestrians walking by day and night. People sat on their porches, nodding and speaking to passersby. Those had been the happiest times.

The Brandon Mill house had been a gift from Stuart's parents and Meredith Hillerman's idea of a way to promote her son's career. If he was to make it to the top in the architecture field, he would need to associate himself with the right kind of people.

In the Brandon Mill gated community, there was a guard at the entrance, a brand new country club with a golf course, a pool and a spa, winding landscaped streets, and enormous high-priced homes, but there were no front porches, and if there had been, nobody would have sat on them. There were no people passing by to nod to. Everyone was in a car driving past each other. It was a community of strangers.

Though she knew she was expected to be grateful, Leslie had always resented the house at Brandon Mill, but there was no arguing with Stuart's mother, who had never clicked with her artsy daughter-in-law. John and Meredith Hillerman represented a clannish breed of Virginia blue bloods that operated under three presuppositions: First, no one calling themselves a Hillerman could afford to be less than excellent in every way. Second, there was a right and wrong way to do everything; and third, she, Meredith, knew that right way. Trying to relate to her mother-in-law's rules of decorum had always felt like walking around in one high-heeled shoe.

Leslie had not been born into wealth. Her parents had worked their way into the upper middle class through hard work and sacrifice, her mother working secretarial jobs to put her father through dental school and then as his receptionist to save money. When Leslie was fourteen, the family was finally able to move into a beautiful home in an influential neighborhood, and she was sent to a private Episcopal girls' school, where she was thrown in with rich girls used to getting their way.

Leslie, who had always excelled in school, promptly fell to the average category. She studied but would never distinguish herself and never feel accepted into the inner circle of who's who, and that was when she started to think of herself as an outsider and an artist. Art class became her haven, where bubbly Mrs. Tweed lovingly nurtured her abilities and her self-esteem.

So when had loving Stuart become so essential? She marveled that she'd never thought to ask herself this question before. Leslie lay back on a boulder jutting out of the water to bask in the sun and to contemplate. She had been happy before she'd ever met such a person as Stuart Hillerman, hadn't she? A vision of TimO, the wild-haired boy, slid into her mind's eye—her first love. Tim Smith was his name. He'd added the O to stand for "original" or, according to her father, "outlandish." Today she couldn't help but smile, but fifteen years ago, it had been a deadly serious affair. There had been nothing sensible about loving TimO, and it was probably the craziest, most passionate, and reckless thing she'd ever done. In a word, she'd been a fool. Of course, even now, love was making a fool of her. Perhaps it always would. She stretched out on the rock, feeling the comforting warmth along her spine. What could she have done with her life had she not always been tangled up with some man? Was it even possible to calmly live out one's potential without one?

The last she'd heard, TimO was an investment banker on Wall Street, but back then he'd called himself a conceptual artist though he'd always been more of a rebel than an artist. She'd met him the first summer out of college, and instead of pursuing a teaching career, she'd taken a hard left turn and traipsed after TimO into the slums, where they'd aspire to live an "authentic" existence. After years of trying to fit in with snobby rich girls who defined a person by the label on her clothes, it had been a liberating experience.

She could still see the shocked expressions on her parents' faces the first time she'd introduced them to this boy with the kinky red hair, looking like he'd stuck his finger into a light socket. For some unimaginable reason, she'd taken them to the opening of his art installation entitled *Concepts of War*, an entire room filled with dismembered G.I. Joes spattered with red paint. How naïve they'd all been back then, but for something like this there is no preparation. It was the early 1970s. Every rule had been thrown out of the play book, and TimO had landed like a grenade squarely in the middle of their well-ordered existence, blasting apart every pillar and creed, including bathing, gainful employment, and matrimony. It was an undeclared war, and he was a full frontal assault against motherhood, civilization, and God himself. Her mother went into mourning but no amount of arguing could dissuade Leslie from her path to destruction, so in desperation, Emily Pierce had decided to get sneaky.

Unlike his wife, Leslie's father, Ed, was a relaxed kind of guy with a great sense of humor, and he and Stuart's dad sang in a barbershop quartet. They'd become close buddies, going on fishing trips and spending time together with their wives. This was how Leslie's parents came to be quite popular within the country club set, and it wasn't long before they met Stuart, newly graduated from college and on his way to a good position with an architectural firm.

The moment her mother set eyes on Stuart, it had hit her like a ton of bricks. Someone like this could surely lure her daughter away from the awful TimO. At the mere thought, her husband had howled with laughter. Leslie liked 'em hairy, he said. The frat boy type with the sleek blond hair and square-cut jaw was sure to be a reject with Leslie the contrarian.

But once Emily set her mind on something, she had all the determination of a pit bull. No, this young man, Stuart, was the answer to all her problems. He was good-looking and had an engaging personality with that easy self-assurance wealth gives to young men, who know they have little chance to fail and so was invited to dinner.

For two years, Leslie had been living with TimO in a bohemian slum paradise, out of wedlock, subsisting on rice and beans and wearing thrift-store clothes. They were "dropouts," escapees of the capitalistic rat race. Despite imminent nuclear attack and her mother's chronic hysteria, Leslie had been having the time of her life. It wasn't that peace negotiations hadn't progressed. Leslie and TimO were actually going over to her parents for strained but civil dinners (topics such as hair and politics being strictly off limits).

That particular night, she'd showed up at her parent's door minus TimO. On pain of being cut out of the will, he'd been ordered home for a family reunion in New Jersey. When Leslie spotted a well-scrubbed guy, handsome as the gods, sitting in her parent's living room, her instant response had been fury. Without wasting a moment, she'd marched into the kitchen, where her mother was slicing a green pepper with characteristic precision.

"It won't work, you know," hissed Leslie, giving the swinging kitchen door an angry nudge.

With a pained expression, Emily reached out and pushed Leslie's thick auburn hair out of her face. "Dear—you look so much prettier with it pinned back." Emily's father had been the town drunk, and she knew all too well how one could be judged on appearance alone, and she'd had to fight every step of the way into the upper middle class. It drove her crazy that Leslie could so blithely toss it all aside in the name of self-expression and some stupid hippy dream. There had been many arguments. To her mind, appearance was a matter of survival in a brutally judgmental world. Leslie, on the other hand, called her mother's obsession with fashion a pathetic plea for acceptance. Even so, beneath all the high-sounding moralizing, there lay a deeper issue, which Leslie had never spoken aloud to anyone, namely the difficulties of having a classic beauty for a mother.

Emily was petite, blonde, with delicate features, and slender hands and feet. Leslie was the feminine version of her father—tall, with sturdy bone structure and dark eyes set in an angular rosy face, with a wide puckish mouth and elfin nose. Officially, Leslie was considered to be cute, a definition that, in her mind, had unfortunately come to mean "not pretty enough." The turning point for Leslie had come one summer afternoon upon overhearing two great aunts lament that it was too bad Leslie hadn't taken after her mother in looks. After that, she'd stubbornly refused all her mother's efforts to make her presentable and resigned herself to being clever instead.

"All I'm suggesting is to put it in a clip!" Emily's eyes widened coyly though she knew quite well this wasn't about the clip.

Leslie reared back defiantly. "I'm talking about that guy in the living room, Mother!"

"What? Is there something wrong with him?" Leslie knew that behind Emily's play at innocence was a brick wall.

"Mother, I already *have* a boyfriend—remember?"

"Forgive me but I *thought* you were so open-minded! Besides, he probably wouldn't be interested in a girl like you anyway." This was a comeback that had come to her in the car, and she'd been looking forward to finding a chance to use it.

Leslie liked to think she was immune now to these subtle barbs, but deep down she wasn't, and it only made her angrier still. "This is so wrong!"

Emily thrust a knife and an onion into Leslie's hands. "Chop," she said.

"I can't believe you would be so manipulative," cried Leslie, chopping now with a vengeance.

"I don't know *what* you're talking about. I just thought it would be nice to have a *normal*—Smaller pieces, dear."

"You know, I take that back! I absolutely *do* believe that you would be so manipulative!"

"I'm just trying to save you from that horrible—" Emily clamped her lips shut. This was not in the script.

"What? You might as well say it!"

"No! I promised your father that I wouldn't!"

"Well, I already *know* that you hate TimO because you can't understand anything or anybody that doesn't fit into your suffocating little middle-class white world!"

Emily's eyes narrowed. "Oh, so it's a crime to be white and middle class now!" Sparks were flying but quietly, for fear their argument might carry.

At this moment, Leslie's father stuck his head in through the swinging door, sniffing around for signs of dinner, but by the pinched white looks, he could see that something was up. "Is everything all right?" he asked.

"No," said Leslie.

"*Yes*, it is," insisted her mother grimly.

"*I'm* going home."

"*No*, you're not! You are *not* going to ruin this evening and embarrass me and our guest," declared Emily, glaring fiercely enough to bore holes right through her daughter's head.

Sensing that Leslie was ready to bolt, Ed slipped an arm around her shoulders and gave a squeeze. He and his daughter had the same comfortable warm brown eyes. "Do you really have to go? I was looking forward to hearing about your new show, and besides, I've missed you."

"But that guy in there!"

His wife opened her mouth but a look from him prompted her to shut it. "Who cares about him? It's me you came to see, right, Lessie?"

This was what she'd called herself when she was but two and signaled the warmest affection between father and daughter. "You can give your old dad a few crumbs of your time now, can't you?" She allowed herself to be gathered into his broad embrace and held close to his calmly beating heart.

"Okay," she whispered.

"Good! Now for heaven's sake, let's eat before I blow away in a cloud of dust!"

"That's not going to happen anytime soon, Daddy!" cried Leslie, patting his protruding belly as they headed laughing into the dining room together.

That first evening, she'd pointedly refused to engage Stuart directly in any conversation. Meanwhile, Emily fell all over herself, digging out all pertinent information about his ambitions to be an architect like his father and grandfather before him. Leslie remained stubbornly unimpressed.

The next time she'd met Stuart was in a bookstore a few weeks before Christmas. She'd turned around, and there he was in line right behind her. It was a long wait to the cash register, and since he'd smiled and called her by name, she couldn't very well pretend not to recognize him. On top of that, he was buying her all-time favorite novel, *A Hundred Years of Solitude*. It turned out to be his favorite novel too. He was buying it for his brother. Conversation flowed easily between them. He didn't seem so primped and squeaky clean this time in a rumpled flannel shirt with a day's worth of stubble on his face. He asked her if she'd like to stay and have a cup of coffee with him, and for a moment, she almost wished she could. She could see disappointment in his eyes when she told him she had to go. She failed to mention TimO.

She didn't think any more about it until sometime after Christmas, when she and TimO arrived at her parents' house for dinner, and once again, there was Stuart sitting in the living room. This time, he had another architecture student with him, a beautiful blonde woman named Alison. She was friendly, intelligent, and clever. Her parents seemed utterly charmed, and for some reason, Leslie instantly despised her.

It turned into an excruciating evening. She couldn't help but compare the courtly consideration Stuart gave to his date (pulling out her chair, pouring her wine, asking her opinion) to TimO's habit of monopolizing conversations and cutting people off. This evening, he broke all the rules and launched into his favorite rant against the greedy capitalistic marketing machine of American society. He was obviously trying to impress Stuart, but all Leslie could think was that he was being utterly rude and self-centered, not to mention dirty and unkempt. Meanwhile, Stuart listened patiently as one would toward a rebellious child. Later, Leslie had yelled at TimO for acting like a jerk and threatened never to bring him home again.

"Why should you care what they think? That's just another bourgeois bullshit guilt trip," he said and dumped himself in front of the television to sulk for the rest of the night.

The next month, her period didn't come. Suddenly her life with TimO started to look less like a noble adventure and more like a nightmare. This was no life for a child. Since TimO's philosophy was that cleaning was just more bourgeois bullshit, the apartment was a pigsty, and though he preached equality for women, he never lifted a finger to wash dishes or clean up. It wasn't his problem if she insisted on enslaving herself to the plastic middle-class image.

A few days later, she discovered that he'd spent all of their food money on Barbie dolls for his newest cynical *Susie Homemaker* installation. She refused to listen to his conceptual framework, and he called her a pouty little rich girl. Out of sheer malice, she dropped the bomb. She could be pregnant, and what did that do to his conceptual framework?

Things promptly went downhill. For an entire week, he was drunk or stoned and feeling sorry for himself, convincing himself that she was trying to trap him. The surly temperament he'd always directed at society and the Man, he now turned against her. Then one night, they got into an argument and he hit her. It was New Year's Eve. New Year's Day, she packed up and moved back in with her parents. She announced that she might be pregnant, and her mother spent the next three days weeping in bed. It was a dark time.

Then in an offhand way, her period made its appearance like a friend who's late but never apologizes. Leslie was saved from her doom, but her self confidence had been shaken to the core. Maybe, she decided, the wild free life wasn't for her after all.

She and Stuart met again a few weeks later in the restaurant where she worked. She had his table. He had a sinus infection, a very red nose, and a silly hat shaped like Rudolf the red-nosed reindeer on his head. She felt an unexpected surge of enthusiasm at the sight of him that immediately plummeted at the sight of Alison returning from the restroom. When he introduced her as the cousin who'd given him the hat, it was like the sun had come out from a cloud, but how had she missed that key piece of information?

After that, it was easy for Leslie to figure out that she actually liked Stuart, and it was a relief that her parents were excited about him. He was smart and ambitious besides the fact that he was clever and extremely charming, and though she hated to admit it, there was the fact of his physical beauty. He was a beautiful man in the way she herself had never felt "beautiful," and of course, it flattered her that he'd taken an interest in her. He showed zero interest in politics, however, and was utterly ambivalent about corporate greed, but at least he could take her out to dinner and actually pay for it.

It also didn't hurt that he was generous, well-mannered, and sufficiently interested in art though in a conventional sort of way. He liked it that she was the offbeat artist type. In fact, dating Leslie would be Stuart's first and only act of rebellion against his own upper-middle-class, country-club upbringing. On the other hand, marrying him was considered to be the first smart thing Leslie had ever done. Even so, she would forever be thought of as the impractical and unreliable artist type while he would play the logical, practical, ambitious one. They got married and moved into the Pink House on Park Street. Those had been the happiest times maybe because they were still nobodies working toward a dream.

Somewhere she'd read that success can sometimes be just as hard on a relationship as failure, and in this case, she would have to agree. Though it was tempting to blame it all on him, over the past several months having nothing but time to dwell on the past, she'd come to see the bitter truth about how she too had played a part in the disintegration of their relationship. Could either one be blamed if they'd gotten so married to their careers that they'd lost touch with each other?

Things had started going south about the time her *Mystic Horse* series really took off. She was painting night and day, making serious money for the first time in her life, and it was exciting—for a while. She was involved in a women's artist collective down in the old Beacon Hotel and, for the first time in her life, was surrounded by women she could trust, women who thought like she did. Meanwhile, Stuart had started working for Weiss Corporation, where he would be taken in a completely different direction.

Originally, Stuart was hired by Lenny Weiss to design an addition to his already stunning house in the near West End. He'd done so well that Lenny's wife, Sherry, pressed for Stuart to be brought on board with Weiss Diversified Inc. Lenny Weiss was refining the art of buying up smaller companies and then gutting them for tax write-offs and expanding his market share. He would be building factories in Asia and wanted Stuart to be on his architectural team. At first, it had seemed like a wonderful opportunity, the one they'd been waiting for, the breakthrough. As their new golden boy, Stuart had been ushered into the inner circle, but it meant longer hours and more traveling, sometimes overseas and often for weeks on end. When he was home, their lives together would become an endless merry-go-round of social events.

Stuart had always been infinitely more social than she'd ever wanted to be, and could she really fault him for being so magnetic that people just wanted to be around him? She'd always counted it a personal failing to be so introverted. Going to parties was good for his career, good for business, so she'd learned to schmooze with the rich clients, faithfully playing the part of the yuppie artist, hiding her dislike of their casual greed and wasteful ways. Greed was in. They bragged about their boats and their trips, their summer houses, their expensive breed dogs. She trained herself to sit patiently and listen, pretending to overlook the flirtatious wives with their empty lives and hungry eyes.

At first, watching him work his charisma from the sidelines, she worried that she was somehow less interesting, less attractive than the women who surrounded him at parties and in his professional world, but as the years wore on, she simply began to feel sour and used up. Maybe it was because that charisma sort of thing always plays better with strangers, or maybe it was just that he always seemed to have more to give to others than to her.

Moving into the Brandon Mills house had really marked the beginning of the end for her and Stuart. The place was huge with vaulted ceilings, glass walls, and bare polished floors that made it feel more like a museum than a home. There were five bathrooms, two living rooms, two dining areas, and intercoms in all the rooms, which on principle, Leslie refused to use. When her mother-in-law was visiting, she relished bellowing across the house that supper was ready, and if she'd had the nerve, she would have hung wet laundry in the kitchen. But perhaps the worst part about it was that no matter how much they turned up the heat, it always felt cold.

Their lives at home had become disconnected, always working and running on different schedules. Meals, if they ate together at all, were constantly interrupted by phone calls from some new client or contact wanting another piece of him. He'd taken to having cocktails with friends after work, a nightcap before bed, and drinking in between. She was an early riser. She did her best work in the morning, so she liked to get down to the studio by about seven. He, on the other hand, stayed up until 2:00 a.m. It was the pressure of the job, he said. He couldn't unwind. In the last couple of years, they had begun moving about the house like roommates leaving notes for each other.

Then there had been the arguments. For example, Stuart had started dreaming about a yacht like Lenny's and a second home in Myrtle Beach—things that Leslie had absolutely zero interest in. She wanted a nice little place in the countryside, maybe near a river or the mountains, a place she could go to paint and to hide from the social whirl. But at this point, Stuart was off in another galaxy, and neither of them was seeing anything the same way.

On top of this, she'd come to feel an almost overwhelming contempt for his friends and business connections that she could barely conceal at parties. Her obedient wife act started to unravel in a major way, and it was not a pretty sight. But though Stuart practically worshipped the man, it was Lenny that she hated the most. He was everything that, in her TimO phase, she would have found deplorable. He was rich, materialistic, and manipulative—the kind of guy who owned people like he owned things, the primary example being Sherry, his gorgeous young trophy wife with the alarmingly prominent breasts. If Stuart had changed, it was easy to blame it on Lenny's influence.

Still, she clung to the old Stuart who had loved her, the one who was true and real, the one that had stripped pink paint off the woodwork and made love to her in the garden under a full moon. When they were alone, it could still be sweet. The only trouble was they were never alone—at least never in the same place at the same time.

Nine months ago, Stuart had asked Leslie for a separation. He said they had grown apart, that he needed some time away. How does going away help us to get more connected, she'd asked, but he'd nothing to say in return. Then he'd left for Asia on business. He would be gone seven weeks, leaving her behind in a state of shock and disbelief, racking her mind for a possible explanation. Maybe she'd taken things too much for granted; maybe she'd been too absorbed in her art, too critical of him. She shouldn't have blamed him for just wanting to succeed. She could have been more supportive but, instead, had stood on the sidelines and scoffed, and now she'd driven him away.

It was odd that prior to this, he could be gone for weeks at a time, and she really wouldn't miss him. In fact, they had always prided themselves on being independent of each other, but now that he wasn't coming back, she was obsessed with him night and day. She found herself clinging to the hope that maybe when he got back, he'd have changed his mind, but he was back a week before he even called, and when he did it had not been a happy conversation. She'd broken down and wept. What had she done to make him leave? She'd begged for them to go to counseling. He'd halfheartedly agreed but then didn't show up to the appointment, leaving Leslie to sit through the session alone. The counselor had had one thing to say: get a lawyer. That was right before Thanksgiving.

It had been a dark winter and a strange, disorderly spring. By April, the temperatures had already climbed into the nineties, promising Richmond another mercilessly hot summer. On a Monday, the water main broke on their street, cutting off all water to the house. By the following Thursday, her studio had been vandalized. It'd probably been just a bunch of teenagers, but they'd thrown paint all over the walls, slashed her canvasses, and, worse, her confidence. Then Stuart dropped the bomb in the form of a letter. He wanted a divorce. The only explanation offered was that neither one of them was happy anymore.

Stuart was obviously having a midlife crisis or at least that's what everybody said. What other explanation could there be for such irrational behavior? The possibility of there being another woman had remained unspoken, but it was in their eyes. All she knew was that she had to get away from Richmond.

The day the letter came, she'd evacuated the house like a refugee fleeing a disaster, taking little more than the clothes upon her back. When word came that Edith Hay, a wealthy friend in the artist's co-op, needed a caretaker for her cottage at River's Bend, Leslie jumped at the chance. It had sat empty for the past several years, but in exchange for minor upkeep and repairs, she could live there rent free as long as she needed it. It was the answer from heaven she'd been looking for, so she packed up her books and her paints and left everything and everyone she knew behind.

Gazing at the quiet beauty all around her, she was suddenly swept by the feeling that somehow she belonged to this river, to this forest, this place. Richmond was nothing more than a gray shadow, a fog. No, she would never go back there. Maybe one of the local schools would be looking for an art teacher in the fall, but regardless, she would find a way to stay.

In her heart, she still hoped that Stuart would change his mind and come back to her. Once he climbed onto that porch and looked out at those distant mountains and the trees and sky, he would fall in love just the way she had. They could be happy here like they'd been back at the beginning in the Pink House on Park Street. This was how her mind worked when it wasn't stuck in the black hole. "Impossible fantasies, maybe," her inner voice told her, "but then again, maybe not."

She was floating lazily down the current, staring up at clouds, when a movement on the riverbank caught her eye. She thought she saw someone half hidden in the shadowy foliage, peering down at her—a man. Her heart turned cold. She sat up abruptly, pulling her knees to her chest, suddenly aware of how vulnerable she was. After a few moments, the stranger tipped his hat and withdrew silent as a shadow.

Leslie did not waste another moment before getting out and putting her clothes back on. He was probably just a fisherman and nobody to be afraid of, but even so, next time she would wear a suit, and maybe her father was right about getting that guard dog after all.

As she came up out of the woods into the yard, she thought she glimpsed a movement in the boxwoods behind the house. Thinking it was most likely her imagination, she went into the house only to be startled a few moments later by the appearance of a young black man politely tapping on the old patched screen door. He was already smiling broadly, like a salesman winding up for the pitch. "Hey! How ya doin', ma'am?" he called out with false gusto. "You must be the lady of the house!" Though he acted like they were old friends, his eyes were wary of her rather frozen reaction. "I'm your neighbor—Linwood Johnson? I live down on Clay Hill Road?" Tall and slender, he was probably midtwenties, with hair sticking out in short whimsical-looking dreadlocks, the sign of a free thinker and a rebel. He was handsome, too, with large expressive eyes and a wide dimpled grin, but the reek of stale alcohol and the dull light in his eyes tainted the natural glow of youth and lent him a subtle air of desperation.

She kept smiling. "I don't think I know that road yet."

"Yeah, well it's just about a mile and half down that way. Um, I came around to see if you needed some help—you know, moving stuff or mowing. Anything. Is that your mower?" He pointed at an old push mower stalled out in some tall grass.

"I'm afraid so."

"Hmmm." He stroked his chin thoughtfully. "That's a real antique." He hastened down the steps so as to take a professional survey of the house and change the subject. "Wow! This place is surely run-down, ma'am! In my humble opinion, it needs a lot of work. No offense but you are gonna need all the help you can get." He flashed a winsome smile, playing the charm card now for all he was worth. "You live alone here, right?" He added this almost as a casual afterthought while examining the loose hinge on the screen door. "A couple screws here and this'll be good as new."

"Listen, why don't I get your number, and if I do need help sometime, I'll give you a call," she said hurriedly. He was being too pushy and she just wanted him to leave.

He looked at her evenly as he sensed the brush off. "You got some paper?"

She hesitated. "Just a minute." She grudgingly went to her studio and grabbed the stub of a pencil and a corner of thick watercolor paper she'd used to test splotches of lavender and gray. She returned to find him inside the hall, squatting in front of the *Snake Woman* painting, where it leaned against the wall. He seemed intensely interested in it.

"That's the very first painting I ever did—a mythological character," she said, scanning the room for an object she could use to ward him off if need be.

"Yes, I know—the Medusa," he murmured. He stood up and looked around. "Are you an artist?" He'd dropped the salesman act and was being genuine now.

"I try to be. Here's your paper." She smiled cautiously. She didn't want to be unfriendly, but she really wished he wasn't standing inside her house.

Meanwhile, he was examining her with an awakened curiosity and then pressed the paper against the wall, writing his name and number with an artful flourish. Beneath it, he wrote "HANDYMAN" and then handed it back to her. "I like to draw too sometimes," he said. "Faces mostly. Sometimes, people I don't even know just appear on the paper and somebody'll come by and say, 'Hey, that's my uncle Harry!' Maybe I'll show you sometime."

"That'd be very nice," she said with a fixed smile.

His eyes had wandered to something behind her. "So you're not afraid of ghosts?"

"No," she said, though a tiny chill sprinted up her spine.

"Well, I guess that's good then." He walked back outside, turning back toward her from the yard, his eyes squinting into the sun. "Don't forget to call me now! Anytime!" She watched him walk back out the dirt lane, waving back when he waved, and thinking that tomorrow most definitely she was getting a guard dog.

CHAPTER 4

Getting a Dog

It was uncharacteristically silent at Frank Hawkins's patched gray double-wide. Not a dog in sight though the trees were peppered with Beware of Dog signs. Leslie honked her horn and waited in the car, like she'd seen country people do.

Immediately, about ten mangy dogs swarmed out through a loose flap under the trailer and surrounded her car in a terrifying din. In a few moments, Frank himself appeared at the torn screen door, buckling his belt under his prodigious belly, and then with a weary sigh, booted his way through the mongrel swarm, barking at the dogs to shut up. The pack eventually melted away to a shady spot at the edge of the woods, where they soon lost interest in the visitor and drifted back to sleep.

She got out of the car but hesitated before sticking out her hand. Did countrymen expect to shake hands with women? "Mr. Hawkins, I believe?"

"Yes, ma'am? Frank Hawkins." He regarded her with suspicion.

"My name is Leslie Hillerman and—" She stuck out her hand.

He took the end of her fingers and gave them a dainty shake. "Lady, everybody knows who you are—especially me! I deliver your mail." He paused and a teasing glint came into his eye. "You seen Henry yet?"

"Henry?"

"The ghost. You believe in ghosts, don't ya?" His eyes narrowed. "Or don't you?"

"I don't know. Do you?"

"Ma'am, all I know is what I hear, and lots of folks wouldn't touch that house with a ten-foot pole. Why you think it's been sitting there empty all these years?"

Like a mischievous school boy he seemed to enjoy making her nervous, and suddenly she wasn't about to give him the satisfaction. "That's interesting but I came to talk to you about your dogs."

His face hardened. "You got a problem?"

"Well, sort of—and since you have such a lot of them—"

"You *noticed*, huh!" His mouth set into a grim line.

"Well, they'd be kind of hard to miss!" He didn't smile at her joke, which gave her the dreadful feeling that this was a touchy subject. "Anyway, I was wondering if you wouldn't mind parting with one. You see, I'm looking for a guard dog and since you have so many—that is if you don't mind—"

"Don't mind?" His face relaxed into a broad grin like sunlight breaking through a dark cloud. "Lady, take whichever one you want. Take six or seven. Hell, you can have 'em *all* for just ninety-nine cents postage and delivery."

"Well, thanks but I only need one. Maybe one of those puppies over there?" She pointed to a tumbling heap of wiggly squirmy puppies fighting in the yard over a frayed length of rope.

"A puppy? Well, sure! You can have a puppy. Buy one and get two free! Or how's about six?"

She laughed. "Well, I think just one will do, thank you."

"Of course, a midnight intruder is not likely to be persuaded by one li'l ol' puppy, Miz Hillerman. You might consider a more seasoned animal like ol' Hooch here." He gestured grandly to a cinnamon-colored hound snoozing in the shade of a trash can. "Come on, Hooch! Introduce yourself to the pretty lady." He dragged the unwilling animal over to where she stood and let go. The dog crumpled into a heap of fur at her feet.

"Hooch don't look like much, but he's an ace watch dog! A perfect burglar alarm. He's lazy, so he'll stick around, and he's got a howl that'll wake the dead!" Frank gave the dog a nudge with his foot, and Hooch rolled over onto his back. "The only trouble with him is that he does like his belly rubs." Frank rubbed the dog's belly with his foot, and Hooch's eyes rolled back in ecstasy. "Of course, his smell alone will drive off even the worst bogeymen. Uh, I don't recommend touching him with your hands, Miz Hillerman. Just use your foot."

After such a hard sell, how could she say no? She took a puppy as well, a small white one with perky upright ears—part terrier and part rabbit, according to Frank, and smart. In fact, he was liable to teach Hooch a thing or two before he was through.

Frank hauled Hooch by the scruff of his neck over to Leslie's car, but the dog stiff-legged the prospect of going anywhere but in reverse. "Hooch, you big dummy! Her place is a whole lot nicer than this!"

"Maybe he just doesn't want to go," said Leslie. Hooch looked up with mournful eyes, trembling so severely that it seemed as though he might collapse.

"Now that's just his big act, Miz Hillerman!" Frank delivered him a boot in the backside, and Hooch lit up into the backseat with ease. "See what I mean? He's what you call an undercover private eye dog! The bogeyman comes, sees this lazy lump of fur, and thinks "Oh that ain't no thing"—but I guarantee, he makes one false move and that hound will be on him like a flash of lightning." Hooch stretched out in the backseat, his chin resting on Leslie's paint box, and let out a perfunctory sigh.

Clearly, Hooch had little patience for puppies, for by the time Leslie got home, the dogs had already engaged in their first skirmish. The puppy, rebounding all over the backseat like a hyperactive moth, had stuck his inquisitive black nose where it didn't belong, and it was bedlam all the way home. But by the time they'd pulled into the yard, the puppy had a name—Elliot.

Showing absolutely no curiosity about his new surroundings, Hooch lifted his leg at the nearest tree and plopped into a patch of mint by the chimney on the shady side of the house. Meanwhile, Elliot zigzagged across the lawn like a madman, sniffing every bush and stone, periodically rushing over to sniff Hooch as well, hoping that perhaps he'd changed his mind. Though Hooch pointedly ignored him, Elliot failed to take the hint. After lying deceptively still for a time, Hooch snatched the upstart by the scruff of the neck and shook him like an old rag doll.

For that, he got a sound beating on the top of his head with Leslie's old umbrella. Meanwhile, Elliot, in his excitement over her dangling sandal strap, sank his sharp little teeth into her big toe. With a scream of pain, she inadvertently kicked him into the mint patch, where he landed with a rubbery bounce, but he was soon chewing busily on a dandelion, undamaged. Leslie sighed. At least he wasn't hurt. Maybe he was hungry. She limped into the house, wondering what she had gotten herself into now.

CHAPTER 5

Lasagna

Pendleton Caughey was sitting morosely on his front porch in the shade of three enormous flowering chestnut trees. At present, the trees were alive with hundreds of honey bees busily mining the blossoms, whose sweet scent penetrated the darkened rooms of his house. His very thoughts were saturated with that hypnotic fragrance, casting the long afternoons into a dreamy haze. In years gone by, sitting here on the porch had always been a quiet source of pleasure, but today it could not mask the desolation he felt now that Libby was gone. It'd been three days, and not once had he gotten out of his pj's nor gone to pick up the mail. He hadn't even bothered turning on his soap, which meant he was feeling just about as low as he could possibly get. Even Peanut looked depressed.

"Hey now, don't let it get ya down, boy. She'll be back. She'll be back." Of course, deep down he knew that when she did, it would only be to collect her mother's silver.

The sound of a vehicle coming up the gravel driveway jarred him from these bleak contemplations. It was Frank Hawkins in his mail delivery car. Panicking, he rose to make his getaway but it was too late. Frank gave him a cheery *toot toot* on the horn.

"Ain't it kinda late to be sitting around in your pj's, old man?" Frank pulled into the yard beaming and then squeezed his big belly out from behind the steering wheel of his little Ford with the U.S. MAIL / FREQUENT STOPS sign attached to the roof.

For your information, I've been sick!" retorted Penny, not daring to look Frank in the face for fear he'd see the lie.

"I was wondering why you ain't picked up your mail. Here." Frank held out a bundle, his eyes glinting with mischief. "I thought maybe you all had gone away on a second honeymoon or something." It had always amused Frank to no end that Libby was young enough to be Penny's granddaughter, and he never let a chance slip by to take a poke at Penny's virility.

"No, that's next week," growled Penny. Frank Hawkins knew all right, and once he got wind of this, it'd be all over the whole county in short order. Penny needed to end this interview and quick. "Well, I gotta go throw up," he declared and headed for the door.

"Want me to call Libby and tell her to come home early?"

There was no mistaking that sly insinuation! "Don't bother," snapped Penny brusquely.

"Well, I just wanted to be sure you were still alive and kickin'," called out Frank cheerily. Getting Penny's temper up always put Frank in a good mood.

"Ain't dead yet," snarled Penny and slammed the door on that heh-heh-heh laugh of his! Sounded like a damn machine gun.

Frank drove off shaking his head. Everybody knew Libby had run off and left the ol' geezer. The library, where she worked, had been a regular soap opera since Tuesday.

Venom had unexpectedly pumped Penny full of energy, and suddenly he felt hungry for the first time in days. "Come on, Peanut. Let's see what's in the fridge." He was actually humming to himself, when he spotted the lasagna right where he'd left it the day she'd dropped the bomb.

A hard fist of pain promptly rose into his throat. *Shut the refrigerator, moron . . . ,* said the voice inside, *you're letting all the cold air out.* This was something Libby would do—stand and stare with the refrigerator door wide open. It used to drive him wild, thinking about the electric bill. He hated waste. He should eat the lasagna before it went bad, but suddenly he didn't feel like eating anymore.

Like a zombie, he closed the refrigerator and headed for the couch to lie down. Damnation, now he was gonna cry! He could feel it coming, a sharp knife rising into his throat. He clenched his eyes shut and squeezed out a few paltry tears. "Damn it all to hell! This hurts," he snarled, the wounded lion, angry now at the pain stuck inside of him. He was helpless, and if he could have, he would have ripped his heart right out of his body, but thankfully after a few false starts, the tears started to flow. He hadn't cried like this in forever. It was like a faucet. He didn't think he even had this many tears anymore. *Look at you, sitting around in your pj's, crying over a woman like a dummy!*

"Let me alone, will ya—for crissake, let me alone!" His agonized cry rang out into the silence of an empty room, but that voice inside his head was relentless. It was going to drive him over the edge.

From his place by the window, Peanut's tail did a slow swish-swash and then froze uncertainly. The grimace of pain on the old man's face softened. "Come here, boy. Come here, old friend." Peanut rose stiffly and limped over to the couch. He put his head on Penny's knee and looked up at his master with brown eyes full of devotion.

A wave of love and pain rose together in Penny's heart. Soon he would have to lose him too. What did this innocent creature know of betrayal? What had he ever done but love him like no human ever had? It was so wrong that he should have to suffer in any way. So wrong! "I hate this world, boy! I hate it!" He stroked the dog's soft furry head, and for one moment, the animal gently closed his eyes, but in the next he was on the alert. Tail taut with apprehension, a low growl rumbling in his throat, he ambled over to his sentry post at the window.

Muttering curses, Penny rose stiffly and went to the window, straining his eyes. He reached for his glasses just in time to catch a fleeting glimpse of the new neighbor lady's car beyond the screen of chestnut trees and aged boxwoods, bumping along the right of way that ran along the edge of Calvin's north field. He shook his head. "What do you wanna bet that dame busts a suspension rod before she's through?" Then an inspiration took hold in his mind.

* * *

Earlier that morning, Leslie had awakened from a dream cocooned in a warm glow—there had been a garden terrace crowded with flowers and a deep conversation with someone who knew her very well. Two words lingered like a fragrance on the air—*"love returns."* She'd lain perfectly still as the words circulated through the dark knots of pain. *Love returns* . . . Could it be the sign she'd been looking for?

She continued to lie in bed, puzzling over the dream until the reality of the day began to press upon her. The gray cloud of depression had just slid into place when she was startled by the toll of the ship's bell at the front door. She waited, hoping that whoever it was would go away, but the clanging only grew more insistent. She hastily pulled on some clothes and ran barefoot down the wooden steps to find an extremely short white-haired gentleman, his dapper mustache twitching inquisitively, peering in through the torn screen door.

"You like lasagna?" he called out in a thick New Jersey accent, holding up a casserole dish covered in tin foil. "I'm your neighbor in the white house behind the boxwoods." He seemed anxious, as if she might tell him to go away, but she opened the door and let him in. "You eat lasagna, right? It's excellent. I made it myself." Without waiting for an answer, he handed her the casserole and moved on into the living room and, like a visitor in a museum, proceeded to explore the contents of the room. It seemed he intended to stay.

"Well, thank you, Mr . . . . ?"

"Caughey—c-a-u-g-h-e-y, as in 'I like coffee, I like tea, I like the girls and the girls like me,'" he called out singsong with a burst of charm and a jaunty wink, "but the pretty girls call me Pendleton."

He suddenly zeroed in on the painting of the nudes, his eyes scouring it up close like a detective searching for clues. "I thought I heard you was some kind of painter, Miz Hillerman. So did you do this?"

"It's one of my older pieces."

He immediately announced that he was going to buy it. "Name your price!" he demanded magnanimously.

"Oh, I'm sorry, but it's not for sale."

"I don't care. There is nothing more beautiful than the human body!"

With a loud crash, a jar of flowers on the windowsill suddenly fell over, the water streaming down onto his foot. "What the hell!" He looked around perplexed. She ran off to get a towel.

"It must have been the wind," she said, hurrying in to dry off his shoe.

"Or a mouse. Mice can be amazingly strong. Nothin' I hate worse than a mouse. Nasty little creatures. Well, anyways, as I was saying—half the stuff they pass off as art these days is pure crap if you ask me! But *this*—this is art, dear lady! Of course, you've got to be careful showing stuff like that around *this* county."

"Why?"

"Baptist country."

"I take it you're not a Baptist."

"Irish Catholic to the bone, my dear. Come from a family of twelve. I was the baby."

"So how is it for you living here?"

"Some of them tried to get me in their church, and I told 'em straight to their faces, 'No way you sons of bitches gonna convert me. I'm a Catholic and if ya don't like it—tough! You can go jump in a lake for all I care.' Them SOBs never bothered me again, I can tell you that. You gotta watch them Baptists. They're the most self-righteous bunch of people I ever met. They won't even drink wine in communion. They think they're so holy. Just grape juice is what they use. Grape juice!" He winced. "I say *that* is sacrilegious because *Jesus* was a wine drinker, and what's good enough for Jesus is good enough for me. Of course, you know damn well when they get home they're packing it away like everybody else, and if there's one thing I can't stand is a hypocrite. I may be a sinner, but at least I'm honest about it, know what I mean?" He paused. "By the way, you ain't Baptist, are ya?"

She admitted to being Episcopalian though the truth was she hadn't stepped foot inside a church since the day she and Stuart had been married.

Mr. Caughey seemed to relax a little when he heard this. "Episcopalian's are okay by me. Some people say they're a bunch of stiff necks, but I know for a fact they drink like fishes—even at their retreats! I had a good friend who was Episcopalian. Owned a string of Laundromats up in Teaneck. Real successful guy. Wanted me to go into business with him. I even thought about it for a while, but the wife I had at the time says no way. She didn't like the guy for some reason. Course, she didn't like none of my friends. It took me a while but I finally got wise to her! Bossiest woman I ever met. Me and her were like two pit bulls, know what I mean? Don't ever marry somebody when you've been drinking tequila." He suddenly looked sad again.

"Would you like some iced tea?"

Penny smiled gratefully. "You bet."

Returning with a tray of iced tea and cookies, she found the little man scanning the painting of the nudes once again, his face just inches from the canvas. "You know, I only wish I brought my glasses," he said.

That night before bed, she discovered a photograph of herself and Stuart stuck between the pages of a book. It was a good one of them both, taken three summers before on the beach at Nagshead in the golden sunlight of late afternoon, his arm around her, their faces tanned and relaxed, hair blowing free on the ocean breeze. It was the image of a happily married couple. They'd had a good time during that vacation and had made love every night. Yes, she did love him still.

The old house creaked and sighed, and from the depths she heard a loud bang. She listened intently but there was only silence. Most likely it was Hooch getting into the trash again. She'd probably forgotten to put the trash can up on the counter, but she was too tired to go down and do anything about it now. She set the photograph on the bedside table, taking one last look before she turned out the light. *Love returns . . .*

She slept heavily, like she hadn't slept in months and awoke late into the next morning feeling instantly out of sorts. It wasn't her way to sleep so late, and the humid sunlight beating mercilessly through her bedroom window promised another blisteringly hot day. No doubt she was going to find the kitchen strewn with trash, she thought irritably as she headed downstairs. What a great way to start the day. But the trash can sitting was still on top of the counter, where she'd left it the night before. However, an iron skillet that hung on the wall beside the stove had fallen to the floor. As she picked it up, she noticed an inscription written on the bare wood lintel. "Built by Joseph Henry Carver, 1938."

Feeling suddenly suffocated by the gathering humidity, she took her yoga mat and went out onto the front porch. Facing west, it was protected from the morning sun and was a bit cooler. *Now this is living!* she thought. *Where you can stand on your head on the front porch in your underwear and not worry about a thing!*

However, no sooner had the thought passed through her mind than Calvin Creed suddenly came bursting around the bend on his old orange tractor. She immediately collapsed in a heap and then made a dash for the door—but too late. He'd seen her all right. She could tell by the way he kept his head discreetly averted when she came back out a few minutes later wearing clothes this time. From where he sat on his tractor, patiently idling, he shouted that he'd come to bush hog her front field and then solemnly touched the brim of his brown fedora and raised the throttle. As the tractor lurched forward, she thought to say that she hoped it wouldn't be any trouble, but her voice was swallowed by the roar of the engine, and he went on without noticing.

For a while, she watched from her rocking chair on the porch, but every time the tractor turned back in her direction, he seemed obligated to nod and touch his hat, causing her to wave and smile in turn. Finally she went back inside.

Later he tapped lightly at the screen door, a great sweating hairy Viking, battered hat in hand, eyes coldly blue. She invited him in for iced tea, which he refused but hung around on the porch as if he was in no great hurry to leave. Not wanting to be rude, she tried to start a conversation, but he answered only in monosyllables and kept looking at the field he'd just mown as if he were only halfway listening.

Finally when she couldn't think of anything else to say, she offered the iced tea a second time, and he surprised her by accepting. His eyes rose briefly to meet hers and then quickly looked away, but in that moment, she sensed a deep loneliness behind the mask of indifference he wore. Though she couldn't be sure, it seemed that now he had something he wanted to say. The conversation stalled out a few more times before he pulled a book out of the front pouch of his overalls and brusquely informed her that he'd finished it. It was the book she'd lent him just two days before.

She couldn't help but laugh as this was a rather dry book of literary essays. Later he would remember the way laughter had brought a deep shine to her brown eyes, lighting up her face like a revelation. Clearly, the corners of her mouth were made for laughing. Though he was slightly perplexed by her outburst of humor, his wall came down, if only for a moment, his eyes melting into a green-blue mist.

Now it was she who looked away, embarrassed by his intensity. "Well, did you like it or—" She feared that she'd seen too much of him.

After solemn consideration, he acknowledged that it was interesting and, for a moment, seemed as if he might have more to say but then simply left it at that. She asked if he'd like to borrow another, all the while avoiding his eyes. He nodded and followed her into the house. Meanwhile, she filled the uncomfortable silence with nervous chatter about the great built-in bookshelves and how disorganized things were with so many boxes of books yet unpacked.

Once inside, Calvin regarded the shelves gravely, running his hand over the edge of the clean varnished wood. The man who'd used to live there had built them, he told her. "He was a writer." He said this almost proudly.

"Then those boxes of books in the basement must belong to him. Do you think he'd still want them?"

Calvin shrugged. He wouldn't know. He'd lost touch with him.

She sensed something sad about this revelation. "Well—let's see what would be a good book to read—" Her eyes lit upon a dog-eared copy of *One Hundred Years of Solitude*. "Ah! Perfect! One of my absolute favorites!"

He rewarded her with a smile, his eyes warming. He'd already read it—three times. Great book, he said.

She gave him a sunny smile but could not help but feel a vague sense of alarm, for there'd been a time when she would have measured the viability of a future boyfriend according to whether he'd read this book or not. Ridiculous as that seemed, she could not help but become intensely aware of his manliness and how very tall and muscular he was, with a scent like cut wood. Against her will, she found herself blushing and, for a moment, not knowing what to say. Meanwhile, he had reached up to the top shelf, the well-formed muscles in his arms flexing as he pulled out a book.

"Oh . . . ," she said. "I haven't read that yet—but go ahead and take it. You can tell me what you think."

CHAPTER 6

Calvin

"Tell me what you think." Words so carelessly spoken played over and over in the back of Calvin's mind, both encouraging and tormenting, for any hope they may have inspired was instantly mocked by the dark conviction of his unworthiness. How could she possibly see anything in him except a crude country hick? As usual, when in the presence of an attractive woman, he'd done exactly nothing to dispel that notion. Maybe Thelma was right. He had about as much social grace as a two by four. His mother's explanation was a bit more forgiving—just that streak of shyness, the curse of his nature.

However, Calvin knew it was far more than just that. It was Annie Clay. He knew he would seem foolish to admit that a broken heart at seventeen could have left such a permanent scar, but that name had remained like a thorn in his heart all these years. He'd learned long ago to act indifferent, but it was just a shield—protection from ever being rejected again.

Still, he remained convinced that Annie Clay had been the one true love of his life. Calvin realized this idea made him hopelessly old-fashioned. People didn't believe in true love anymore, but she had seen into his soul and known him through and through, and when they'd finally made love on a magic summer evening in a field under the stars, it had been as if they were one person, bonded and pure. She was a year older than he, and before she'd gone off to college, they'd sworn to stay true, to write each other every day until he could join her the following year. Then disaster had struck. His father, always so hale and hearty, had fallen dead in his tracks, carrying in a load of firewood. In a matter of moments, Calvin's bright future was snatched from him forever.

Ruby was paralyzed with grief, and the thought of her only son leaving her alone was enough to send her into the hospital the very week before he was due to leave for college. Unspoken pressure from the family compelled him to postpone it for a year. He was praised for putting family before self. It was the noble thing to do, looking after his mother and the farm.

Not long after, Annie's family moved to the West Coast. She wouldn't be coming home to Olympia for Thanksgiving or Christmas ever again. They promised to write, to save money for him to fly up for visits. They would cling to hopes and live on dreams until they could be together again.

Then since Calvin didn't want to listen to common sense, his mother did something that, at the time, appeared to be more prudent than sneaky since this infatuation was just puppy love and nothing more. A man never marries up and she just wasn't his kind. Everybody knew it except Calvin. And all those crazy notions that that girl had put in his head of Calvin becoming a writer needed to be nipped in the bud but good. Better now than later, she'd told herself. He was just setting himself up to be hurt. Besides, though he had a partial scholarship, there was no real money to send him to college, and what would happen to the farm without him? Willow Oaks had been in her husband's family for three generations! She needed Calvin at home and that was the bottom line.

To this day, she'd never told a living soul that she'd intercepted their letters, but God forbid Calvin should ever find out what she'd done. As far as he knew, he'd written his heart out in letter after letter and never heard anything back. As far as he knew, Annie Clay had just dropped off the face of the earth without a word of explanation.

The one time Annie did call, he was so hurt and confused that he could barely speak, and she seemed distant and distracted by roommates giggling secret jokes in the background. He withdrew into monosyllables. He'd never liked talking on phones anyway. After a very impersonal conversation, they'd hung up without either one having said anything meaningful, and that had been the last he'd ever heard from her.

His mother said the girl had probably found another sweetheart and most likely just didn't want to hurt his feelings. In anguish, he'd stormed out the screen door, cats and dogs flying every which way, and never spoke of Annie Clay again. But that didn't mean he wasn't thinking about her day and night. For a year, he groped through a black depression, his confidence shattered. He would never trust a woman with his heart again. All thoughts of college or of ever being a real writer were gone, and he set about training himself not to care, not to want, not to dare.

Calvin's family had once been fairly well-to-do farmers. Now they were land rich and money poor. Last week, his oldest sister, Thelma, had started pressuring Calvin to sell off some of the wooded acreage so he could invest in a restaurant scheme with her husband, George. That section was hilly and not much good for planting anyway. If he was smart, said George, he could clear cut the trees first and then sell it off in ten-acre plots. That way he could get paid twice for the same piece.

Cal thought about it all of ten seconds before saying that he guessed he wasn't too smart then because he had zero interest in raping the forest for any amount of money.

Thelma had flown off the handle and accused him of being backward and ignorant. Or was he just plain stupid? "You know what I think, George?" she said. "I think Calvin just plain likes being poor."

With a look, George sent her back to her chair. "Now listen, Calvin," he continued calmly, "we're just trying to help you. We know you don't much care for business, but I'm telling you this restaurant deal is too sweet to pass by. Now I'm giving you a chance of a lifetime to get in on the ground floor. Why, you could see your profits quadruple within, say, five, six years. And let's face it. Nobody's makin' it as a farmer these days. What are you gonna do down the road if you don't have some investments?"

A big friendly red-faced man, George was known to be a smooth talker. Ruby always said he could have been a real good salesman, either that or a preacher. However, though he generally thought of himself as having the answer to every question, he was, unlike his wife, capable of listening to a guy disagree without jumping down his throat.

As usual, Thelma could barely restrain herself, rolling her eyes and tapping her pencil like sixty as Calvin made a foggy attempt at defending his position, which was, as usual, that the forest needed to be left wild and natural, not cut into lumber. When he was done, she blurted out that maybe he cared more about chipmunks than he did about his own mother and that she and George (once again and for the very last time) had washed their hands of trying to make Calvin a success! He was spoiled, that was all, and stubborn as that smelly old goat of his.

"What do you expect, him having a whole string of big sisters doting on them golden curls he had, remember?" mused Ruby dreamily. "What a waste of them curls on a boy. Oh, but he was cute, wasn't he, Thelma?"

Thelma cast her mother a withering look. She wasn't in the mood for fond reminiscing. "Don't blame us. You spoiled that child more than anybody, and I ought to know!" Poor Thelma had suffered the classic fate of the oldest daughter. From the time she was six years old, she'd carried the burdens of that family right alongside her mother without ever having gotten proper credit.

Meanwhile, George and Calvin were looking at each other in glum silence. This was almost an exact replay of the time they'd tried to convince Calvin to open a horse-boarding business. He hadn't been interested in that either. He didn't want to be tied down and having to please persnickety horse people, who were, in his opinion, some of the worst kind of people in the world.

Calvin didn't need to be a mind reader to know what George was thinking right about now. It always made him feel damn lucky to be single whenever he got a close up on George's life with Thelma. Though he liked his brother-in-law well enough, he could only wonder at what lapse of judgment had ever gotten him tangled up with an overbearing woman like her!

For sure, Calvin counted his lucky stars that he'd steered clear of the polished dainty white fingers of that red-headed vixen from Dixie Springs, the one he'd gone out with all of three times before she was already planning the guest list for the wedding. It hadn't been long before he'd discovered that all she cared to talk about was shopping and TV shows, and that bored him to tears, so he'd cut it off quick. Then she'd come storming over, crying and sobbing and throwing herself around all full of accusation and blame, like he owed her something. When she saw it wasn't having any effect, she'd turned to sweetness and light, acting like a seductress in a bad movie.

Over the years, Thelma had tried and tried to match him up with one woman or another, all to no avail. Renovating her brother's life was her eternal mission in life. In her mind, the bottom line was that every man needed a woman simply to be civilized, George being her prime example. Why, if Thelma hadn't gotten her hands on him, no doubt he'd still be a dry-wall finisher, drinking beer at the Dew Drop Inn, but now look at him—an independent contractor.

Of course, since Calvin was a 100 percent stubborn mule ingrate, there wasn't much she could expect. No matter how many perfectly good girls she'd introduced to him, he insisted on acting bored and stupid as a plank, driving off every last one of them. She still couldn't quite forgive the way he'd treated the last one, that lovely soprano from the Bethel Church choir. He said she'd talked too much! Why, what else could the poor soul do with a man who never said a word? So what if she was a teensy bit overweight! At least she had personality, which was more than she could say for him! But as usual, he'd muffed his chances, and Thelma just had to wash her hands of him *completely*—again.

This was the year of the twentieth Olympia High School reunion, and beneath his stoic reserve, the apprehension was stirring his old wound. Thelma had been hounding him to go, go, go, and as many times as he'd thrown the invitation in the trash, she'd fished it out and stuck it back up on the refrigerator.

He had lots of reasons, all equally painful. Why go and be compared to all the successful classmates, who'd had the sense to move out of Olympia and make a life for themselves? As long as he kept to himself on the farm, he was content and knew well and good not to disturb that. Over the last two decades, his days had settled into a calm sameness, and he'd actually learned to enjoy physical labor. He'd never be the workhorse his father had been, but he didn't mind the farmwork now. Being out of doors in the solitude of nature actually suited his nature. It gave him space to think, and though at first he'd rashly vowed never to write again, it hadn't been long before characters and stories started forming in his imagination, and the words once again started to flow.

He wrote at night out in the old workshop. At one time, it had been his father's woodshop, and indeed, all these many years it was still referred to as Daddy's workshop. Aside from having painted it fire-engine red, a highly controversial topic still bemoaned by his mother and sister, the workshop had remained, in part, undisturbed in that all his father's tools, his white work coat, even his hat, still hung in their customary places. However, it was Calvin's sanctuary now. Relics of nature, feathers, and bones, and unusual sticks hung from the rafters without any pretense of order. Yet the overall effect was one of a harmonious and, indeed, artistic clutter. The workbench had been converted to a desk, where he kept an old Remington manual typewriter amid stacks of books in various degrees of disarray. Calvin had never made it to college, but that hadn't stopped him from getting an education. In his reading chair, a rust-colored recliner salvaged from Thelma's house, Calvin had read everything one would find in a college curriculum, from the classics to the twentieth century, foraging widely into history and philosophy as well.

There was a small potbellied woodstove for heat, and here he would hole up to write late into the night. He never showed anyone his stuff, but the shelves were stacked with manuscripts all in stages of incompletion. Every now and then, his mother would urge him to send something off to a publisher, but he'd always snap back that he wasn't ready yet. Inside, he suspected that he probably never would be. As much as he craved having a reader, like any writer, he feared it too. His father had bullied him into secrecy long ago, and that had made it deeply necessary for Calvin to disguise those parts that felt so intensely, that wept for beauty, that questioned things others took for granted. He wouldn't dare expose his dreams to the cynical eyes of the world at this late stage. To open himself to judgment and criticism would be too painful.

Annie had believed in him though, long ago. In her eyes, he was going to be a great novelist, and she would be a painter, and they would live in the country and create. That was her dream, and he'd borrowed it for a while, but he knew now that it was a dangerous dream. Better not to hope so high. Life had taught him that much. The outer world was a race to the finish line, and he was too far behind to ever catch up now. Better to remove himself, better to submit to his fate, to lay down in the tracks of his ancestors. He was a solitary farmer with a secret foolish dream and nothing more.

But there was a problem facing him now. Something about Leslie reminded him of Annie in a deeply disturbing way. Like Annie, she was a painter but it was more than that. There was something about the light in her eyes, the way she looked into him, not at him . . . like she really wanted to see *him*. He'd learned a long time ago that people didn't look at each other that way in Olympia. What they saw was just a seeming. They didn't bother to look past what they'd already decided they were *going* to see. He called it being pig brained, and those sorts of people wouldn't recognize the beauty of a piece of poetry if it bit them in the rear end. Without meaning to, they'd stomp your soul to pieces and never even notice. That's why he kept to himself. It was for protection from an ignorant and brutal world, but now his instincts were telling him that she was different, she *could* be trusted—to see.

He hadn't met another woman, who inspired this kind of feeling since Annie Clay, and he'd started pining like a sixteen-year-old kid and thinking dangerous thoughts, like how he could make her see him for who he really was and the most terrifying notion of all—what would happen if he let her read his novel?

The mere thought of this filled him with a sickening dread deep in the pit of his gut, but that didn't stop this crazy notion of him creeping over before dawn, laying it on her porch, and then beating a hasty retreat before she had a chance to know any different. There'd have to be a note, of course, saying something simple like *"Here is a little something I wrote. CT Creed."* Of course it wasn't little, so he went back and scratched out the word "little" and then added *"PS: if you don't want to read it, that's okay."*

Depending on what hour he was in, the idea either sounded pretty good or completely mad, but every time he tried to give it up, he'd wind up thinking about all the times he'd let his chances slip through his fingers. For all he knew, this could be the last one, and no matter how crazy it was, something told him he just had to do it. He had to take a chance, and if he failed, well, then he failed; and if she thought he was a fool, well, then she thought he was a fool. Of course, he really couldn't argue that one. He probably was a fool but this time he had to try. So he went into Richmond to find a print shop, changing his mind at least a dozen times on his way into town.

The manuscript sat around in a manila envelope for an entire week, concealed beneath a stack of magazines so he wouldn't have to keep looking at it and be reminded of what he would rather avoid. Nonetheless, he found himself circling that envelope all week. Finally, out of sheer disgust with himself, he surrendered. Come hell or high water, at dawn he was going to walk, not drive (the truck would make too much noise), over to Leslie Hillerman's house and leave it on her front porch. If luck was with him, she'd be fast asleep. He visualized his plan of action over and over again until he felt satisfied he could pull it off without a hitch. The only thing he hadn't planned on, however, was Gulliver.

After he set the envelope on Leslie's porch, he turned around, and there in the gray light of early dawn was the plump little goat under the clothesline, chewing complacently on a pink slip. Muttering vile threats,

Cal meandered casually in Gulliver's direction. He knew better than to make a direct charge. That would only cause the bold creature to dart maddeningly out of reach. Damn his curly hide! It was moments like these he thought about selling him to the old Greek down the road. At least he'd get a few bucks for him.

When Calvin got within a few yards, he stopped, pulled out a piece of chewing gum, and slowly unwrapped it. As expected, it wasn't long before Gulliver's inquisitive little face appeared at his elbow. Cal bided his time. If he made his move too soon and missed, it would all be over. Cal waved the gum in the air, Gulliver's bright little slit eyes following it up and down, bleating a loud protest. Cal winced. If she wasn't awake now, it would be a miracle! He took a swipe at the shirt and the tug of war began.

Meanwhile, the lady painter appeared on the porch, looking groggy and confused, her long auburn hair a profusion of disarray. She yawned and rubbed one eye. "So this is the goat, huh!"

Gulliver bleated politely and would have looked sweetly innocent were it not for the pink slip dangling from his jaws. With a burst of resentment, Calvin yanked it loose, ripping off a long strip of lace in the process and, with sheepish apologies, handed it over to Leslie. Hell, he'd let the Greek have him for nothing! Casting his eyes humbly down gave him a clear view of her bare feet peeking out from beneath the pink blanket she was wrapped in. They were sturdy sun-browned feet with straight even toes—practical feet, like her hands.

She smiled in the midst of another monumental yawn with assurances that no harm had been done. Meanwhile, Gulliver had clattered up to the yellow rocking chair and started to nibble on the corner of the manila envelope. "What's that?" Her eyes lit with interest.

"Oh no, you don't!" Grabbing the envelope, Calvin delivered Gulliver a hard kick in the ribs and sent him clattering down the steps into the mint patch, where he stood, bawling reproachfully.

Leslie cringed. "Oh, dear, is he all right?"

"Don't worry, that's just his little act. He likes to play the victim when he knows he's in trouble, but we'll see how smart he is when he *winds up Sunday dinner at the Greek's!*" The stout little goat broke off a sprig of mint as if he couldn't care less.

Leslie erupted with hoots of laughter, which surprised Calvin as he hadn't intended to be humorous. She had a comfortable earthy laugh. "So is this for me? It's heavy!"

His heart immediately turned to stone as she took the manuscript from his hands. The moment of truth had come. He wondered if it would look strange if he just turned around and walked away, but she broke into a broad grin. "It's a book, isn't it! And you want me to read it!" At least, she seemed pleased, though he reminded himself it could have been faked out of politeness.

Suddenly and not a moment too soon, Hooch came skidding down the hall with a blood-curdling howl. The smell of goat had finally penetrated his dreams. Hands on hips, Leslie gave him an arch look. "Just a little late, aren't we? O trusty watch dog!"

CHAPTER 7

Hooch Gets the Boot

Later, as she was preparing for bed, Leslie nestled close to Elliot's small furry body. Calvin's manuscript with the chewed corner lay on her side table, but she was too tired to read it now. It would have to wait until tomorrow. She thought about this inscrutable Calvin Creed character, hiding behind that furious-looking beard of his. Why had he chosen her of all people to read his manuscript? She hoped it wasn't too terribly bad. It would be so awkward to have to pretend.

Somehow, without there ever having been a clear decision on the subject, it just came to be that Elliot slept curled on the pillow opposite Leslie's head. She knew this was probably a mistake but if she tried to put him anywhere else, he cried the whole night through. If she hadn't fallen foolishly in love with the little beast, she would have to say that getting this puppy was among the worst mistakes of her life. At night, he ruined her sleep, and by day, he was driving her out of her mind. That day alone, he'd yanked a lamp off a table by the electric cord, left the *Sunday Times* in shreds, and tried to bury one of her shoes in the flower bed.

As for Hooch, the original plan had been that he would be an outdoor dog, but with thunderstorms threatening almost every night, he had frantically clawed his way right through the screens. (Later he would learn the subtler art of wedging his nose into the crack and nudging it open). She didn't dare shut the inner door, for the night breezes cooled the house, and thus, he was free to come go at will. The compromise solution was a bed made out of old blankets in the studio with the firm understanding that he was not to get onto the furniture or to come upstairs at any time. These were the two absolutes that Leslie was determined not to concede since a bath had done nothing to improve his smell. Aside from insisting on eating both his and Elliot's food simultaneously, he was far too lazy to bother getting into things. At least during the day, he preferred to remain inert, rotating between patches of sunlight and the shade of the mint patch, poking his head out of the greenery like a sphinx. It was in the dark of night when he roamed the house, perusing the trash according to his whim, (she now had to set the can on top of the counter) and, lately, leaving suspicious dents on the couch along with a lingering odor.

Early the next morning, Leslie was dragged against her will up through layers of sleep by a noxious odor and an unrelenting squeak. It was Elliot wrestling with that squeaky plastic mouse that had sounded so cute in the store. Deciding that it was not so cute anymore, she'd wrenched it from his mouth and dashed it vengefully to the floor. Elliot immediately took a nose dive right along with it, his little tail whirling with delight. After a thud, followed by a terrible silence, the squeak of the rubber mouse resumed from below. Sleep mumbled another invitation, and she'd closed her eyes to drift once more—but what *was* that horrible smell?

In the next instant, the answer came in the form of an angry outburst from below. Apparently Hooch had sneaked up under her bed and didn't like the plastic mouse any better than she did. With a shriek, Leslie bolted out of bed, raining blows down on his thick scull before he murdered Elliot. Tail between his legs, Hooch beat a hasty retreat down the steps only to be discovered a few minutes later snoozing on the couch. If he'd had the sense to be repentant, he may have saved himself but, instead, acted nonchalant as she drove him off the couch and out into the mint patch. In a fit of fury, she ordered him into the car and promptly drove him over to Frank's place. It was officially time for a divorce. In the rearview mirror, she could see him skulking in the back seat, ears flattened, disgraced, forlorn, and humiliated.

As she pulled into the dog-infested yard, Frank was just getting back from his mail route. Without a word, she opened the back door of her car. He took one look at Hooch and shook his head. "Let me guess. The honeymoon is over."

Leslie recited the list: sneaking onto the furniture, ruining the screen door, hogging the food, and vicious attacks on the puppy, not to mention that he rolled around in manure every time he was bathed.

Frank gave her a look. "That's just instinct, Miz Hillerman! To hide his scent! Besides you don't want the other dogs to think he's a sissy, do ya?"

Leslie arched an eyebrow. She was not about to change her mind. "I think Hooch will be better off someplace else, Mr. Hawkins."

Frank Hawkins frowned. If he wasn't careful, that "someplace else" was bound to be his. Allowing that maybe she didn't know what an ace tracking dog she had in Hooch, he made her an offer, an even trade—three of his dogs for Hooch. "Now which ones do you want?" When she held steadfast, he poked out his lower lip and put on his saddest face. "Now come on, Miz Hillerman. Let's be fair."

"No, I've really got my hands full with the puppy," she said, but the truth was she'd just found out that her mother's best friend had a year-old yellow lab with papers that she was willing to give Leslie for free.

He heaved a dramatic sigh of resignation. "Well, no harm in trying. Say good-bye to Miz Hillerman, Hooch." Hooch waved his tail uncertainly. Somehow she couldn't help but think that he looked defeated. Leslie felt an unexpected twinge of sympathy, which she quickly quelled. Dogs did not feel defeated, she told herself.

As she pulled out of the yard, Frank made one last attempt with that sly persuasive grin of his. "You sure that little rabbit dog of yours is gonna be enough protection for ya now?"

"I'm sure."

"You're sure you're sure now! I mean, really sure!"

"I'm really, *really* sure."

Though she told herself not to, she glanced back to see Hooch sitting stoically beside Frank, his large pink tongue hanging out, his lips drawn up into a smile; however, she couldn't help but feel it was a forced smile. All the way to the grocery store she was haunted by visions of those big brown eyes. She'd never really noticed how sweet and trusting they were.

On the edge of town was a strip mall consisting of a grocery, a pharmacy, and a pizza place—flat roofed and boxy soulless structures, the kind that look worn-out after only a few years. Here in the sprawling gravel parking lot, old farmers lonely for company would sit in their cars to watch the people come and go; and in the far corner a gang of youths collected, leaning against their cars, waiting to hook up with some excitement. She kept her eyes averted as she passed them on her way in. She was feeling introverted at the moment and wanted to get this over with fast. Everyone seemed to know everyone around here, and she felt self-conscious and out of place. On the way out, one of them separated himself from the group and fell in step with her as she headed across the parking lot with two sacks of groceries and a gallon of milk.

"You want me to carry that for ya?" It was the young black man, who'd showed up at her door that day wanting to mow her lawn.

Her heart filled with dread. At the moment, she wasn't in the mood to fend off any propositions. "That's okay, I've got it."

"You sure? Looks kind of unwieldy." Without waiting for a response, he took both sacks of groceries out of her arms. "You can carry the milk," he said, heading for her car.

"Thanks," she said when he set them in the backseat. "Um, I'm sorry. I've forgotten your name!"

"Linwood Johnson."

"That's right. Linwood."

"You never called me."

"Oh, well—"

"If you'd have called me, you'd know my name better. But that's okay. I forgive you." He gave her a severe look. "So I bet you lost the paper with my number, didn't you!"

"No! I still have it."

"You sure now?"

"I'm sure."

"Don't forget me now." He sauntered away, cocky and confident, as he rejoined the group of guys, some white but mostly black, in baggy pants riding low over their hips. They were smoking cigarettes and looking tough for the young girls parading for their attention in tight revealing clothing. Linwood slapped hands with a tall beefy guy with long red hair wearing a head scarf like a biker pirate and then with a sleek-looking black with braided hair, wearing sunglasses and dressed all in white. She drove away perplexed. He seemed nice enough but something about him made her uneasy.

Returning home, there was an unexpected stab of pain at the sight of the empty mint patch by the chimney. The house seemed lonely and vacant, and she found herself wandering from room to room, unable to concentrate on anything. Even Elliot seemed strangely subdued and sat steadfastly at the screen door as if waiting for someone to squeeze through the hole.

Later, after a half-hearted attempt at painting, she ate a light meal and headed up the steep wooden steps to her bedroom under the sloping eaves. She wrote a short poem about loss, gave Elliot a pat on the head, and then turned out the light.

Invariably, the moment it was dark, the old house would start to talk, exuding creaks and sighs like a weary old woman settling in for the night. This was the danger zone, when Leslie's mind would start to roam. For months, her thoughts had been locked in a dark tunnel, fixated on Stuart, causing many sleepless nights; but this night, against her will, she found herself wondering about the ghost.

Suddenly, with a paralyzing chill, she heard a low screech as the front screen door slowly opened and then banged shut. That was no mouse. Her ears strained to penetrate the silence over the loud thumping of her heart, and then out of the stillness came the rhythmic *click, click, click* of claws on the bare wooden steps. Relief flooded her entire being. This was no ghost either—just Hooch.

Entering the room, he immediately proceeded to scratch himself thoroughly, his rear leg banging reflexively on the floor and then yawning noisily, settled in beneath her bed with a contented sigh. Leslie smiled. "Good night, Hooch." There was the slow sleepy thud of his tail against the leg of the bed and then silence.

Sunday morning, the one morning of the week that Frank did not have to haul himself out of bed to deliver mail, the one morning of sweet refuge from the world, the phone had to ring. "Hello!" he barked, squinting mightily at the clock and hoping it didn't say what he thought it did, namely 6:00 a.m.

"It's me." It was Clarice.

"Sweet Jesus, woman! What happened? You win the lottery?"

"It's kind of urgent. I was out walking last night and I found this poor dog—"

"Lord a' mercy, woman!"

"And she looks like she hasn't eaten in weeks. She's so skinny you can see her ribs, Frank."

When had he heard that one before! "Well, take her to the animal shelter, Clarice. That is what it's for."

"So they can put her to sleep?"

"How do you know some little kid ain't gonna come and take her home and make her a pet?"

"Nobody is going to take *this* dog home. She looks like she's been through the holocaust. Besides, I think she has a litter of puppies somewhere."

"Oh no . . . I can see it coming . . . and the answer is no. No. No, and on second thought, no!"

"But Frank—"

"And in case you didn't hear—no."

"Well, I can't keep her here, Frank! You know there's no animals allowed in my building!"

"Then why in God's name did you move there in the first place, woman?"

"Would you please stop calling me 'woman.' It's demeaning!"

"Demeaning? But that's what you are, Clarice! A woman who left her husband with a million cats and dogs, and now she wants him to take on even more!"

"I took this place because it was the only one I could afford!" Her voice sounded unnatural when she yelled.

"Well, guess what—that is not my problem. We're getting divorced, remember?"

"Frank, this is a poor defenseless animal that we're talking about."

"I know all about them poor defenseless animals, Clarice—seeing as I've got about fifty of them eating me out of a house and home." He took a swipe at a gray striped kitten attempting to scale the lampshade.

"That's not fair, Frank. I'm paying for all their food."

"Yeah, well how about paying for the babysitter? I charge fifty bucks an hour."

"Frank, I promise this is the last time I ever ask you to do me a favor again!"

"No, Clarice, and don't ask again!" He hung up, basking in the rush of pleasure it gave him, however fleeting. Then his mind slipped back into its familiar gloom. Up until now, he had been so angry with Clarice that he'd been able to forget how much he missed her, but the sound of her voice had shaken something loose. He stuffed it back in quickly before anything drastic happened, like tears. No, it was his anger that kept him going. Without that, he'd be laying around in his pj's like Pendleton Caughey.

The phone rang four more times while he was showering and making breakfast, but he didn't dare answer it. He'd never been able to say no to that woman for long. Sooner or later, she'd talk him into it, and he wanted it to be later.

CHAPTER 8

Pages on the Water

Fairly quickly, Leslie's days had fallen into a quiet routine. In the morning there was yoga and exercise and then cleaning up around the house and some work in the gardens. Each afternoon, she'd make herself sit in front of her easel, but after one look at the dismal gray face in the self-portrait, she invariably decided to head for the river instead. As a sort of guilty compromise, she always carried along her paints and brushes. The show at the Klausen Street Gallery was coming up in the fall, and she needed to get something going, but once she got down there, time would start to slip away and there she was—just a body without purpose, floating in the merciful river, soaking up the life of the sun.

Today, as usual, nothing had gotten done. Instead of painting, she'd lain on the sandbar and attempted to read Calvin's manuscript, but a conversation she'd had on the phone that morning with her mother kept interrupting her concentration.

Emily was worried. She'd accused Leslie of living in a fantasy world if she thought she was going to be able to survive out in the country, living only off of her art. Leslie had turned a deaf ear. Not that this didn't worry her too, for she had always depended on Stuart to bring in the real money. Her art had never been more than the equivalent of a part-time job at best. Certainly, it had never brought in enough to live on. Still, the thought of putting it all aside and going out to get a full-time job somewhere was suffocating.

"Teach. Get a job in a school teaching art. You've done it before!"

"That was an after-school program, Mother. I'm not even certified. No one will hire me. Do you realize how many certified art teachers there are running around, dying to get hired?"

"Well, what are you going to do?" Emily was also convinced that it was a huge mistake for her daughter to give up the house in Brandon Mills. "At least, you would have a decent roof over your head!"

"That's Stuart's house, Mother. His parents gave it to *him*, not me."

"And he left *you*, remember? You have a right to that house! Besides, I cannot believe that Stuart would leave you out in the cold. He knows you're not capable of taking care of yourself!"

"Mother! I can take care of myself just fine, thank you!"

"Living in that squalid shack?"

"It is not a shack," cried Leslie, rearing back angrily. "It's historical!"

"It's a relic! Oh, Leslie, what am I going to do with you?" Leslie could just see her mother throwing her hands in the air.

"Nothing. You can't *do* anything with me, Mother! I'm an adult, remember?"

"I just wish you'd start acting like one. Women have to look out for themselves in divorce situations. Look at my friend Mindy Evans and," she added, tolling the bells of doom, "remember your aunt Faye!" This was family shorthand for disaster.

"What you think, you become, Mother! It says it right in the Bible! So if you keep looking for the worst possible thing to happen, then you're going to make it happen!" This was usually where their arguments ended up, but no amount of Biblical references would convince Emily that she wasn't just being realistic.

However, the real poison pill wasn't delivered until the very end of the conversation. "So," her mother had asked, "have you seen *her*?"

Though Leslie knew it had been whispered about, so far Stuart had said nothing about there being another woman, but now even her mother thought that that was what was happening. From the moment her mother had given it voice, a black hole had opened up inside of Leslie's chest, a whirling vortex of chaos and disaster. In a desperate attempt to grab the reins on her emotions, she had to ask herself what it was that was really bothering her. Deep down she could see that yes, it was loss, and all the old standards: fear, abandonment, guilt, and rage, but to her surprise, beneath it all, she had discovered the sting of failure.

It had always been a point of pride for her mother that no one on her side of the family had ever divorced, and Leslie had grown up assuming she would follow in her parents' footsteps and have a good solid marriage. Not that there weren't plenty of skeletons in her father's family, but Leslie was not to take after "that" side. The very worst threat her mother could ever make was that Leslie was acting "just like Aunt Faye," her father's renegade sister, the would-be artist run amok with three husbands and a string of uncontrollable brats, the scourge of every family gathering. For Faye, life was one big party and she was the star attraction. Among her many flaws were smoking, drinking, and swearing, though it was probably Faye's fashion sense that was, more than anything, her most unforgivable transgression, for Faye was famously and divinely gaudy in every respect and not afraid of rhinestones either.

Secretly, however, it had always pleased Leslie to be compared to her aunt. She liked to think that she could be an artist and a rebel though she had always failed through lack of courage to be truly flamboyant. Dampened by an equal and opposite need to please her parents, she'd settled on being rumpled and chronically late.

For most of her life, being an artist was completely out of the question—at least as far as her mother was concerned. She'd sent Leslie to the Episcopal girls' school, cultivating her for a strategic marriage. Meanwhile, Aunt Faye was quietly subverting these plans by giving her niece art sets for Christmas and, when she was older, taking her to galleries and showing her off to her cast of eccentric bohemian friends. It was Leslie's first taste of that forbidden world, and after that, the tame orderliness of her parents' lives could only suffer in comparison. Artists and eccentrics were passionate and authentic, daring to walk on the edge of life, living the way they wanted to, unhindered by petty rules. Her parents were just drones for a conformist mass society.

As the years wore on, however, Aunt Faye's glamour had worn thin. No amount of makeup could disguise the baggy eyes and harsh lines around her mouth, and with a voice like rusty nails, even her laughter sounded sad. She was the last to realize the party was over.

Since Leslie had chosen to move to the country, her mother's favorite subject seemed to be Faye's miserable poverty and how she'd been reduced to having to live off her children, going from house to house like a vagabond, a burden to everyone. The image had stuck in Leslie's mental eye like a small thorn. Faye had "fiddled her life away" in Emily's words, and now she was paying the price.

Though outwardly Leslie stubbornly fended off her mother's sly insinuations, on the inside she, too, was filled with doubt. Was she going to end up like Aunt Faye, penniless and alone? The thought made her squirm. She forced her eyes open and was determined to look at the clouds, the river, the trees—anything but the chaos inside.

Suddenly from the corner of her eye, there was a fluttering movement, like a covey of white birds taking flight; however, these were no birds but the pages of Calvin's manuscript being wafted on the wind far and wide across the river, swiftly flowing downstream.

She made her way dispiritedly back from the river, carrying the soggy remains of Calvin's manuscript and dreading the thought that this could be his only copy! Was this, she wondered, worse or better than obsessing about Stuart?

She was so deep into her thoughts, however, that she didn't notice she had taken the wrong path; for suddenly she found herself at the top of a hill in what appeared to be a small cemetery with five crumbling headstones covered in lichen and all but overcome by vines. The letters had been worn smooth by time, but she could still make out the names: James Earlie Harris, 1903 and Mary Emmalyn Harris, 1915. There was no birth date, just the day of death. Alongside were three smaller markers for young children, all of whom had died within a week of each other, the youngest being but three months old. A wave of sadness swept through her as she tried to imagine the terrible grief laid into that ground so long ago.

Further down the overgrown path were the remains of a small wooden house, where this family must have once lived, though it seemed impossible that anyone could have ever lived in such a tiny and remote place. The house had but two rooms with a small porch, the roof of which had caved in on one side. The front door now hung lopsided on its hinges, revealing a darkened musty interior filled with dead leaves and broken tree branches. A bare wooden table and two broken chairs and a rusted iron bed frame were all that remained of the furniture. Beer cans, empty packs of cigarettes, and old shotgun shells littered the floor as well as a recent edition of *Time* magazine, featuring Ronald Reagan and Gorbachev shaking hands. A shovel leaned against the wall in one corner. Someone had been here not too long ago, and this made her feel strangely uneasy. The wind sighed through the trees, causing a tree branch to scrape against the dirty windowpane.

She stepped outside and was startled to see a small wiry man wearing a brown fedora standing among the trees about thirty yards off. She hesitated and then waved, and he nodded and tipped his hat. She wanted to explain that she was lost and hadn't meant to trespass, but when she called out he just strolled away as if he hadn't heard, whistling a melancholy tune, his hands tucked comfortably into his pockets. She tried to catch up with him but he quickly disappeared from sight. All she found instead was an old lawn chair sitting at the edge of the bluff and, through the trees, a clear view of River's Bend far below.

Well, well, well . . . , she thought to herself in wonder. At least she knew how to get back home even if it was straight down and through the briars.

Arriving at the house scratched and sweaty, she was stunned to find the front door standing wide open. Frantically, she searched her memory. Could she possibly have left it like that? It was such a peaceful scene—the sun shining, the birds twittering in the trees—but a quiet insinuation of danger made her blood run cold.

Suddenly the stillness was jolted by a loud bang from upstairs, followed by another, repeating again and again. The dogs instantly charged up the steps in a wild outburst of indignation. She hesitated and then slowly followed, not sure she even wanted to know what was up there.

From the top of the steps, she could see that the door of the guest room stood ajar, revealing only the sloping ceiling and a corner of the bed beyond. Whatever it was, it was in that room. Growling low in their throats, the dogs paced anxiously between her and the door while the horrible banging persisted with an almost demonic intensity. Summoning all of her courage, she gave the door a nudge with her foot, and it slowly creaked open. There, to her relief and dismay, stood Gulliver, Calvin Creed's miniature goat, butting his own reflection in the full-length mirror!

With terrible bleats and howls, goat and dogs came trampling back down the steps in disarray, Gulliver bolting out the front screen door with the dogs nipping at his heels. They chased him around the yard a few times until he found a distance they would tolerate, and that is where he stayed, munching complacently without a single sign of remorse. Apparently, Hooch was not the only animal who knew how to get into this house.

The dogs eventually grew bored and retired to the shade for a nap. She tried to shoo him off, but Gulliver was only interested in doing the exact opposite of what she wanted him to do. Chasing him proved to be utterly futile as he would only coyly bide his time than skip maddeningly out of reach the moment she came near. However, when she tried ignoring him, he boldly began munching on the daylilies, and that was enough of that! Leslie grabbed a carrot. It was time for a little goat psychology.

No one was around when Leslie walked into the Creed's side yard with Gulliver trotting close behind, staring fixedly at the carrot poking out from beneath her arm. Except for a flock of chickens calmly pecking at the grass, the place was deserted. Country music blaring from a cluster of small out buildings drew her to the one painted fire-engine red. The door was open. She stuck her head inside. No one was there, but she recognized Calvin's old brown fedora flung carelessly on a box of odd pieces of lumber. From the rafters and on the shelves that lined the walls was a collection of very old-looking tools, but this was obviously more than a toolshed.

Under a dusty windowsill adorned with an arrangement of feathers, stones, and a small set of antlers was a workbench where an old-fashioned Remington typewriter sat beside stacks of typewritten pages. The walls were lined with shelves filled with books of all kinds—philosophy, history, poetry, and classic literature—but what drew her eye were the small hand-carved wooden animals perched here and there. She reached for the figure of a sleeping dog, its tail tucked over its nose and the small framed black-and-white photograph beside it. It was an older man in a striped suit and a fedora hat, his hand resting on the shoulder of a blond-haired boy. They both had the same square cut chin and the same sheepish grin. At their feet was a dog identical to the carving she held in her hand.

Suddenly Gulliver clattered in and leaped nimbly into an old rust-colored recliner in the corner. Next to it was a small side table piled high with more books. He nestled in like he owned the place, and in a matter of moments, a small black terrier scampered in and hopped up beside him. Suddenly there was Calvin in the doorway, stopped dead in his tracks, bare chested and muscular and glistening with sweat, his shirt rolled up and slung over one shoulder. His eyes traveled immediately to the sleeping wooden dog in her hand.

Her cheeks flushed bright pink. She felt like a thief caught in the act. "Nobody was around and I heard the, um, radio so I—" She held up the wooden dog. "Did you—"

He cast a sidelong glance at the photograph of the man and boy. "My grandfather carved it." He modestly turned his back before slipping on his faded T-shirt.

"Oh!" *Could this be Henry*, she wondered, *the man who'd died at the foot of the stairs?* She leaned in to take a closer look and, with a little shock, realized that he looked very much like the whistling man she'd encountered in the woods.

They both wound up staring at the photo for an inordinately long time, as neither one could think of what to say next. At the moment, all she could think about was that she may have just seen a ghost, but she wasn't about to admit it. Instead, she gestured at the general clutter, "So I suppose this is where you do your writing."

He walked over and switched off the radio, standing, she noticed, directly between her and the typewriter as if to shield her from seeing anything. Because she hadn't mentioned his manuscript, he could only conclude that she hated it and was too polite to say so. When he turned back around, his eyes were an icy blue, peering from out of the furious tangle of hair and beard with all the wariness of a wild creature hiding in the underbrush. "It's just scribbling."

Suddenly it became clear that he did not want her here. "Well, I'm sorry to interrupt," she said hurriedly. "I was just returning your goat. You're not gonna believe this, but I found him upstairs in my spare room, butting his reflection in the mirror!" She tried to laugh it off, but apparently, Calvin did not see the humor of it, for his face only grew dark.

"Gulliver!" There was no mistaking the man's tone, and the goat instantly made a beeline for the door. Growling his displeasure, Calvin lit after him with a vengeance, the little black dog on his heels, yapping excitedly.

Outside, in her shrill crow's voice, Ruby was already sounding the alarm. "Calvin! Get that goat before he eats my pansies!" Leslie found the old woman sitting in her rocker on the back porch, looking like a shriveled, indignant bird. Why, if Calvin's daddy was still alive, he would never have put up with such shenanigans! Animals were animals and stayed in the pasture, not in the doggone living room!

Presently, Calvin appeared from around the side of the house, his hand under the goat's collar, yanking him roughly toward his pen. The goat bleated pitiably but Calvin's face was set in stone.

Ruby's bitter diatribe continued. Not only had the goat poked his head into her kitchen but when she'd gone to sweep him out, he'd also tried to eat the broom! And when was Calvin going to get those baby chicks off her side porch? Her house was not a barn or a zoo either! By now, Calvin was loping back across the yard in his long-legged way, his shoulders hunkered down, dark clouds filtering across his brow. Leslie noticed the book she'd loaned him peeking out of the front pocket of his overalls.

"Whoever heard of such! Goats getting into the neighbor's house," cried the old woman when she'd heard Leslie's story. "He was looking for Sonny, that's what. *He* was the one taught Gulliver all them sorry tricks!"

Calvin gave Leslie a baleful look. "She never liked Sonny because he had a ponytail."

Ruby looked smug. In her estimation, Sonny had been a worthless old hippy, but just to spite her, Calvin had insisted on being his friend.

"He happened to be more intelligent than everybody in this county put together!" he muttered as a side note.

"Just because somebody reads a lot of books don't mean he's intelligent!" Ruby went on in scandalous undertones to add that nobody ever could figure out how the man had made his living because he never seemed to have a job.

"He was writing a book, Ma," groaned Calvin, rolling his eyes. Clearly, this was a long-standing argument between them.

"And nobody ever saw the first word of that book now, did they! *And* you should have seen his clothes! He looked worse than Calvin!"

"He wanted to live a simple life. He got his clothes from the thrift store and grew his own food from his garden. Is that such a crime?" countered Calvin, his exasperation rising.

"But dealing drugs is! Oh! What he put his mother through—" She shook her head mournfully. "He's in prison, you know. Busted!"

Leslie had to suppress an urge to laugh, hearing that word coming out of Ruby's lips.

Meanwhile, Calvin had looked away, ashamed that he'd allowed himself to get pulled into an argument in front of Leslie, but the subject of Sonny had always been like dynamite between him and his mother. The moment she'd seen that ponytail, her mind had shut like a steel trap, and she'd refused to allow that there could be anything good about the man. She had never been able to understand that Cal had found in Sonny something very rare indeed—a kindred spirit.

Sonny was a good twenty-five years older. He'd "gone hippy," as he'd always put it, relatively late in life. Before that he'd actually been an investment banker on Wall Street and, on the day he was thirty-seven years old, just walked out and left it all—a spoiled wife, a million-dollar house, a sports car, and a mistress. "I was a different man back then," he'd used to say. He'd had it all, but the day he threw it away was the day he started to learn happiness. "Life, my friend, is an art."

He'd started drifting around with artists and adventurers, gone down to South America on archeological digs, even worked on a ship that sailed around the world. That was how he'd ended up in Thailand for a while, studying under a Taoist master. When his mother's health started to fail, she'd convinced him to return to Virginia and take up residence in her weekend getaway, River's Bend, which she'd just bought from the Creeds.

He moved in, planted a garden, and started writing a book. Evenings were spent on the porch with Cal, telling stories. Sonny was a marathon talker. He could go on for hours. There seemed to be no limit to the man's curiosity or experience, and in the stories he told and the books he lent, Calvin traveled the world back and forth through time and on into the universe, something he craved in the stagnant backwaters of Olympia.

Then three years ago, a helicopter had spotted Sonny's tiny marijuana patch down by the floodplain. It was just for his personal stash, he'd always said, but that was how he'd wound up in prison, where he'd been ever since. It had been a huge scandal. The locals now cast him as a villain, and everyone said they hoped he'd be put away for good. Only Calvin had been sorry to see him go. To his knowledge, Sonny had never hurt anyone.

The argument was now about whether Sonny was coming out of prison soon or not. Ruby was convinced that he had fifteen years to go and demanded to know who had told Calvin otherwise.

"Like I already told you half-a-dozen times, Jimmy Crocket down at the feed store says he's supposed to get out any time now."

"*Who* told you?"

He leaned down and shouted in her ear. "Jimmy Crocket!"

Ruby's shriveled eyes widened. "That old fool? Your daddy never had two cents worth of good to say about him either!"

"As if that has anything to do with anything," grumbled Calvin under his breath.

"Calvin, speak up and stop mumblin' so a woman can hear you proper!" She turned to Leslie for sympathy. "He's such a tur-r-r-rible mumbler!"

"Is he?" said Leslie, fighting back a smile and trying to think of a good exit line.

"Oh yes, just tur-r-rible." Suddenly the old woman switched on the charm. "Well, my show's comin' on. Now don't stay a stranger, hear? You come over and visit an old lady now and then." She reached out and grabbed Leslie's hand and pressed it warmly, her eyes bright as a bird's.

"I will," promised Leslie.

A radiant smile transformed Ruby's creased face, revealing the beauty of what once was. "I like you," she said. "Don't you like her, Calvin!" This was more of a statement than a question, as if there were no doubt that he did.

Calvin shuffled his feet, visibly taken off guard. He mumbled something resentful under his breath.

"Calvin! You are such a mess!" cackled Ruby, bubbling over now with good humor. "What am I gonna do with him, Miz Hillerman?"

Leslie cast a diplomatic smile in his direction and started to go and then, on second thought, turned back. She had one more question. "Mrs. Creed—have you ever actually *seen* your father's—ghost?"

Ruby's eyes opened wide and her voice fell to a whisper. "You seen somethin'?"

Leslie frowned. "Well—"

A reverent glow lit her face. "You'll hear him whistlin' along about evenin' time mostly," she said softly. "That's when the veil between worlds gets thin."

Calvin rolled his eyes heavenward. "Ma! Good grief!"

"Oh, now there's nothin' to be scared of, honey!" purred Ruby. "Daddy wouldn't hurt a fly. He does rearrange things now and then, and if you don't like it, just tell 'im to stop. He'll listen."

"Don't listen to her," said Calvin disgustedly.

Ruby gave him a blank stare and then turned to Leslie. "Like I said, just tell him to stop if he bothers you." Suddenly she let out a heart-stopping shriek. The goat was out again!

It wasn't until she was halfway home when Leslie realized she'd neglected to tell Calvin about the manuscript getting blown down the river. Though she dreaded it, she knew she would most likely keep "accidentally forgetting" if she didn't call him the moment she got in the door. However, going into the house was a bit more difficult now that she had reason to think that there actually could be a real ghost roaming around inside.

Even so, everything seemed quietly normal, and she was just about to pick up the phone when she noticed her diary lying mysteriously face down in the middle of the living room floor. After a few moments of mental racing, she made the firm decision that it had to have been the goat that had knocked it off. However, the tattered work glove, which lay beside it, was a bit more of a challenge. It was hunter orange and not easy to overlook; yet here it was, and she could not, for the life of her, remember having seen it before. For a moment, she had the distinct sensation that she was not alone in the house though she quickly pushed that thought aside because, of course, it was Calvin's glove! Who else's could it be? He'd left it here by accident the day he'd been mowing, and the goat had been chewing on that too! This made her feel much better, as she refused to consider the possibility that there could have been a ghost involved.

Back in the sixth grade, Leslie had made a clear determination on two key points. One was that she would never be a "primper" glued to the mirror like the girls teasing their hair and practicing sultry expressions like the models in the magazines. In fact, she was so intent on not being like them that she purposely ignored the mirror as she passed by, thus having the tendency to appear slightly disheveled and unput together, something that would plague her poor mother and later cause serious disaffection with her mother-in-law.

Her second guiding principle was that she would not be an "ewie" girl, meaning that she would not scream and get hysterical about such things as mice or spiders. This extended to the subject of ghosts as well. At junior high school sleepovers, she had always found it somewhat degrading to be expected to scream and clump together in fright over a spooky movie and, on such occasions, tended to find an excuse to go to the bathroom until the other girls returned to their senses. It wasn't that she never felt fear but her self-respect would never let her show it.

Now she was faced with a clear choice between living in fear of the ghost *and* depression over the divorce or just the depression over the divorce. She decided that she could handle the depression because she had to but couldn't afford to be afraid of the ghost. She liked this house too much, and besides, she had nowhere else to go. So the decision had already been made even before she ever found the diary on the living room floor.

"Look," she said, addressing the ceiling as if that were the most likely place for a ghost to hang out, "I'll try not to get in your way if you try not to get in mine. Then we should get along fine!"

Though she didn't hear an answer, she figured that no news was good news and that her negotiation had been accepted. Which was how she forgot to call Calvin and tell him about the manuscript blowing down the river—again.

CHAPTER 9

Going Episcopal

Frank went outside the double-wide to see what had stirred the dogs into such a fuss. It turned out to be Calvin walking up the road, carrying a bucket and a fishing pole.

"Catch anything?" called Frank as he made his way down to the road.

"Just a couple of bass." Calvin had already started moving off but in the direction of Leslie Hillerman's driveway.

Frank looked puzzled. "Hey! Last time I checked you lived that a-way!" He waved his arms like a flag man on an air strip.

Cal paused with a scowl. "I know where I live, Frank." He resumed walking.

"Ohhh! I see. Heading over to Miz Hillerman's again, huh?" Frank flashed him a sly grin. Cal didn't respond. "You never gave *me* no fish. What if *I'm* hungry? You know I don't have Mama cookin' for *me*!" He poked out his lower lip and rubbed his big belly suggestively.

"You can get your own damn fish." Cal kept walking.

"Better watch yourself now! I hear you was over there drinking and bush hogging, now you're giving her fish. I smell romance in the air."

"It was iced tea and you can just shut the hell up!"

This set off an explosion of laughter. "Iced tea! Ohhh! A sure sign love is in the air!"

"Lucky for you I'm standing over here, Frank—or you'd get your fish all right! Right in the—"

Suddenly a blue 1973 Lincoln Continental thundered out of Pendleton Caughey's driveway, horn blaring, dogs swarming in from all directions. Peering over the steering wheel and laughing like a madman, Penny swerved with sinister intent straight into the center of the pack.

Roaring with indignation, Frank laid hold of a rock and hurled it at the Lincoln's rear bumper with all his might. Stepping on the gas, the little white-haired man sped off with an impudent squeal, leaning on his horn all the way around the bend. Frank stood in the middle of the road, impotent with rage.

"You psycho, son-of-a-bitch maniac! No wonder your woman left you!" Frank glared in consternation as the automobile vanished out of sight. "That man has gone completely out of his tree!" As an afterthought, he threw another rock for good measure. Calvin quietly cursed from the ditch. It had been a narrow escape. He made sure he got away before Frank had a chance to launch into his damned Yankees tirade.

Since five thirty, Penny had been awake, caught like a rat in a maze of indecision. For some reason, he'd gotten the crazy notion of going to church. This was very unusual. He'd never worried much about being a "bad" Catholic and going to hell. By now, he figured he didn't have much chance of going to heaven anyway. However, he reasoned that if Jesus really was all he was cracked up to be, surely he could let some things slide. So he was surprised that morning when it came to him so strong, the thought of going to church. The urge that had, for one moment, felt like a warm bright feeling had quickly turned into a dark lump of guilt. He knew that once you let an idea like that get into your mind, it would hang on you all day like an unpaid bill.

There was only one Catholic church in the whole county, and he'd been there exactly once, after which he'd vowed never to go back again. The priest there was as gay as a three-dollar bill, and it brought back bad memories of priests, who couldn't keep their mitts off the young choir boys. Even so, he'd been feeling so awfully low he was driven to desperate measures. All morning he'd spent getting dressed and undressed, one minute thinking that he was going come hell or high water and the next deciding to forget it.

And then a compromise solution slipped in. *How about going to the Episcopal church across the street?* Deep down he knew that God wasn't buying the excuse that it wouldn't count since it wasn't Catholic, so like a man going to his own funeral, he put himself in the car and started off, though pretending to run over Frank's dogs did give his spirits a temporary lift. He hadn't laughed like that in forever, and that little boost had carried him all the way into town.

Olympia was a small town built alongside the James River way back when the main system of transport had been bateaux floating cargo downriver to Richmond. At the turn of the century came the trains, making Olympia the hub of the county. However, in the 1950s, Eisenhower's interstate highway system soon left it behind in a mad rush to the future. Eventually the passenger trains ceased to run, and even the freight trains didn't stop in Olympia anymore. The train depot closed down, and a series of floods coming one after another dealt the final death blow, drowning out what businesses were left and leaving the town discouraged and exhausted. Buildings were left to decay along Main Street. Only the churches and a handful of homes nesting in the hills were left intact.

For someone wanting to go to church, Olympia boasted three major religions: two Baptist churches, one white and one black; St. Stephens Catholic; and St. Andrews Episcopalian. The blacks had their church higher up the hill, hidden in a grove of trees. It was a simple wooden structure that did not even look like a church except for the plain wooden cross above the door. However, they were the only ones to have seat cushions and air-conditioning, since they stayed in church most of the day.

On the far side of town (which wasn't very far) was a newer brick building with Greek columns. This was Zion, the white Baptist church. Beside it was their fellowship hall, a long low building covered in white sheet metal reminding him of an oversized toolshed. If there was one thing Penny couldn't stand, it was a white Baptist. In his mind, they were sanctimonious and their taste in architecture merely confirmed his theory.

The Catholic and Episcopalian churches stood directly opposite from each other. St. Stephens Catholic was a fairly plain white structure with a modest steeple and a bargain basement stained glass window on the front, all in all, not anywhere as prestigious looking as its rival across the street. St. Andrew's Episcopal Church was an imposing brick structure on the edge of the bluff, overlooking the river and reminded Penny of a medieval castle with its bell tower rising like a turret on the front and exquisite stained glass windows all around. It was nestled in a dignified cemetery, contained by a brick wall, topped with wrought iron fence, and shaded by stately oak trees. Despite the outward trappings, however, the Catholics easily outdid the Episcopalians in church attendance ten to one. At nine o'clock, their parishioners' cars so clogged up the narrow streets that the Episcopalians were forced to hold their services an hour later just so they would have some place to park.

The minister of St. Andrew's had thought long and hard about this situation and had come to the conclusion that this was not entirely a matter of creed or dogma. He had strong suspicions that it had more to do with the fact that St. Andrews did not have bathroom facilities in the main building. Parishioners in need were forced to trudge a block up the hill and another block over to the old rectory to use the toilet, and in most cases, this was becoming a real problem. Certainly none of them were getting any younger. The average age of the congregation was hitting somewhere around seventy, and each year, the population grew smaller and smaller. Reverend John Weston himself had just passed his seventy-fifth birthday.

This year it had coincided with the yearly congregational meeting. This was a day he dreaded, for he had the unpleasant task of drawing up a list of the parishioners' names. In years gone by, he'd been accused of padding the list with the names of anybody and everybody who'd ever stepped foot in the door. This year, he'd overheard the senior and junior wardens both chuckling like it was some kind of joke! But how, he'd wanted to know, could he present a list of just fifteen people? How would that look to the diocese, to the bishop? He just couldn't do it! Besides, though some of the members listed may not have appeared for several years, who knew what might bring them back? The Lord works in mysterious ways! That's what he would say if anyone dared to question the logic of this list. With that decision, he had printed up his list totaling forty-two names.

Inside, the church was elegant with red carpeting, a real pipe organ, and stained glass windows that were opened on warm days to the birdsong and the scent of honeysuckle and boxwood along with the visit of an occasional wasp. Above the altar was a stained glass picture of Christ praying in the garden at Gethsemane, a dove descending in a shaft of heavenly light.

Penny stood uncertainly in the narthex. Several people, mostly gray-haired women, were scattered among the pews, hunched over in prayer. The minister was nowhere in sight. A stale sacred hush prevailed over the sanctuary. Presently, Scottie, the minister's thirty-five-year-old son entered solemnly from the vestry room behind the altar, bearing the church flag. Clearly, he had Down syndrome and was as bald as a billiard, wearing a white robe that made him look like a medieval monk. He marched down the center aisle and into the narthex and stood next to Penny. The two men stood together as Scottie gazed adoringly out of puffy oriental eyes, his moist lips moving as if he were about to say something.

Penny smiled uncertainly. "You'll have to speak up, son. I'm deaf as a cob," he croaked, his voice sounding louder than he'd intended. Several amongst the congregation turned to stare.

"Sweet," said Brownie softly, his small brown eyes still as pond water. He smiled the smile of a little child. "Sweet," he said again. His small agile tongue darted out of his rosebud mouth, and then he clamped it shut with a smile, as if satisfied that his message had been delivered.

The organist hit the opening chord. The congregation stood up as Brownie began his stately procession down the aisle, bearing his flag proudly to the altar. He solemnly positioned the flag in its stand and stood in front of the altar, bowed three times, saluted the American flag, and then sat on one of the carved wood benches just below the altar.

John Weston suddenly appeared at Penny's side. He'd been outside the building, relieving himself in the boxwoods behind the church. He touched Penny's shoulder lightly and whispered, "Glad you could make it." Then he opened his hymnal joining in on the first verse as he swept down the aisle in his long white robes.

Penny slinked into the back pew, thinking ahead to a fast getaway before the last hymn was over. From across the aisle, a good-looking older man by the name of Farley Jacobson was eyeing Penny with a friendly bemusement.

Penny scowled. "Take a picture. It'll last longer," he muttered to himself. He'd never met a six footer that he didn't dislike. Meanwhile, Farley Jacobson grinned and nodded as if he were reading his mind.

Just as the first hymn was ending, Pete Talley shuffled in with his old sausage of a dog, Jimmy, following sedately on his heels. At age ninety, with snow-white hair growing abundantly on top of his head and out of his unusually large ears, he was the oldest man in Olympia. As the self-appointed town historian, he still had an iron grip of a handshake and, if given half a chance, could hold his audience captive for hours on end with stories of Olympia in its heyday back when the trains still stopped in town, back before the floods of '69, '73, '77, '78, '79, and

'81 . . . before they'd finally given up and moved the depot up to higher ground, where it presently sat collecting cobwebs.

Pete loved to recite to disbelieving newcomers the list of all the businesses that had since been boarded up and or torn down. Three saloons, three general merchandise stores, a post office, town hall, Masonic Lodge, and, the grandest structure of all, a house of ill repute. Being that he was also just short of being stone deaf, these conversations were inevitably one-sided.

Pete delivered Pendleton Caughey a resounding clap on the back and then sat a few pews in front of him. His dog, Jimmy, lay down in the open doorway and drifted off to sleep. In a bored "let's just get this over with" manner, the minister mumbled through a litany of prayers and lengthy confessions. For Penny, it was all a blur until they came to the Lord's Prayer, and suddenly there was an unforeseen lump in his throat the size of a golf ball. Though his lips were moving, not a sound came out. Tears blurred his vision and dripped down his cheek into his collar, where they tickled like crazy, but he dared not wipe them away. He didn't want Farley Jacobson to see that he was crying; so he waited until everyone was fidgeting with the hymnals, getting ready for the next hymn, before he surreptitiously brushed his hand across his face.

The sermon was interminably long and difficult to follow, John Weston being famous for going off the subject and never finding his way back. Somehow he'd gotten into the subject of government regulation and the price of septic tanks. Three-fourths of the way through, a freight train came roaring through town, blasting its horn. Pete's dog woke up and started to howl. Weston waited patiently until the ruckus subsided and then, to everyone's disappointment, resumed his dissertation.

"And so, we cannot forget that while to a lot of folks a toilet may spell the difference between the so-called high life style and the so-called lower class, substandard, so to speak—and there's nothing wrong with that. Nothing wrong with that. Don't get me wrong. Live and let live is my motto, but even so—even so, to my way of thinking, this is not how a true Christian is gonna be thinking, see? Now you may sit there and say, 'John, who are you to be standing up there and telling me how a true Christian ought to be thinking?' And I'd have to agree—to a point. But here's the thing, see—a true Christian, and I mean a *true* Christian (and that's the whole difference, the meat of the subject, as the little lady on TV says, 'Where's the beef?') . . ." He paused here, waiting for a laugh, and when it didn't come, he went on. "A true Christian is *in* the world but not *of* it. Now what does this mean? I want you to think about this. Don't just toss it off as John Weston's bugaboo. This is your business—your business too. We're all in this together, and when the ship sinks, everybody gets wet! In a sense, this whole subject keeps getting flushed down the tubes so to speak because nobody wants to face it. Now you may wonder, what in the heck is this man trying to say? Well, I'll tell you what I'm trying to say. I can't do it alone! That's it in a nutshell! We need each other! I need you and you need me, but you can't just sit there and wait around for somebody else to do it all for you! A church is a body! Not just an arm here and a leg there! Not just a head on a platter either! I may be the head of this body, but folks, we need hands and feet too!"

Penny was now actively plotting his escape. John Weston, however, had apparently run out of steam.

"So to wrap it up on a more positive note, let's just say this: Man does not live by bread alone. What this means to me is don't get hung up on details like toilets for instance. Don't let that get in your way. We have to grow. We are called to grow in Christ. Okay, so if that means walking up the hill to go the bathroom—so be it! Pick up your cross and follow me!" He dropped his head abruptly. "Go in peace to love and serve the Lord. Amen."

There was a general sigh of relief as the congregation rustled around, preparing for the last hymn. Penny checked his watch. What the hell, might as well stay for the last song.

"Since we're running a little late, we'll just sing the first verse of hymn 104," announced the minister. The organist ran through the intro and a chorus of scraggly voices limped into "A Mighty Fortress is Our God." The only one who didn't get the message was deaf old Pete Talley, who went ahead and sang the second verse alone. No one made a move to stop him. The sound of his clear sweet tenor voice in that aged sanctuary felt more holy than all the words and prayers that had gone before. Tears flooded Penny's eyes a second time that morning. He'd finally gotten what he'd come for.

CHAPTER 10

The Fish

Monday night, there was a huge thunderstorm. Penny Caughey called it a real gusher. The dogs were petrified and wouldn't come out from under Leslie's bed all evening. Then around midnight, with a little squeal, the luminous clock on her dresser died. The power was out. Without the night lights glowing in their sockets, the house fell into pitch darkness lit only intermittently by violent lightning. Of course, the moment the power went out, she felt a desperate need to pee.

High winds buffeted the trees into a frenzied dance outside her window, and she prayed one of them wouldn't crash into the house as she slid out from beneath the covers onto the cold bare floor. Feeling her way blindly through the dark, it occurred to her that this was the perfect night for ghosts, and for the rest of the night she was haunted by mysterious creaks and thuds and countless imagined phantoms drifting past her door. When the first streaks of dawn arrived, she hadn't gotten the first wink of sleep.

The next morning, the power still hadn't come on, and the pump was out. Whatever water was still in the pipes quickly ran out. Both Pendleton Caughey and Frank Hawkins drove over to make sure she was okay. The word was that there had been a twister in the western part of the county. The power was likely to be out for a couple of days. She moped around, feeling hopeless and gloomy and then went out to buy jugs of water, a couple of flashlights, and some candles. At least the humidity had lifted. She bathed in the river that evening and ate her dinner by candlelight and stared at the moon until her eyelids grew heavy. Convinced that she would surely sleep better this night, she went to bed, but no sooner had she started to drift down through the layers of sleep than did she hear the sound of footsteps on the staircase. This time they sounded all too real. "Hooch?" she called hopefully into the listening darkness, but Hooch was busily scratching himself under her bed. The wind moaned like a grieving woman. Somewhere a door slammed shut, and the house groaned deep in its bones. A presence was standing in the doorway, watching and waiting. Suddenly all resolve to live pleasantly side by side with a ghost went out the window, and she spent the rest of the night wide awake and sweating under the covers.

The second day of the power outage, the heat started to rise along with her temper. By afternoon, the house would be like an oven, so she set off for the river, feeling very resentful that it should be so hot and sticky when she would rather just vegetate in the house. The dogs were already in the water when she got there, paddling in their dogged fashion to the sandbar, where they would lie about and collect fleas.

Wading against the current on her way to the tiny island took whatever strength she had left, so when she got there she just wallowed in the shallows like a beached porpoise until the little fish nibbling at her legs drove her up back up onto the sand. There she slept until the sun had moved behind the trees, waking with a loud groan. Now she'd done it! She was sunburned for sure! She laid there for a while longer, miserable and drifting in a wooly mind fog. She was dying of thirst but too exhausted to make the effort to get her water bottle, which when she finally did open her eyes, was discovered bobbing merrily down the river along with her towel.

It took a moment before it fully penetrated that the island was actually shrinking because the river was rising. Soon the little sandbar would be swallowed completely! Calling the dogs to follow, she launched into the swiftly moving current, now a tumultuous murky brown and full of broken branches and dead leaves, whereupon they were promptly swept downstream alongside an old bleach bottle and a rusty paint can. The dogs fought valiantly against the fierce current as they turned onto shore, where her old cotton dress and a pair of holey tennis shoes should have been waiting on a nice flat boulder. However, now the boulder was underwater, and her dress and her shoes were well on their way to Richmond.

Barefoot and dressed only in a faded pink two-piece with big-eyed fishes wearing sunglasses, she headed up the deer path into the meadow on the flood plain, gingerly trying to avoid walking on sharp sticks and stones. She felt like something the river had chewed up and spit out.

When a rabbit darted out of the brambles and zigzagged across the field, the dogs tore after in a howling burst of enthusiasm and vanished into the brush. After a few minutes, Hooch reappeared, panting heavily, his long pink tongue drooping, but Elliot was not with him. "Where's Elliot?" she wanted to know, but Hooch just gave her a guilty sideways look, his big nose tucked between his paws, tail swishing vaguely across the grass.

A yelp arose from beyond a bank of dogwoods and wild roses. It was Elliot in distress. He'd somehow ended up on the opposite side of the creek. Most likely, he'd walked across on the fallen tree trunk, but no matter how she tried to persuade him, he refused to come back over. Leslie had always been afraid of heights, but the creek was running far too wild and deep, and she had no choice. She edged her way along the trunk of the fallen tree, but when she stooped to pick him up, he turned and ran off through the bushes. Cursing her bad luck, she followed the ingrate back through the brush only to stumble upon the most magical little glen she'd ever seen. It was an absolute fairyland nestled among the trees. For the first time in six months, she felt inspired to paint, but her enthusiasm was short-lived; for at that moment the snarling, snapping, stinking mongrel horde swarmed in from out of trees to surround them.

She screamed as Hooch charged valiantly into the breach, teeth bared, ferocious and brave and horrifyingly outnumbered. He stood nose to nose with the leader of the pack, a big shaggy-looking thug, both dogs bristling with danger, tails taut as bow strings. Suddenly with terrifying snarls, they reared up on hind legs, jaws at each other's throats. Then two other males started to move in for the kill, but to her relief, Frank Hawkins appeared out of nowhere, running at a full gallop, waving his arms and roaring like a grizzly bear. "Get the hell out of here before I chop you up for cat food! Go on now, git!"

The mangy crew started to melt away, tails tucked between their legs. For good measure, he struck one of the stragglers on the rump with a big rock. It ran off yelping. "Don't worry, Miz Hillerman. They're all bark and no bite!" He said this by way of apology, but she was in no mood to acknowledge it. Instead she erupted in a fury.

"You have no right to let your dogs roam like a-a-a pack of wolves! It's dangerous and it's irresponsible!"

Frank's eyes narrowed. He hadn't slept much either and was cranky to boot besides the fact that it was pure rebel blood running through his veins, so he didn't do well with city women telling him his rights. "Let me tell you about rights, lady! See that pink ribbon on that tree branch there? That's the property line. Right through there and up the hill past that big ol' oak tree . . . which means *you're* trespassin' on *my* land. Those dogs are protecting their territory, Miz Hillerman. That's just their nature, and I can't do nothin' to change that."

Leslie's eyes lit like coals of fire. "So you're saying that you are just going to keep on letting your dogs terrorize the neighborhood and—and everyone else be damned?"

His eyes widened and then screwed down even tighter, the steam rising. "*Your* dogs run loose!" He waved a cautionary finger under her nose like a lawyer in a courtroom. "But yet you want *me* to keep *my* dogs locked up. You can't have it both ways, Miz Hillerman. It's either one or the other."

She drew herself up with all the self-righteous indignity she could muster for a woman in a pink bathing suit with fish wearing sunglasses. "I wonder how you'll feel if those dogs ever really *do* hurt someone, Mr. Hawkins! Let's just pray that it isn't a small child!" She stalked off without waiting for a reply.

Meanwhile from the top of the bluff, a man watched unnoticed.

Still brooding about the encounter with Frank Hawkins, she headed back up toward the house. She should have threatened a lawsuit. That would have shut him up good! Her right foot hurt. During her dramatic exit, she'd stepped on a sharp stick, and now it was vigorously oozing blood.

From the edge of the trees, Leslie caught sight of Calvin sitting forlornly beside the old water pump set in a slab of concrete in the middle of the backyard. Her heart sank. She was in no mood for conversation, especially with someone who required so much effort, but it was too late to hide. He'd already seen her and had lurched to his feet in his sheepish way. It had been an exhausting trip from the river. Pausing to catch her breath, she waved and called out a half-hearted hello.

For a moment, he found himself staring as she emerged from the shadow of the trees. Her dark hair framing her face with graceful confusion lent her an accidental loveliness of which she was totally unaware—a goddess, barefoot and all but naked, blithely revealing herself to him, the gentle curve of her breasts, the generous line of her hips, her long shapely legs. Every detail would be indelibly printed in his imagination.

"I'm having a terrible day!" she cried woefully, looking down at her feet and legs streaked with dirt and blood. "I feel like a drowned rat."

It wasn't until she started walking again that he noticed her half limp, half hop. "Do you need some help?" He hastened down to offer an arm, and she gratefully leaned against him, stooping to hold up her foot like a wounded paw so he could see. "I stepped on a stick or something." They proceeded slowly up into the yard. She rattled on about having fallen asleep and how the river rose and carried off her shoes, her towel, and her favorite dress; about the terrifying dogfight and her argument with Frank Hawkins.

The two of them processing so slowly across the lawn, arm in arm, suddenly created the disquieting notion of a bride and bridegroom, prompting her to limp faster.

"Don't you think you better slow down?" he said. "I mean, that looks like a pretty bad cut. You might need stitches."

"No—I don't think so. Do *you* think so?"

"I'd have to take a look at it," he said. They were silent until they arrived at the water pump. She sat on the edge of the concrete slab and stared sorrowfully at her filthy feet. "I do hate to use the water I bought at the grocery store to clean *these* up."

"Water from the store!" He gave her a quizzical look. "You're sitting next to a pump. Why use water from a store?"

"You mean this thing actually works?"

"It worked five years ago. I don't see why it shouldn't work now." He started pumping slowly at first, the rusty old handle complaining with a metallic shriek, and then faster. At first nothing happened, and then presently a gush of foul reddish brown water spurted out, but as Calvin continued stalwartly pumping, the water soon ran sparkling clear.

She told herself that it was only with an artist's eye that she noticed how finely made his arms were, the sinewy muscles developed from years of chopping firewood, rippling with the smallest of movement, the fine broad shoulders, the easy graceful way he moved. But it confused her, and she felt slightly resentful at the thought of being attracted to anyone but Stuart because Stuart was going to return. *Love returns*. The dream had told her. Besides, even if there were to be another, it would not be such an unlikely one as Calvin Creed. She was embarrassed in front of herself to even be having such a thought.

When she looked up, she found him looking at her as if reading her mind. Mortified, she quickly cast her eyes down. "So do you think the power will come back on soon?" she asked, more or less to change the subject inside her head.

"Most likely it will be soon but you never can tell."

"I hope so." She sighed. His eyes were amazingly blue though and so beautiful that she had great difficulty avoiding them.

He knelt in the grass before her, hesitated, and then held out his hand. "Give me your foot and I'll wash it off for you." When she lifted her foot, images of Prince Charming putting on Cinderella's glass slipper flashed unbidden through her mind. Inside her head, she heard a voice cry, "Ridiculous!" Even so, the moment he touched her foot, a tiny electric thrill went straight to her womb. It shocked her because it was so unexpected, and once again, she felt resentful of the seemingly arbitrary nature of this response. All the while, he held her foot so gently, stroking the mud and blood away from the wound with his fingers.

When he was almost through, she mumbled a grudging thanks and then lurched to her feet, saying she could do the rest. She tried taking over at the pump handle, but it was too hard to clean off her legs at the same time, so he went back to pumping as she turned her bare legs to and fro under the cool gush of water. For the first time, she was the one off balance and unable to think of anything sensible to say, so she babbled on about what an idiot she'd been for not having thought about using the pump all this time. She tried not to look at him.

The cut turned out not to be very deep, and the bleeding had all but stopped, but she still needed to protect it. He went to his truck, where he kept a first aid kit, and then deftly bound up her wounded foot, after which he filled a couple of buckets with water—for flushing the toilet, he said almost cheerfully. He'd carry them upstairs for her, too, and even offered to fill up bottles for drinking water, but she erupted with a harsh laugh, saying she was not an invalid and that she could do it herself. She instantly regretted being so abrupt, as he immediately withdrew back to a guarded distance behind his beard.

For his part, he could only think that he'd gone too far somehow, and she had put him in his place. He would gladly have left right then if it weren't for the fish. He'd brought them by way of compensation for the trouble Gulliver had caused, but all he managed to say was, "I brought you some fish," in the bluntest possible way.

"Oh! Did you catch them in the river?" She asked this not because she really wanted to know but because she didn't know what else to say. Making conversation with Calvin could be such an uphill climb.

He shook his head. "The pond," he replied.

"Oh! You have a pond?" She said this as if it were the most interesting thing she'd heard all day.

"You can't really see it from the road," he added.

"Oh—yes—well—" The conversation dangled precariously. She tried to look interested in the three shiny bass swimming around in a bucket. "You know I've never cleaned a fish before."

"I'll take care of it," he said brusquely and, without further explanation, reached into the bucket, closed his hand carefully around the first fish, and lifted it out. It wriggled at first and then became calm, as if under a spell. He lifted the knife.

"But it's still alive!" she cried, suddenly alarmed.

For the first time that afternoon, he looked amused. "Actually it's kinder this way. Cut the spine and they don't feel a thing."

With such a lean and muscular body, he would make a good model for a painting. It was safe to think this, now that she had established a certain distance. Of course, he would probably think it a strange proposition, so she wouldn't mention it. Instead, she commented that this concrete slab seemed a pretty good spot for cleaning fish.

At first he said nothing and she wondered if he had even heard. What she couldn't know was that at the mere mention of the concrete slab, his tongue had darted to the tooth he'd chipped on this very cement slab when he was twelve years old and chasing Peggy Grable around the yard. Falling flat on his face in front of her was still one of the monumental humiliations of his life and that tooth a permanent warning against ever chasing a woman again.

"Actually," he said after an awkward gap, "this is where my granddad taught me to clean my very first fish." He didn't follow up with anything further, and the conversation lapsed once more into tedious silence.

She had gone back to the house to get a plastic bag for the fish and to throw on an old paint smock when the phone started ringing. It was Stuart. Her spirits rose and then were immediately dashed, for there was no mistaking the tone of resentment in his voice. The house was now on the market, and he'd been trying to reach her for over a week. Did she ever check her answering machine or was she going to dump all the responsibility for selling the house on him? If so, he didn't appreciate it.

Her throat closed over angry tears and she said nothing. He took it for stubbornness and launched into a tedious recitation of everything he had to do, meaning he had carried her weight long enough, and if she wanted her share out of the house, she had better get with the program.

The truth was she didn't want to deal with the realities of selling the house. It made everything seem far too final, but she couldn't tell him that, so again she said nothing.

"Well, I just thought you should know," he said finally. "Look I've been going through some boxes and found some old photos. I thought maybe you'd want them." For the third time, she didn't answer. He sighed loudly. She knew that sigh. It meant he was getting frustrated and that gave her a curious pleasure. "So do you want them or not?"

"I don't know," she said barely above a whisper.

Through the back screen door, she could see Calvin had finished and was sitting with arms propped on his knees, patiently waiting for her to bring him a plastic bag. Elliot was in his lap and Hooch lay at his feet. A covey of crows descended with rude ejaculations upon the flower bed. For a moment, he tilted his face into the sunlight. Was he praying?

Stuart's voice rose in irritation. "So what am I supposed to do with them until you decide?"

She could tell that he'd been drinking. There was that slurring of certain words, however slight. Stuart had always been able to drink vast quantities without showing any outward signs of drunkenness, at least not to anyone, it seemed, but her. However, in the past several years, it had started to take a toll in ways that perhaps they'd both refused to see.

"I don't know," she wailed. "Throw them in the trash—I don't care anymore!" She hung up the phone and burst into tears.

Suddenly, she was startled by a hesitant tap on the screen door. It was Calvin on the back porch, holding the fish. Sobbing, she fled to the living room, knowing very well that it was too late to hide. She couldn't stop crying now even if she wanted to.

He found her sitting on a chair, covering her face the way a child would, with her paint-stained practical hands, the nails trimmed to the quick, shoulders heaving with tears of desolation. He stood helplessly by, not knowing whether to go or stay.

"Look, I don't think I want the fish anymore," she said finally in a muffled voice, wiping her eyes with the paint-stained corner of Stuart's old white shirt.

He awkwardly held out his pocket handkerchief. "It's clean," he said gently.

"Who carries these around anymore?" She gave something between a laugh and a sob, delicately wiping the tip of her cherry red nose.

He looked abashed. "Well, I guess I do."

She gave a weak smile, hugging her bare sun-browned legs to her chest and resting her chin on her knees. "My grandfather always had one of these in his back pocket, ready to wipe away—my—" Her eyes glittered with a fresh wave of tears. She gave a ragged sigh.

Though Cal tried to keep his eyes on the floor, her face was so open, so beautiful with emotion that he could barely keep from gazing upon her. Suddenly realizing he was still wearing his hat, Cal sheepishly pulled it off. She gave a fond laugh. "You *are* old-fashioned, aren't you, Cal?"

She'd called him Cal. He ventured a fool's smile but her expression only dimmed.

"That was my husband on the phone—my *ex*-husband, I guess I should say." She stared bitterly at something he could not see. "He's selling the house. I thought I hated that house but now—I don't know—" There was a long silence before she continued. "I guess it makes me feel like it's—really over, you know? I mean I guess I was still hoping—" Her voice broke. "I've been such a fool."

"Nobody's a fool for having a heart," he said gruffly and then abruptly made for the door.

When he was halfway across the yard, she called out from the front door, "Thanks for the fish, and sorry about all the—drama!"

He turned and raised his hat. "Don't be sorry," he said and then kept on walking. By the time she remembered the orange glove, it was too late. He'd already gone around the bend in the road.

Out in the yard, the dogs stirred as Frank Hawkins's mongrel horde started howling in the near distance. Suddenly she felt danger all around her. Surely, they would not dare approach her house! She stood at the door and called in the dogs. Meanwhile, standing among the trees, the shadowy figure of a man watched intently and then hoisted a shovel to his shoulder and quietly withdrew from sight.

CHAPTER 11

Linwood

The old black man lay flat on his back perplexed. He'd just been awakened by a terrifying thump on the roof and a mysterious voice calling his name. "Clarence! Clarence," it said, "it's time to come on." Then it seemed the archangel Gabriel himself had come sliding down a blinding shaft of light with the heavenly choir singing "Glory, Glory, Hallelujah!"

Clarence was understandably surprised. "You know, I'd love to go, but I can't get out of this bed to save my soul. There's a storm comin' and my artheritis is killin' me!"

"Don't worry about that!" spake the Angel, "If you've got a rat problem, we've got the solution!" And the heavenly choir chimed in, "Pest away, pest away! We got a way to put the pest away!"

Needless to say, this had left poor Clarence more confused than ever, and he was about to say that though they did get a few mice every now and again, ordinary traps usually worked just fine, but the angel Gabriel rather rudely interrupted with the number to call—1-800-457-4990. Then he said it again: 1-800-457-4990! Though Clarence wasn't what anybody would call a religious scholar, he was pretty sure angels didn't use telephones, and that's when he *really* woke up.

It took him a moment to register exactly which world he was in and, to his disappointment, realized that it was this one. It had all been nothing but a dream, and that heavenly light shining down on him had been just plain sunlight coming through a big hole in the roof that his lazy-assed grandson had patched last week. Apparently, now it had finally blown off just like he had predicted.

A voice on the radio beside his bed went from the Pest-Away commercial to the next song entitled "Lovin' Jesus that Ol' Fashioned Way." The wind moaned around the eaves as a dead leaf floated down through the hole and landed on the old man's chest. Painfully, he lifted his hand to remove it. The arthritis was so bad right now that he could barely move. A storm was surely coming. Where was that boy anyway?

Out in the bare dirt yard, Shortie, the stub-nosed three-legged stray started howling. Please God, let that be Linwood with the medicine! Sure enough, in a few moments the door opened, and Linwood filtered into the room, sullen and empty as a shadow.

"You got my medicine? And wipe those feet!" Linwood's boots were caked with mud. The old man knew better than to ask where he'd been.

"Here." Stony and indifferent, Linwood dropped the pharmacy bag down on his grandfather's chest and turned away. With one foot, he slid the cement block away from the refrigerator door so he could open it. Since the floor sloped downhill, it had a tendency to swing open without something propped against it. Linwood pulled out a Budweiser.

"I told you that patch you put up there wouldn't last. Look at it! It just blew off! Now what are we gonna do? There's a storm comin', sure as hell, and that rain is gonna come pouring in here."

Linwood barely looked at the hole. As usual, nothing seemed to matter to him. He sat at the table and, taking a pencil in hand, idly traced the outlines of a drawing he'd started earlier in the week. It was a copy of a picture in a magazine of a basketball player rising up for a hook shot. He'd finally gotten the arms in perspective with the rest of the body.

"You know you ain't rich enough to set around drawing pictures all day, boy!" His grandfather scowled. "Don't you just sit there like you don't hear me! When are you gonna care, Linwood? When are you gonna do something right?" In the old days, he would have slapped that look right off the boy's face, but he could barely move now, and even if he could, it would hurt those old hands more than that belligerent young face.

Without a word, Linwood grabbed the sketchbook and went back outside, which is where he stayed most all the time now, even on the coldest days. There was a seat from an old school bus set up under the trees, where he and his friends hung out to drink and smoke cigarettes and pot.

Even the TV was broken now and the old man was left alone all day long. The two had lived in this tiny shack ever since Linwood was eight years old, when his mother had run off with a man who didn't want little kids hanging around. Now Clarence knew that those had been the good years. Too bad he hadn't realized it back then. Linwood really hadn't been such a bad kid and not as much trouble as Clarence had advertised. Sure, at the time the boy had put a crimp in his step, talking up a storm, and tying him down when he could have been so free. Funny! Now Linwood was pretty much all the old man thought about—where was Linwood, what was to become of Linwood, and when was he comin' home?

Now Linwood kept his hair in what they called dreadlocks. He fancied himself a Rasta. Whatever that was. In his grandfather's opinion, he looked like something dragged out of the bush, but he'd learned pretty quickly to keep that opinion to himself or Linwood would go and never come back, and those had been his exact words.

Most of the time the two never spoke, but the old man could see more about Linwood than perhaps Linwood could see about himself. He could see that Linwood had just passed that point of being too old to be young and too old to be hanging around all day unemployed. He'd been barely surviving on odd jobs—mowing lawns, cutting firewood, or bringing in the hay for the elderly farmers in the area. For a few short months, he'd worked on the maintenance crew at the boarding school up the road but claimed that the boss hated him because he was black, and so he'd quit. Most likely, by his attitude, he'd called that down upon himself, but it was such a pitiful salary they paid up there—more of an insult than a wage.

Linwood had always been that way. All through school, he'd been in trouble, a quitter before he even started, labeled uncooperative, a problem kid, sleeping in class, playing too rough in the hallways. He didn't even graduate. When he was eighteen, he'd gotten caught in a drug raid and spent sixteen months in prison. After that, he'd acted proud of his time in the big house. If only he could see what a fool he was. Still, it hadn't been fair—just a small amount of marijuana in his pocket—but the law didn't give any breaks to poor blacks from this side of Olympia.

Clarence didn't like the crowd he was running with at all. Never had. Linwood seemed to have unerringly bad judgment when it came to people—just like his mama. Not that Clarence had been much better at that age. When he looked at his grandson, he couldn't help but see himself, but times had been different back then. The Depression had made people more sensible. There were none of these high-flying notions of driving around in a Mercedes bought with drug money. This was an ugly culture. Ugly. Oh, how Clarence pined for his boy to come back to himself. He felt the squeeze on his heart, and the tears streamed out the corners of his eyes. When would Linwood wake up?

Meanwhile, outside in the little patch of shade, Linwood stared blindly out at the road. There was a wall blocking his path and he felt it more strongly every day. His grandfather had always told him he was headed straight to hell, but if the truth be told, he was already there. Now, however, for once, he had a plan. Storm clouds darkened the western sky. The wind smelled of rain and he remembered the roof. Damn! He'd have to do something about that. He got up and went looking for a piece of plastic and something to hold it down.

CHAPTER 12

Pit Bulls for Sale

Strolling down the rutted dirt lane at twilight, a rare contentment settled in Leslie's heart like a nesting bird. In her hand was a letter she'd written to Stuart in the dark hours of a hard night of truth and pain. She felt she'd turned a corner and finally understood where their relationship had gone wrong. Suddenly it was clear how they could find their way back to each other.

It was after she'd awakened in the middle of the night from a dream about the child. It was the one she'd never been able to have, and it was all so real. She could still feel his chubby little body in her arms, his sweet-scented curly head against her cheek and the painful, sweet longing that she thought she'd put so carefully behind her. Suddenly, the whole scenario of their marriage opened up before her like a movie, and she and Stuart were characters with hidden motivations and buried feelings.

She saw that from the beginning, it had been assumed that she and Stuart would have children, though at first, truthfully, she'd been ambivalent. Motherhood was a mere abstraction, and though she'd always liked children well enough, it had never been anything she would have put at the top of her to-do list. Making art was what she was about, and when she still wasn't getting pregnant after several years of carelessness in the birth control department, she wasn't exactly upset. Maybe relieved would have been more accurate.

Stuart was the one who'd pushed the whole subject—that is, in the beginning. He came from a family that was big on the production of a male heir to carry on the family name. In fact, it had been brought up as one of the toasts at their wedding reception. It was thought that she and Stuart were waiting for him to get established in his career before starting a family, and then when five years had passed and there was still no sign of a baby, his mother had started to drop insinuations that it was Leslie who was holding out against having a child.

It wasn't until later after years of half-baked trying that it became clear that it was Stuart's doing. He was infertile. Leslie could only guess at how devastating this was for him because he'd withdrawn into an inscrutable silence on the subject. Only once when he'd been drinking a little too heavily did he say anything. They'd been alone on a terrace, watching a friend helping his little son tie his shoe out in the yard.

For once, Stuart had been able to look her in the eye. "I know you want that for yourself," he said, "and I wouldn't blame you if—"

"Blame me for what? Stuart! What are you talking about? We'll just adopt!"

He'd cringed at the word, looking into the distance. "It wouldn't be the same, Les." After that, he never said another word about it but went on acting as if everything was great as usual, though something irrevocable had changed between them. Now she could see that he was keeping his true feelings hidden. She tried very hard to reassure him that it didn't matter to her, but when she turned thirty, something unexpected happened. Suddenly there was this inexplicable, irrational longing for a child. Maybe it was just the idea that it was something she couldn't have, but nevertheless, she began to have vivid dreams about one particular child, a blond, curly-headed cherub of a boy. Sometimes he was older, and sometimes he spoke to her, but she always awoke feeling as if she'd been with an old friend. This joy confused her, and she'd found herself enviously watching the mothers and their young children at the park or in the malls. She began to believe that there was a particular child somewhere, somehow, who was meant to be with her.

From the beginning, though Stuart had agreed to the adoption, she knew his heart wasn't in it. Still they'd filed all the papers, gone through all the interviews, and for two years, they waited. Then without telling her, he'd had it withdrawn. On the day she found out, she'd run out into the rain and sat under a tree crying. He'd stood in the door and watched. "You're being stupid!" he'd said. "Come in the house. You'll get pneumonia!" But he'd offered no reason for what he'd done and no apology.

So much about their relationship had ended up that way—buried out of sight, out of mind. Like his parents, Stuart had never been one to delve into feelings or to be patient enough to listen to anyone else's. He preferred happy talk and keeping things upbeat. Self-examination was lumped in with moodiness or biochemical influences, and Leslie's moods were like stones better left unturned. If she made the mistake of letting them show, she was liable to feel the cold shoulder or left behind while he went off and played golf.

At this point in her ruminations, she heard a loud thump from downstairs. Thinking it was Hooch rummaging through the trash cans again, she trudged wearily down the steps to check, but the trash can was still on top of the counter, undisturbed just as she'd left it before going to bed. On her return, she noticed a book had fallen from the shelf and was lying open on the floor.

The curtains stirred gently on a pleasant sweetly scented breeze. Could the wind have pushed it off, she wondered. The book was one that had been in the house when she arrived, a Bible, and as she picked it up, her eye rested on these words:

"Remember ye not the former things, neither consider the things of old. Behold I will do a new thing; now it shall spring forth; shall ye not know it? I will even make a way in the wilderness, and rivers in the desert."

A choir of insects chirped comfortingly in the velvet darkness as she looked up to see a pale sliver of silver moon hanging like a jewel in the night sky. Peace flowed into her heart like a sigh. The inscription penned in a very careful hand on the inside cover read *"Given to Joseph Henry Carver on his Confirmation Day, 1903, St. Andrews Episcopal Church, Olympia, Virginia."*

The house settled its bones with a creak and a sigh, and the unmistakable aroma of pipe tobacco drifted on the gentle air. Tears sprang to her eyes. Yes, she could leave the past behind. They could make a new start, this time with greater understanding of each other. "Thanks, Henry," she murmured softly. Somehow she knew that this had been his gift to her and a sign.

She sat down and poured herself out in a letter, saying all the things she'd never been able to say before and all that she had realized that night. In the final paragraph, she made a proposal. Let him come to

River's Bend for a weekend, just one weekend. They could talk, really talk, and try to work things out. *Love returns,* she thought, sealing the envelope. She'd had a sign after all. *Love returns.*

Back at the mailbox, two men were in the midst of an argument. One of them was Frank Hawkins pontificating with broad expansive gestures, and the other a stranger she did not immediately recognize.

"All he's thinking about is making a buck and to hell with everything else!" she heard the stranger say.

"It's his land. Who am I or you or anybody to tell him what to do with it?" Both Frank and the other man stopped short at her approach, and that's when she realized that he was none other than Calvin Creed, looking very naked minus the beard.

"So," he continued, addressing Frank as if she weren't even there, "you're saying that just because somebody owns a piece of property they can just trash it no matter what the impact is on the ecosystem?"

"Hey! I didn't make up the Constitution."

Since she dreaded having to speak to either one of them, she was perfectly content to be ignored and so put her head down and made a beeline for her mailbox.

"Well, I think the Indians had it right! It's barbaric to own a piece of nature."

"Creed," smirked the mailman, "I always knew you were a communist at heart."

"Why does everything have to come down to that?" Calvin's voice rose sharply. "This is about the web of life, Frank! You just can't chop a forest into little five-acre plots. It's an interdependent system! You're a hunter! You of all people should know that!"

"Yeah, and it still sounds like communism. Come on, admit it! You want the government running everything!"

"Hey, you work for the government—not me!"

Leslie stole a hidden glance at Calvin's face. Without the hairy camouflage, he was astonishingly handsome. Leslie tried not to stare.

"So what are you gonna do, chain yourself to a tree?" sneered Hawkins. "Can't stop progress, man."

"And you call destroying natural habitat progress?"

"Keep in mind that just because somebody calls themselves a scientist, it don't mean they know what the hell they're talking about!"

"And just because you can make money from something doesn't make it right either!"

For years, Frank and Calvin had been arguing like this on summer evenings, standing at the mailboxes in the dust of the road. It was a tradition, and though they normally disagreed on every possible subject, they'd learned to enjoy sharpening their wits against the loyal opposition, and even when things got heated, before it was over, they could laugh it off and part as friends.

What had ignited tonight's argument was the news that a land speculator was getting ready to clear cut 120 acres of mixed trees, including some very old oaks that had stood for over half a century on the fringe of Frank's property. The county was dotted with such stretches of blighted wasteland.

"And I bet you send money to Green Peace too!" continued Frank disparagingly.

"So what if I do?"

"Then tell me this—is an owl more important than a human?"

"What's good for owls is good for humans, Frank."

"So what you're saying is we should all eat mice!"

The sun had dipped below the horizon and the sky was a deepening purple. On the horizon, Venus stood out like a diamond tucked into the curve of a pale crescent moon. The debaters started off on their separate ways. Usually the only thing that could break them up was the sun going down. From the top of the rise, she heard Cal call out, "Better get a beach chair and some suntan oil, Frank 'cause at this rate, the oceans gonna rise!"

"Hell, that ain't so bad!" Frank shouted back. "Beachfront real estate! We'll be rich!"

Their laughter rang out into the gathering twilight and then faded into silence. The fight would wait another day.

Calvin stood in his yard for a long moment, gazing at the moon. Leslie still hadn't said the first word about his manuscript, which could only mean that she hated it and was avoiding him.

He stroked his naked chin. The beard had come off as a result of losing a bet he'd foolishly made with Thelma over the name of an obscure character in an old movie. It was a stupid thing to do, but he'd been so sure he was right, and the chance to make her eat her words had been too much of a temptation.

Getting him to shave had been a real coup for Ruby and Thelma. Maybe now Thelma could fix him up with a normal woman.

A few days later, Ruby called Leslie with the news that Gulliver had turned up dead in Calvin's south pasture. Calvin was pretty sure it had been Frank's dogs that had done the deed. More than once, they'd come around before to harass the goat. It was a right ugly job, too, she said—all torn up and ripped apart. Cal was just sick about it.
Frank said it was probably that bobcat that had been prowling around lately. Of course, Frank was never one to admit having done wrong. He was far too proud for that. Leslie told her all about the incident down at the river, and both women agreed it was high time something be done about the situation. What if it had been a small child? Leslie suddenly felt an upsurge of unity with the old lady. There was nothing like a common enemy to bind people together.
Even Penny Caughey had become an ally. He'd called the sheriff, but there was nothing in the law that would force Frank to pen up the dogs though if a dog came onto his property, he had every legal right to shoot it. The next day when he went down to the mail boxes for his mail, he was carrying a .22 rifle.
Why did he have a gun? Frank wanted to know. Penny answered that it was protection from that pack of wild dogs Frank let run loose. After what they'd done to Calvin's goat, he didn't trust 'em—not that he ever *did* trust 'em, he said. Penny ended with his standard threat, namely to blow the brains out of any dog that dared to step foot on his property. Frank casually replied that if that were the case then maybe he'd just shoot old Peanut, who was, at that moment, lounging under Frank's tree on *Frank's* property. A few more ill-advised words were batted back and forth. Before it was over, Penny had vowed to report his portly neighbor for animal abuse, and Frank had accused Penny of threatening a postal worker (a *federal* offense)! A few days later, a sign appeared on a tree outside of Frank Hawkins's house, advertising PIT BULLS FOR SALE.

This promptly ignited a firestorm of controversy. Angry messages lined up on Frank's answering machine, but he was making himself scarce and did not deign to answer. Penny was officially on the warpath, calling Leslie every fifteen minutes with some new drastic counteroffensive, including poison and pipe bombs. (But aren't you afraid they'll put you in prison? Leslie would ask). Between him and Ruby calling up every day, reciting (over and over and over) all the horror stories of pit bulls attacking innocent children, Leslie didn't dare answer her phone either. But even so, she found herself brooding about it. In the country where everybody waves at everybody, Leslie was now driving past Frank's place, looking straight ahead though she need not have bothered. Frank had already turned his back and was looking the other way.

One afternoon soon after, she'd literally collided with Calvin coming out of the drugstore. She hadn't seen him since Gulliver had died, and she said something predictable and sympathetic. Without the dense growth of beard, his face looked naked and vulnerable, but his eyes were guarded and distant as ever. Wasn't Frank's Pit Bulls for Sale sign outrageous, she added; but to her surprise, instead of agreeing, Cal just threw his head back and laughed. Frank was way too lazy to go to all the trouble of actually doing it, he said. No, this was just his way of getting everybody upset, and it was working.

"You don't seem very angry about his dogs killing your goat," she said almost accusingly.

"What's the use of getting angry? It just makes everybody feel worse." He suddenly seemed bored by the subject.

Leslie found this attitude oddly annoying. She'd just spent the better part of three days obsessing about the evils of Frank Hawkins and wasn't in the mood to give him a pass. She asked him if he wasn't even just a little irritated, as that would have comforted her some. After a thoughtful pause, he agreed that, yes, he was a little irritated; however the mildness of his tone gave her no satisfaction whatsoever.

"Well, don't you think you should at least *tell* him?" She pressed him now, a little heated.

"Frank knows what I think," answered Calvin calmly, his hand on the door.

"So you're just going to let this go! I mean—how is he ever going to learn if you don't tell him?"

"People like him just need a little space but he'll figure it out." Calvin gave a curt nod and went into the store, leaving Leslie to steam in her own juices. Here was the victim of the crime completely placid! Maybe Ruby was right; he *was* contrary.

CHAPTER 13

The Revelation

It was after dark when Leslie returned from what had become a very traumatic cocktail party at the home of one of her mother's dearest friends. It was in a neighborhood of fine older homes in the near West End of Richmond, with tree-lined streets and lovely gardens. It was comfortable and gracious, exquisitely decorated with a tasteful array of modern and antique furniture, thick Persian carpets, and original art. On the wall was an oil portrait of a long-haired, blue-eyed daughter with her horse; another, a cozy husband and wife scene at the lake place, all casual signs of comfortable wealth. These were not the nouveau riche but people brought up with means and social eminence over generations. Both were well-known in the corporate and civic realm, their names attached to hospital buildings and cutting-edge private schools for underprivileged youth. Of all her mother's country-club friends, Leslie had always respected and admired Jill and Langdon the most. During Leslie's "rebellion," as it was now called, Jill had been something of an ally, stepping in to reassure Leslie's mother that an apple never falls too far from the tree.

For the first time in almost a year, Leslie was in a great mood, and she was looking forward to relaxing in their beautiful backyard, landscaped with garden terraces hung with Japanese lanterns and twinkling Christmas lights. Then she spotted Lenny Weiss, Stuart's boss. Even from behind, she would have recognized his bald head anywhere with the fringe of hair dyed black as shoe polish. Immediately, her good mood took a nosedive. Lenny was one of the last people on earth that she would ever want to see anywhere, much less here. He was standing in line at the butler's pantry, waiting for a refill of his drink. Though he'd lost weight, he'd visibly aged since the last time she'd seen him, and there was a wounded hangdog expression on his face, but she wasn't about to hang around to find out why. In hopes of dodging him, she veered toward the Florida room, but he'd seen her and, in a matter of moments, latched onto her like a drowning man clinging to a life raft.

Where had she been all this time? He'd been dying to talk to her but hadn't known how to reach her! Had she moved? As much as she'd always disliked him, it came as a shock to see this cocky little man so diminished. His voice, loud and abrasive as ever, made her wince at every word being broadcasted across the room. He would make a scene before he was through and she did not want to be in it.

When she told him that she was living in the country, he smiled grimly. "Had to get away, huh! Tell me about it. I went to the Bahamas. I just got back but it's worse than before, I think. Worse than before. Like a knife through the heart. I loved her, you know." He looked away, tears standing in his eyes. "I know people used to talk, like she was some kind of gold digger, but she was better than that. I always thought she was better than that. I guess I was wrong, huh."

Leslie was now utterly confused. Should she know something about Sherry? Suddenly the look on Lenny's face made her heart go cold.

"You don't know, do you! Oh my God. You mean to tell me that bastard didn't even have the guts to tell you?" Leslie cringed, sure that everyone in the room was now listening.

"Tell me what?" she was saying, not sure she even wanted to know the answer to that question.

Lenny's round face twisted into a vindictive leer. "Him and Sherry were having an affair. Oh yeah—I finally found out about it! For three years, they've been going at it right under our noses!" He shook his head in disgust. "Bastard. Lying bastard. I mean, he was like a son to me!"

Struck numb with shock, she turned away, muttering that she had to go and then plunged blindly through the crowd of bodies and voices for the door. Suddenly she had to get out of there. He called out from the front steps as she headed for her car. Where was she going? What about her number? How was he going to reach her?

"Sorry," she shouted without looking back. "Sorry—"

She'd left without telling anyone, gotten into the car, and just driven due west until the city lights and the traffic had thinned to nothing, leaving her in the protective cover of darkness. The lonely searchlight of her headlights roamed the long winding stretch of road ahead as her thoughts tumbled in a chaos of emotion. Stuart and Sherry together? She'd been such a fool. Everything was clear now—all Stuart's incomprehensible behavior, why he had so heartlessly cut himself out of her life. He'd had three years to prepare for this. For him it was old news. Of course they'd had to conceal their affair even after the separation because of Lenny, because of Stuart's job. Now that he knew, Stuart would lose his job for sure. That accounted for the anger about selling the house. He needed the money.

And the letter she'd written—how naïve had that been! They must have gotten a big laugh over that one! What a fool she'd been to think they could get back together! What a stupid romantic fool! Love returns! Bitter, furious tears blinded her eyes, and she hoped to God she wasn't driving off into a ditch.

Her mind flashed back to the last time she and Stuart had been to a party at Lenny's. Reckless from one too many glasses of wine, Leslie had made a point of seeking Lenny out. She had an important question to ask him. How, she wanted to know, in the age of hostile takeovers and sending factories overseas for cheap labor, could he gut perfectly healthy companies and still look himself in the mirror? Lenny had given her a patient, fatherly stick-to-the-artwork-honey sort of look. That was just the nature of the beast, he said. Business wasn't run on niceness.

"I see, so it's all hail the almighty bottom line and the little guy be damned, right?" Whereupon she confided to an innocent bystander at the cheese board that the real reason he built factories overseas was so he wouldn't have to pay his workers what they deserved and so he could buy another monstrosity of a house that he didn't need.

On the way home, Stuart had been furious. What the hell had she been thinking?

"Just because they have money doesn't mean I can't say what *I* think!" A dog raced alongside the car, barking ferociously. Its owner whistled from the front steps of a house.

"You're not the social activist you pretend to be, Les! You're one of them whether you like it or not! Shall I remind you that the only reason you're able to stay in your little artist ivory tower is because of the lifestyle which Lenny provides us."

"You say it like I'm some kind of kept woman. I've lived in the slums. I know what it's like to be poor."

"Like your parents haven't always been there ready to step in and save you from yourself!" His face twisted into mockery.

"Okay, so you want me to make more money? Is that what you're saying? I've told you a hundred times, I'll be happy to go waitress somewhere." She hated it that she sounded like a petulant little girl. This was one of her hot-button issues. Above all else, she craved respect, and deep down she knew that what he was saying was true, and it hurt her pride.

"That's not what I'm saying!"

"I think that *is* what you're saying! That I have no value unless I'm making money!"

"When did I ever say that?"

"All the time, you're pressuring me . . . keep those paintings coming, Les . . . But is that going to sell, Les? You can't look at anything without seeing it as a-a-product with a price tag. I mean, to you, art has nothing to do with beauty or-or even artistic value!"

"Les! You are the worst kind of self-righteous bigot!"

"Bigot?"

"Yeah, bigot! I can't believe you said those things tonight. Just because they're rich, you think that you're better than them?

"Oh, please! He's just a greedy little SOB with a gold-digging wife!"

"Oh, so now we're attacking Sherry, huh!"

"Oh, please!"

"You don't even know her, Les. I mean, if you gave her half the attention you paid to her maid, maybe you'd find out she really isn't so bad!"

"Come on! Why do you think she married Lenny if it wasn't for his money? It sure wasn't sex appeal."

"Some women are attracted to older men."

In light of the fact that Lenny was half a head shorter, bald, and overweight, Leslie could only howl with derision. "And I suppose that's why she's always checking out other guys—including you, I might add!"

"God, Les!" His voice sounded angry. "Would you stop!"

"Well, it's true. She has a huge crush on you, and if you can't see that, you're blind."

He put on the turn indicator and pulled into the left turn lane—no one in sight in either direction but they sat there, waiting in a heavy silence. "Yeah, well she's a lot smarter than you give her credit for—and sensitive too," he said finally.

"I've never trusted women who are too perfectly coiffed," sneered Leslie.

"You know that chip on your shoulder is really holding you back, Les."

She brooded, knowing how bitter she sounded, but she refused to let him see how ashamed she felt. "Okay, so maybe I'm jealous of all the attention she gets for just being pretty," she said finally.

There was another silence. "So do you need me to tell you that you're pretty?" He had the tone of strained patience.

"Not when I make you!"

His voice hardened. "Stop being adolescent."

Perhaps that's when she'd first realized how much he had changed. There would have been a time when she and Stuart would have joked about these people behind their backs. Now he really did want to be one of them.

When she got back to River's Bend, a full moon had just risen over the trees, casting long shadows across the yard. The dogs came charging out from behind the house, barking ferociously until they smelled who she was, and then it was all warm wiggles and cuddly whiney complaints.

The moment she opened the door, Elliot jumped up on her leg and put a big run in her stockings as Hooch nearly knocked her off her feet, pushing his way past both of them on his way to the couch, where he was not supposed to be. She was too tired for a battle of wills, however, and pretended not to notice until she remembered how bad he smelled.

When she commanded him to get off, he merely eyed her indifferently. "I said get off!" She smacked his backside with an umbrella, and with an injured look, he plunked heavily to the floor and then ambled over to the easy chair. "Wait just a minute, mister! What do you think you're doing?" He paused, one paw on the seat cushion, and then with a sigh as if to say "so close and yet so far," he opted for plan B and headed for the stairs.

"Nuh huh! You are *not* going underneath my bed! Not the way you stink!" She was just about to kick him back outside when there was a loud crack of thunder. Now no amount of shoving and blows could persuade him to go outside.

"Then it's into the cellar with you, my man! Go on! Down!" She yanked open the small cellar door under the stairs, and for a moment, they both stared down into the dank ominous darkness below. He looked at her as if he couldn't believe she was serious, but she was angry enough now to be heartless.

"Go! You are not going to smell up my house!" She gave him an extra whack with the umbrella for good measure. Like a man headed for the gallows, he descended, step by step, his toenails click-clicking on the wooden steps. She slammed the door behind him for extra good measure.

Elliot, meanwhile, had already vanished under the couch. Good, thought Leslie. At least he will stay out of my hair for a while. She plopped down on the couch, exhausted. The phone rang in the hall. She waited to see who it was before picking up. She didn't want to talk to anybody. After a blank silence, Calvin's voice came onto the answering machine.

"I finished the book and brought it back, but you were gone, so I left it on your porch." His voice became muffled as he addressed someone in the background before hanging up, at which point, Leslie heard a bloodcurdling howl from the cellar, followed by a murky silence.

She stood at the door, peering down into the darkness below. "Hooch?" There was no sound from below. She called out more sweetly this time. "Come here, Hoochie boy!" But again there was no response. It seemed very odd that he wasn't clamoring to come back up the steps. What was that infuriating creature up to now? She had just decided to go down to investigate when with another monumental clap of thunder all the power went out.

"Not again! Not now of all nights! I just can't take any more!" she wailed, feeling frantically around for the flashlight she'd left by the telephone and banging her hand painfully against the chair. As she pointed the beam down into the cold dank stairway, that old vision of Henry falling down these very steps and breaking his neck leaped unbidden into her mind. Okay, so we're not going down, she thought just as there was the sound of an alarming crash coming from the basement.

"All right, I'm coming! I'm coming!" Firmly pushing aside all trepidation, she began the slow descent down the creaking stairs, following the shuddering beam of the flashlight to the dank earthen floor below. In the next moment, all Hooch's mischief lay revealed. He'd knocked over a dusty old shelf full of clay gardening pots and canning jars and was contentedly occupied with chewing open an old sack of fertilizer.

"Stop!" she screamed. "That's poison, you idiot!" As if something had yanked the feet out from under her, she went sprawling face first onto the floor. The flashlight promptly flew out of her hand and broke, plunging her into inky darkness.

Stunned, she lay on the cold earth and took an inventory of body parts, hoping that her nose wasn't broken because no doubt her foot was. She'd clearly heard the crack of a bone but strangely there was no pain. In fact, there was no sensation at all. It was completely numb.

Thunder rolled like a giant bass drum, shaking the very earth beneath her as Hooch shoved his wet nose into her face, washing her in his stinky breath. Not caring how bad he smelled, she threw her arms around his neck and sobbed.

If only he were smarter, like Lassie. She tried to envision him running over to Calvin's house and Calvin saying, "What is it, boy? What is it? Something wrong, you say? Show me where she is, boy!" But knowing Hooch, he'd just plop down and take a nap. No, she was going to have to drag herself up the steps to the phone. Then she remembered. The power was out and the phone would be dead. Well, no matter! She would drag herself up the stairs and out to the car, and if she had to, she'd drive herself to the hospital (and for the time being, she would not think about spiders or rats).

For a few moments, the thunder subsided, and in the silence she heard a creaking on the cellar stairs. The hairs rose on the back of her neck. Hooch uttered a low ominous growl. This was not the haphazard creaks of an old house settling in for the night but systematic, like an old person slowly making their way down the steps, stopping now and then to catch a breath, and she had no doubt that once again that presence was waiting there in the darkness, watching. She could almost imagine that she could hear it breathing.

After what seemed like an interminable silence, suddenly there was another deafening roar of thunder, along with a shocking explosion of glass. She screamed and Hooch erupted in a bloodcurdling howl, and though later she would dismiss it as only imaginary, she could have sworn she heard the muffled cry of a human in pain.

A few moments later, she heard Elliot's frantic barking and the sound of footsteps overhead, followed by a man's voice, a very real voice, breaking through the darkness like a beam of light. "Miz Hillerman?"

"I-I'm down here!" She wanted to sound brave, but to her own ears, her voice sounded thin and childish. "I think I may have broken my foot!"

Instantly a flashlight bounced down the steps. "I'm coming," he said. The light flicked around the room until it found her curled up in the far corner of the cellar. She'd been going exactly in the wrong direction! A stab of electric pain shot up her leg. The shock was wearing off and her foot was starting to wake up.

"What the hell happened?" From beyond the beam of light, he was but a shadow, but she already knew that it was Calvin Creed.

Suddenly she was sobbing and shivering, trying to explain about the dog and the lights going out and falling in the darkness and the horrible cracking sound. Could it be broken? He knelt beside her and gently palpitated her foot. It was already an angry blue-black and swollen.

"Looks like it," he said. He handed her the flashlight and told her to hold on tight and then squatted down and, with perfect ease, gathered her up into his arms. His clean earthy scent instantly calmed her. She trained the narrow beam of light on the rickety wooden steps.

"Let's hope those steps don't collapse," she said, gritting her teeth against the jarring pain. "I've put on a little weight lately."

He laughed. "Maybe we ought not to think about that just now." His mouth was so close to her ear that she could hear his every breath. "Ready? Here we go."

Halfway up, Hooch decided in his inimitable fashion to squeeze past, prompting a loud shriek from Leslie and fervent curses from Calvin who, nonetheless, continued stalwartly on. Once upstairs, he set her down on a chair and then disappeared into the kitchen for ice only to return with a bag of frozen peas. It was all he could find. "Hold this against your foot. It'll ease the swelling. The phone's dead so there's no point in trying to call rescue. Anyway, they'd be coming all the way from Wade's Creek. It'll be just as quick for me to take you myself." He put on his poncho and went out to move the truck up near the porch. Outside, the rain was pouring down in heavy sheets. He returned, dripping, covered her with an extra poncho he always kept in his truck and carried her out into the storm.

The windshield wipers were weak and the visibility so poor that it was an effort just to stay on the road. The defroster didn't work either, but the rain was so heavy they didn't dare crack the windows, keeping Leslie busy wiping away the fog as he strained to see the road. The roar of the engine and the pouring rain made talking difficult. She decided that this was actually a good thing. There was no need for awkward conversation now.

"This is kind of like a disaster, isn't it?" she shouted at one point.

He grinned, flashing white teeth in the light of the dashboard. "We'll make it," he said. He drove with determination, the oncoming headlights sporadically brushing his face with strokes of illumination, revealing a gentle face set in composure, a good face, she thought. As the truck chugged doggedly through the storm, she thought that if there was anything good about this situation, it was that Stuart had temporarily been wiped from her mind.

It wasn't until they were on the way back from the emergency room four hours later that she thought to ask how it was he'd happened to come by her house at that particular moment. It was the book he'd left on the porch. It was going to storm, and he was afraid it would be ruined by the rain. She hadn't answered her telephone earlier so he'd assumed she wasn't home. When he'd gotten to her house, the front door was standing wide open, the lights were off. He'd called out, but there was no answer, and Elliot was acting so upset that he knew something was wrong.

"Maybe the angels sent you," she said though she hadn't ever particularly believed in angels.

"Maybe they did." She couldn't know what he was thinking at that moment, but the look he gave her sent a tremor through her body that took her by surprise.

CHAPTER 14

After the Fall

Leslie and the dogs spent the next week at her parents' house. From the start, things did not go well. First of all, her mother immediately noticed that she wasn't wearing Nana's cameo necklace, and Leslie had to admit she'd lost it. Then she'd made the mistake of confiding to her mother about Stuart's affair. At first, Emily refused to believe that her adorable, charming Stuart, the son she'd never had, could have betrayed her only daughter, and even when she finally did accept it, Leslie couldn't help but feel that in her mother's eyes she somehow was to blame. Indirectly, Emily hinted that perhaps if Leslie had worked harder at being liked by her in-laws, this might never have happened. After all, Leslie had never made a secret of her contempt for their way of life. This propelled them into a fierce argument, ending in a sullen peace with Leslie staying in her room for half a day until her father came and dredged her out.

But the most difficulty surrounded the dogs. The first night, Emily insisted they stay in the garage, where they howled all night long, keeping everyone awake. In the middle of the second night, her father tapped discreetly at the guest room door, where Leslie was sleeping. "Don't tell your mother," he said as the dogs padded in and instantly fell asleep on the powder blue rug. After that, her father smuggled them in each night, careful to return them to the garage before Emily woke up each morning. All would have been well if it hadn't been for Hooch's smell and Elliot's little accidents.

For eight days, Emily roamed the house, sniffing with an evil eye, on the lookout for suspicious wet spots. She sprayed air freshener incessantly to the point of asphyxiation and exhausted herself waiting on Leslie hand and foot. Soon everyone's patience had worn thin. True to her ways, Emily carried on as if nothing were the matter.

Finally, an argument broke out between the two women over a peanut butter and jelly sandwich, which Leslie was trying to make. Though completely exhausted, Emily felt compelled to seize the knife and do it herself, followed by a tug of war and then an argument over who was more exhausted and who was being more stubborn.

Leslie threatened to go back to the country. Emily got hysterical. Who would take care of her? Finally, her father came to perform his usual function of tamping down the flames, and a more reasonable plan was hatched. Leslie would go back to her country house, and her mother would drive out three times a week and make sure everything was okay. Back at River's Bend, they set up a bed in the living room, stocked the refrigerator, and said good-bye. Her mother was still worried, but Leslie made a good show of sounding more confident than she felt.

It would be a long and empty afternoon with nothing to keep her from sinking into a gloomy obsession about Stuart and Sherry. Every show on the antiquated TV set looked like it was set in the middle of a blizzard, and reading made her head hurt. By late afternoon, she'd sunk into a restless depression, and doubt had started a full-scale attack. She would never make it on her own, her mother was right, and she should have fought for the house in Brandon Mills. It was time to stop living in a fantasy and get real, and if this meant going back to the city then she just had to accept it.

About four o'clock, with surrender weighing heavy upon her, she'd just picked up the phone to call her parents when the cellar door slowly creaked open. She froze, fully expecting someone or something to appear at the top of the stairs, but nothing happened. Sooner or later, somebody was going to have to close that door, and it might as well be now. With a sigh, she hoisted herself to her one good foot and crutched her way over to the dreaded door, and that's when she saw what she realized she was meant to see—a dusty porcelain plaque hanging on the inside of the door. For some reason she'd never noticed it before nor the poem written on it.

The Shadow of the Rock

The Shadow of the Rock!
Stay, pilgrim, stay!
Night treads upon the heels of day;
There is no other resting place this way,
The Rock is near,
The well is clear;
Rest in the Shadow of the Rock!

The Shadow of the Rock!
The desert wide
Lies round thee like a trackless tide,
In waves of sand forlornly multiplied.
The sun is gone,
Thou art alone;
Rest in the Shadow of the Rock!

The Shadow of the Rock!
All come alone;
All, ever since the sun hath shone,
Who travelled by this road have come alone.
Be of good cheer,
A home is here;
Rest in the Shadow of the Rock!

Tears of gratitude sprang to her eyes. Though it had been hanging here in the dark for who knows how long, she knew that, in this moment, this message was for her; and it was telling her that she wasn't alone. She was being helped.

She limped out to the porch and sat in the cooling shade of the wisteria vines. With a sigh, the wind moved and set the trees into a slow dance. The sun had dipped low in the western sky, and in the hush of late afternoon, the fertile beauty all around flooded her with a surge of comfort. No, this was her sanctuary. It was okay to be here and she didn't need to know why.

At that precise moment, Calvin's sister Thelma arrived out of nowhere with a parade of covered dishes and a chocolate cake. She whirled around the house, a tornado of orderliness, quickly setting everything to rights. She even cut zinnias from the yard and put them in a vase on the coffee table and then made tea and proceeded to talk Leslie's ear off for about an hour and a half. To start with, she couldn't believe Calvin had driven Leslie to the hospital in that ramshackle old truck. According to her, why—it was a miracle they'd made it there alive!

Then she went on to discuss in minute detail every medical complaint of every person in her family, followed by the latest news on the pit bull situation. She never did trust the man that could be so nosey about other people's business. After all, why did Leslie suppose that Frank Hawkins had become a mailman in the first place, if not to peep into other people's mail when he had the chance! Thelma was annoyed that Leslie seemed doubtful of this and went out of her way to explain that lots of people failed to lick their envelopes properly.

"Anyway, Penny says he's going to take that man to court if he doesn't do something about those dogs, and I hope he does! I mean, do you hear that racket every night and day? Poor Mama! I guess it's a blessing she's about stone deaf."

Leslie nodded. No matter the subject, she was glad for the company. On her way out, Thelma promised to get the ladies in her church to help out.

The next afternoon, Pendleton Caughey arrived on her front porch looking very trim with a tool belt strapped to his waist. He mentioned that he'd run into Thelma and heard the news about Leslie's calamity and announced that he had come to fix her rotten front porch steps. It was a hazard for anyone with two good legs, let alone a woman on crutches. What was wrong with her landlord that she hadn't fixed it already?

Grateful for the company, she sat in her rocking chair and watched while he set to work. The good thing about Penny was that she didn't have to worry about trying to think of anything to say because he handily did all the talking. He talked mostly about the past, a life lived in constant defense against hostile sons of bitches, be they human or canine. In his mind, there was little difference between them except that he generally favored dogs over humans. He pointed to his bumper sticker which read "The more I know humans, the more I like my dog." His view was that unlike humans, dogs could be trusted. If they want to kill you, at least they're honest about it. During the course of the day, she also discovered that he was an unapologetic Jew and "nigger" hater. Whatever the subject matter, it would always eventually work its way back to how they were bringing the country down.

When she commented that it was a good thing he wasn't president, he burst out with great cheer. "You're damned right. They'd assassinate me in a heartbeat."

He was determinedly slow at his work, making great long pauses between every nail and measuring and remeasuring before every cut. "Measure twice, cut once" was his motto; though to be more accurate, it should have been "measure once, talk, measure twice, talk some more, and then forget the measurements and have to do it all over again."

The end of the first day left her convinced that she could do with a little less company, but he was back again the next day, hammering away bright and early. She was trying to come up with an excuse for going inside to hide, when suddenly he turned to a slightly more interesting topic—his wife, Libby.

Their entire marriage, he said, had been a complete and utter sham. Oh yes! She'd played him for a sucker, and if he'd have known then what he knew now, he would never have married her in the first place. She was a spoiled little princess, and he used the word "little" in a figurative sense, being that the woman was fat and getter fatter by the hour! And selfish? Why, with her it was always me, me, me. He went on to rant and rail against what he called the "me generation."

"In my day, we wasn't allowed the luxury of always getting our way. If that's what was cooked for dinner, you damn well ate it or you starved. If we got too full of ourselves, my father would knock the hell out of us! That's what he would do. Why, even my own kids—if they ever tried to give me that 'me-me-me' crap, they'd see the back of my hand right now! There's nothing I hate worse than a spoiled kid."

On the second day, she was startled by the sudden appearance of the young black fellow, Linwood, peering in at her front screen door just as he'd done the first time he showed up. She let out a ridiculous little shriek, and he jumped.

"Sorry about that, ma'am!"

"Oh! Hello, Linwood." she said, composing herself and glad that she'd made the effort earlier to change out of her nightgown.

He looked at her crutches and her cast. "Broke your foot, huh? Wow! Too bad! Does it hurt?"

"Some but it's better than it was."

"That's good." For some reason, he looked almost guilty. "Listen, your grass is getting pretty high. You want me to cut it?" When she hesitated, he added that he'd do it for nothing.

"Oh no. You don't have to do that. I'd pay you."

"How about an art lesson and we'll be straight? I wanna know how to paint. I can draw but I can't paint."

"Well," she hesitated, moved by the hope reflected in his eyes. "The thing is I don't know how much I could show you in one lesson."

"Well, I'll mow your lawn twice and you can give me two lessons." He smiled that broad dimpled smile.

She laughed. He was a real charmer, all right. "Okay, but do you have any paint? Paint is expensive."

"I'll get some." She watched as he commenced to mow the lawn with the old push mower, and though it was obviously not an easy task, he had far less difficulty than she'd had with it back before she'd given up entirely.

After he finished, she paid him; and they were still standing on the porch, discussing the art lesson when Penny's car appeared, advancing slowly around the bend, as he always took great care driving over her potholed lane. He was there to work on the steps, he announced brusquely as he disembarked. Immediately, the young man's smile disappeared and he retreated behind a sullen mask of indifference.

Penny was visibly displeased, and he looked past Leslie as if Linwood weren't even there. "What's he doing here?"

"He was mowing the lawn!" Leslie answered defensively with an apologetic smile in Linwood's direction, but the young man looked off at the trees.

"Mowing the lawn, huh!" He gave Linwood a hard look.

Turning toward Leslie, his eyes trained low, Linwood mumbled something that sounded like "thanks" and then slunk off down the road with a slouching gate that gained arrogance the further off he moved.

"Why," cried Leslie furiously, "did you talk to him like that?"

"You don't want his kind around your place," replied Penny calmly. "Can't trust them kind of people."

"Them kind of people?" Leslie was seeing spots; she was so angry. "You mean because he's black!"

Pendleton J. Caughey seemed not the least bit bothered that she was angry with him but glared right back at her just as fierce. "No, it's because he's a jailbird, okay? That's what he is! A jailbird and you better be careful! Did he come into your house?"

She paused. "No," she lied. "He just—mowed the lawn."

"Well, if he comes back, whatever you do—don't let him in. Tell him to get the hell away or you'll call the cops."

"That is ridiculous. I won't do that!"

"If you have a lick of sense, you will! You're a single woman living alone in this isolated place! And a cripple to boot!"

"He's seems nice to me."

"And I'm sure the Boston Strangler seemed nice too. You're just the type his kind is looking for—all sweet and trusting. But I'm telling ya, you better listen to me because I know what I'm talking about! Do not let him in."

Leslie remained aloof on the subject, but truthfully, she didn't know what to think, and some intuition told her that maybe Penny was right.

On the third afternoon, Penny started to give Leslie compliments. First, he complimented her paintings. This time he had his glasses on, and the way he examined the nude portraits made Leslie feel strangely undressed. "I always say, there's no greater masterpiece than a naked woman," he announced at least five or six times and then adding with a slow suggestive wink that artistic women made the best lovers. She could only manage to say that she was glad he enjoyed art.

Then he complimented her eyes. "You know, I like a brown-eyed woman. Everybody's always making such a big deal about blue-eyed babies, but give me a good brown-eyed girl any day."

"Would you like some . . . coffee, Mr. Tea? I mean some tea, Mr. Caughey?" cried Leslie, grabbing for her crutches and giggling a little from embarrassment.

He arose swiftly, closing his hand over hers. "Honey, it ain't tea that I want—and call me Pendleton." She lurched from her seat, stumbling onto her broken foot with a howl of pain.

"Oh, baby! Are you all right?" he crooned, his hands all over her.

"You must be so thirsty!" she exclaimed, giving him a well-placed shove. "I'll be right back." She crutched in desperation to the kitchen, but he dogged her every step, cornering her by the refrigerator. "This is real cozy in here, I'd say. I always like a woman who can cozy up a place."

"That's a very nice thing to say, Mr. Caughey," she answered brightly, keeping her head low and trying to squeeze past him.

"I keep telling you to call me Pendleton," he murmured huskily, following her to the sink. "Looks like you've got a leaky faucet there, little lady. Guess I've got my work cut out for me." His mustache twitched meaningfully, at which point a coffee can full of paintbrushes inexplicably fell off the overhead shelf and onto Pendleton Caughey's head.

"Oh, Mr. Caughey, are you all right? I'm so sorry!" she cried meanwhile crutching as fast she could back out to the porch.

He followed, vigorously rubbing the spot where the can had hit. "Babe! You gotta be more careful when you put things up there like that," he said, noting when they got to the front door that she had forgotten something. Suddenly they were both wedged eye to eye in the doorway, wrapped in the flowery scent of his aftershave.

"What?" she asked.

He grinned, his eyes glowing like a cat that had just cornered a mouse. "The iced tea, babe! You went all the way into the kitchen and you forgot about the iced tea, but never mind, I'm not thirsty no more." His voice became low and intimate. "If I didn't know better, I'd almost think you was trying to avoid me—Leslie." The way he said her name felt almost obscene.

"Of course not," she answered, leaning as far away from him as possible without falling over. To her great relief, Calvin's dilapidated old truck suddenly came barreling around the bend. "Oh, look! Calvin's here!"

"How's it goin', Cal?" Penny called out cheerily, casually slinging his arm across her shoulders.

In her hurry to move away, Leslie stepped down on her broken foot, yelping with pain.

"Oh, baby, baby, are you all right?" Once again, Penny's hands were all over her.

Barely able to keep from slapping him away, Leslie insisted that she was fine. Meanwhile, he made a big show of helping her to the porch swing and then planted himself right beside her with a proprietary air.

Calvin approached the house solemnly, bearing a casserole dish covered with one of Thelma's handmade quilted ducks, his face a mask of indifference. Acting like he owned the place, Penny rose and took the casserole into the kitchen. Meanwhile, Calvin coughed stiffly and looked out at the field.

"Mr. Caughey's come over to fix the steps," offered Leslie by way of conversation.

Calvin glanced at the steps without seeing. "That's fine," he said.

He stubbornly resisted her efforts to draw him into conversation about the book she had lent him, only saying that she didn't have to worry. He always returned books.

By then, Penny had returned. "How do you like Leslie's new steps, Cal? Pretty nice, huh?" Without waiting for a response, he started reeling off the long list of repairs that he planned on making to the house. By the time Penny veered onto the subject of the correct and incorrect ways of pouring cement, Calvin was staring off into the field again. In a moment of desperation, Leslie made the mistake of jumping in with a question about Frank's Pit Bulls, and it wasn't long before an argument soon boiled up between the two men.

Penny called the sign a clear declaration of war. "And if it's war he wants, then its war he's gonna get," he declared. "I've got my rights too, and I'm telling you right now, I'll set me a chair down there on the edge of my property line, and so help me if one of them mangy mutts puts one paw over that line . . . Kapow! I'll blow his head off. And you know I'll do it!"

"And just which line are you talking about?" answered Cal quietly. The property line had been a hotly contested issue for years. Frank claimed that the dirt road that ran to the river was solely on his property and that Penny's property came to the *edge* of the road. Penny claimed his property line ran down the *middle* of the road. Both men had spent many hours searching for the mythical iron stake driven into the ground that reputedly would end the discussion, but neither had ever been able to find it.

"So you're just going to roll over and let him do what he pleases? Come on, Calvin! He killed your damned goat! Be a man for crissakes!"

Cal set his jaw, pulling his brown felt hat down low over eyes, which had turned a steely blue. "If you give things a chance to just simmer down some, Frank will come around to reason, but if you go down there with guns blazing, you *are* gonna set off a war, and I don't want any part of it!"

"Ah, don't be a Virginia weeny," sneered the older man.

Leslie placed a restraining hand on Penny. "Please! Let's not argue! I already have a headache!"

"Sorry, babe! You should have told me! Here! Let me give you a head rub!" Despite her protests, he slid behind the settee and began vigorously rubbing her temples and pulling her earlobes, boasting that he could cure any headache, any time.

Meanwhile, Calvin fell into an inscrutable silence.

"How's this feel, babe?" crooned Pendleton.

Leslie pushed Penny's hands aside with finality. "Yes, I feel much better now. Thanks." She detested being called "babe." "So, Calvin—"

"You'd best bush hog that field before the briars take hold," interrupted Calvin tersely and then abruptly headed to the truck and took off.

Watching the blue truck disappear up the dirt lane, Leslie felt an unexpected surge of disappointment. How was it that a man could carry someone in his arms and then, two weeks later, act like a complete stranger?

Meanwhile, Penny stood shaking his head with a satisfied chuckle. "A real moody character, that Calvin—temperamental as a woman. The least little thing you say and he goes off on a sulk. A real mama's boy."

The next day, Ruby phoned with exciting news. There'd been a shootout at the mailboxes. No one was hurt except for Frank's PIT BULLS FOR SALE sign. Armed with his .22, Penny had gone down to pick up his mail. On the way, he'd suddenly heard a whole series of pistol shots in quick succession.

"Ruby! You can't be serious? They didn't actually shoot at each other, did they?" broke in Leslie.

"No, now wait a minute. I'm getting to that! Don't you ruin my story now," chuckled Ruby, clearly enjoying the drama of it all. "So where was I? Oh, yes—the pistol shots! Anyways, Penny he comes down to the end of his lane, and the shooting stops and what do you know but Frank is standing there in the middle of the road, with his hand behind his back, just a-grinning like an ol' bullfrog. And Penny says, 'I thought I heard a pistol going off down here.' And Frank, he says, 'I didn't hear nothin'.'" In the background, Leslie heard a dog barking. "Git that dog out of here, Thelma! I'm talking to Leslie!" cried Ruby excitedly. "Now where was I?"

"Frank said he didn't hear nothin'—I mean anything," prompted Leslie, feeling more like two gossips out of middle school.

"Oh yes . . . well then Penny says, 'What's that you got behind your back, Frank?' And Frank, he's just a-grinning you know how he does, and real innocent he says, 'Oh, nothin'.' But Penny says to Frank, 'Well, I wasn't born yesterday, and I know damn well there's something behind your back! And I'll just bet you I know what it is!'"

"Mama! Such talk for an old lady!" cried Thelma from the background.

"Oh, hush, Thelma! I'm just telling what Penny said!"

"Go on, Ruby!" urged Leslie, feeling anxious now to hear the rest.

"Anyway, so Frank says, 'The hell you do!'"

"Mama, I declare!" wailed Thelma.

"And then Penny says, 'I'll bet you fifty dollars it's your repeater pistol. And don't you try to hide it, either.' So Frank brings out his pistol real slow. 'I was target shooting,' he says. 'I figure I better practice,' he says, but Penny says he could see there was blood in his eye. Well, when Penny heard that, them cold prickles went shooting right up his spine, and he says, swear to God, Frank was this close to shooting at him right then and there!"

"No!"

"I kid you not! I would have run helter-skelter right then and there, but you know Penny Caughey—he's a regular ol' pit bull himself!" Ruby shrieked with laughter at the thought. "Why, he just stood up there and says, 'Go on, take your best shot, ya coward!'"

Of course, Frank he just laughed his head off—you know, the way he does when he's got ya cornered, and that just made Penny so mad, he took and shot a few holes in the pit bull sign. Well, that wiped the smile right offa Frank's face, let me tell you!"

"Mama! Hurry *up*! I gotta use the phone!"

"And then Frank, he whips around and he points that gun—"

"Mama! This is an *emergency*!"

"And Penny says, swear to God, for a minute he thought he was going to shoot Peanut!"

"Mama!"

"Would you stop your whining, Thelma! Give me a break!"

"So then what happened, Ruby?"

"Well, that was pretty much it. Penny got his mail, and he yelled at Frank and told him that if them mongrels steps one foot on his property, why, he's going to blow them all to kingdom come . . . and I don't blame him!"

As much as she hated to admit it, Leslie was a bit disappointed that the story hadn't a more exciting ending but said she was glad nobody got hurt.

"Me, too . . . but that Frank Hawkins! Somethin' needs to be done about that man! He's a regular lunatic! No wonder his wife left him! And readin' private mail too!"

"One night, those dogs ran through my yard, and thank goodness Hooch was in the house!" said Leslie by way of agreement.

"Oh, Lord, or they might have done him like they done Calvin's Gulliver! I never liked him much, but that was a bad way to go, even for a goat."

"Mama, for heaven's sake! I have got to use the *phone*!"

"I gotta go now. I'll talk to you later!"

Meanwhile, Leslie's anger started a slow burn.

CHAPTER 15

The Stray

The reunion was drawing near. Thelma had made another bet with Calvin, namely that he would be too scared to go, and he wasn't about to lose this one, too, or he'd have to have a buzz haircut. Still, the nagging anxiety had played a steady drumbeat ever since. Would Annie Clay be there? He didn't know if he could bear that.

Cal was drinking coffee out in the backyard under the maple tree. In practical terms, the backyard really was the front yard because nobody ever used the front door. There was no sidewalk leading to the front door nor even a worn foot path. It was rarely even opened, except, of course, on the day the wind had blown it shut and shattered the glass. On the other hand, the backyard was a wide swath of pounded dirt tamped down by generations of many feet from where the vehicles were parked and where chickens roamed and pecked.

The stray cat that had been hanging around the place for the past several weeks peeked from behind the wheels of the old orange harvester. She was a pretty long-haired yellow cat with wide-set pale green eyes, and she was mewing at him again. He called her Scaredy because she was a timid thing. Even so, she seemed equally fascinated by him and would periodically come almost close enough to be touched and then take off like a shot. "Come on, little Scaredy! Come on! You don't have to be afraid of me."

He'd had been trying to tame her with food every day, and today was the closest he'd come to touching her. By now he knew not to reach for her. She would come to him on her own terms. "Come kitty . . . come," he crooned softly. She stared wide-eyed. The slightest move, he knew, and she would vanish like smoke.

Something about the way she had of moving close, as if she wanted attention and then running away as soon as it was offered, suddenly reminded Calvin of himself. With a rueful smile, he pulled an old envelope and a pen out of his shirt pocket. He was in the habit of keeping something handy in case he got a stray thought worth writing down.

> Come close
> For what I dare not say
> Come closer
> And then run away
> O frightened creature
> Of my heart

Calvin stared at the words he'd written and then quietly ripped the envelope into small pieces and tossed them into the burning barrel. The mere thought of Thelma or Ruby's prying eyes catching hold of this was like a scrub brush on a burn.

At this very moment, Cal was supposed to be working on a new coop for the baby chicks he'd bought a few weeks back, but his heart wasn't in it today. In fact, he didn't feel much like doing anything this morning, and it was all because of Leslie Hillerman. It wasn't that he wanted to be thinking about her—it was just that he couldn't stop thinking about the searching way she'd looked into his eyes at the drugstore—what had she seen? He dreaded to think that his true feelings might have shown. And what did she think of him? He wouldn't dare to guess about a woman like that. For a time, he'd thought maybe there was a way to escape, but from the moment he'd held her close, he'd known that it was too late. He hadn't felt this way since—well, not for a long time, not since Annie Clay. He couldn't hide it from himself any longer. He'd fallen flat on his face in love with the woman.

He'd been thinking about Leslie night and day with a yearning that was nothing short of pain ever since Sunday, when he'd discovered that son-of-a-bitch Pendleton with his arm slung across her shoulders, acting like he was king of the hill, the cradle-robbing bastard! Cal had seen the way Penny treated his young wife, Libby, running her down in front of people like the little tyrant he was. Cal knew the type well—the man who must drag others down so they can feel big. Cal was still burning in the fires of humiliation after driving off, all tongue-tied and twisted up inside with Penny's mocking laughter stinging his backside like poison quills. Well, if she wanted a man like that, then let her have him. Calvin had no time for either one. This was a lie, of course, but it felt good, at least temporarily, just to pretend.

What was it anyway about that white-haired old blowhard that could attract young women to him? Calvin couldn't see anything attractive about him whatsoever. Then again what was there to interest Leslie in a thirty-eight-year-old farmer, who still lived with his mother?

Calvin knew the answer to that question without even thinking. His tongue wandered over the chipped edge of his tooth, reminding him that she was nice to everyone, so why should he think that she felt anything special toward him? After all, what did he have to offer a woman like her, who had been places and done things that he knew nothing about?

And now to make matters worse, he'd gone and showed his novel to her. His darkest secret self was in that manuscript, all the pain and beauty of his existence, and he'd showed it to her! What a fool move that had been. That she'd said nothing about it was absolute proof that she thought it was no good. God, he hoped he'd never have to see her again.

As a boy, Calvin had learned to keep his dreams of becoming a writer to himself for fear of his father's scorn. Writing and literature and reading books was for girly men. It was honest labor that his father believed in, and he ruled the roost. There wasn't room for any other way but his. It never would have occurred to him to think that Calvin might possibly be a different kind of a person with different kinds of dreams. Now after so many years, they'd begun to seem foolish even to Calvin, and he had come to accept his fate as a solitary man in a solitary world. Not to say that in his small world he had not found some measure of contentment, and so long as he never allowed himself to wonder if maybe—just maybe—things could have been different then he was safe from the bitterness of regret. *That* beast would eat him alive with anger and shame over the monumental failure in making his escape.

For years he'd pined for that girl—Annie Clay—and it had only been with great difficulty that he'd finally buried the pain. He would be a fool to let this woman Leslie get him all worked up now, but there was something about her. She was different. For one thing, he hadn't met a woman since Annie who loved books like he did, and then there was the fact that she was an artist—but it wasn't just that either. It was the way she listened and the way she sort of stretched herself out to people, trying to really understand them. And it was the warm light in her brown eyes, so ready to smile, so eager to be delighted. It was a childlike eagerness she had, and she wasn't too proud to be vulnerable or even foolish. He wasn't used to that in a woman. His mother and sisters were so full of their own opinions they couldn't care less about what anybody else thought or felt.

It worried him, this nervous excitement he felt at the mere sight of her. It made him angry, too, that after all these years, he'd allowed himself to slip once more into the trap of love. Still, he'd carried her in his arms, and holding her body close had felt so amazingly right.

He was pulled out of this dark reverie by the arrival of Linwood Thomas coming up the lane on foot. Damn it all anyway! He was supposed to work on the fencing tomorrow, not today! Calvin felt the walls closing in on him. Ruby was already breathing fire down his back about getting another coop built for the chicks, and it couldn't be put off until tomorrow or the next day but had to be done *today* because, according to her, it should have been done *yesterday*.

Calvin felt the pain of being stretched between two tasks, neither of which he wanted to do, but he didn't want to disappoint Linwood after he'd just walked a couple miles to get here. Living in the country with no car, no job, and no money was no joke. Jail time and a couple of DUIs hadn't helped Linwood's situation either.

"Hey, Linwood!" Calvin caught the kid's attention just in time before he went up to the house and knocked on the door. At this point, it was better for Ruby not be stirred from her recliner, or she'd be out there fussing.

Linwood merely nodded disinterestedly. He'd been solemn after being in jail but seemed even more suppressed than usual. Calvin still thought of him as a kid though Linwood was past twenty-five and already showing signs of age. His brown skin had lost its luster, and the gray shadows under his yellowed eyes showed signs of too much drinking—a common fate for the young black men in the area. By way of proof, the sour smell of old liquor lingered on his person as he drew near.

Calvin felt a sinking sadness to see Linwood in this condition. He'd known him all his young life and been friends with his grandfather, who had always worked alongside Cal's father around the farm. In some ways, Clarence had shown more interest in Calvin than his own father, who'd been all work and no play. There was always a lot of laughter when Clarence was around, and he was a good storyteller.

When his daughter fell in with a rough crowd and run off, Clarence had taken over raising her young son, Linwood. After that, the boy was always tagging along. Calvin remembered him as being a cute little kid, very loveable, always smiling. Cal was twelve when Linwood had first appeared in their yard, the first small child he'd ever really known. He remembered how he'd carried Linwood piggyback, swinging him around, tickling him, and making him laugh while the men worked. Linwood had attached to Calvin like a baby duck and wanted to do whatever he did. It had made Calvin feel good.

But when Linwood went through puberty, he'd started doing drugs, hanging out with a disaffected group, bitter and cynical about whites. From then on, he was distant and sullen. His grandfather was not an educated man and didn't know how to get his grandson to advance himself. When Linwood rebelled, Clarence did what he knew to do, and that was to come down hard on him, but it had only driven him away. In his older years, the old man had become so crippled up with arthritis that his old sunny disposition was hard to come by.

Lately, since doing time in prison, Linwood had started coming around again but only out of necessity. He was looking for odd jobs, trying to make ends meet. Calvin still periodically brought Clarence vegetables from his garden and even bought groceries now and then, when it seemed they were struggling, but it was only for the old man's sake. Linwood's stony indifference put him off, not to mention that he could still be seen hanging out in the grocery store parking lot with all the wrong people.

So here stood Linwood on the wrong day, probably not too excited about working but needing the money, no doubt. The question was for what? Calvin wondered if the young man wouldn't be wasting it on drugs or alcohol, when the old man was in need. Linwood had started to feel like a burdensome relative. He was certainly no fun to have around, working in a very sullen and disinterested way.

Because Calvin's father had been so domineering, always ordering people around, Calvin never had taken pleasure in telling people what to do. However, with Linwood, it was a necessity, as he seemed incapable of doing anything without being told in minute detail. Or maybe it was that he just wasn't willing. Calvin started to understand how a good-natured man like Clarence could have lost his patience with the kid. But it turned out that Linwood wasn't here to work on the fence. He wanted to know if Cal had some roofing paper he could use for the hole over his grandfather's bed. Meanwhile, Thelma had roared into the yard in her husband's truck with the ridiculously oversized tires, drawing Ruby out into the yard with her cane. When they saw Calvin sitting under the tree, they both aimed their trajectory straight at him, indignation shooting preemptive sparks, Ruby's shrill voice piercing the distance.

"What the heck are you doing sitting around under a tree for? I thought you was going to get my coop built today? Hello, Linwood. How's your grandpa?"

"He ain't doin' so good, Miz Creasey."

"Well, that's fine. Say hey to him for me." Ruby had long since dispensed with the effort of actually hearing what people were saying and usually just forged ahead with the conversation whether she'd heard them or not. "So Cal—when *exactly* are you going to get them chicks off my side porch? They are getting too big and they smell!"

"I said I'm gonna do it."

"When? Half the day is gone. Your papa would have had it done by now!"

"I *said* I'm gonna do it."

"Of course you will, only that's what you said last week and every day since."

"Well, there's other things that have to get done around here, you know."

"Like what?"

"Like the fence for one."

"The fence? What about my house? I am not going to live in a chicken coop, Calvin!"

"If you'd have listened to George in the first place, you wouldn't be in this predicament!" Now it was Thelma's turn to weigh in on the subject. Her husband was a "big idea" man. According to him, Calvin had built his cheap wooden chicken coop too small in the first place. Now here he was just a few years later with a fallen-down chicken coop and having to build another one. He should have built a nice big one of cement block on a cement pad. George was all about cement. He guaranteed that it would "last longer than you do!" He'd just built his own new house with a concrete basement down the road. It was ridiculously huge, in Calvin's opinion, but far be it from him to say so. He just shrugged it off, like he shrugged off everything else having to do with Thelma and George.

"And promise me you won't use that horrible old rusty sheet metal again to cover the walls," added Thelma with a stern eye.

Ruby threw up her hands and rolled her eyes, "Oh, that sheet metal—"

"There's nothin' wrong with the old sheet metal." Calvin had never understood Thelma's obsession with everything having to be brand new. What was wrong with using old cast-off materials? It was cheap and pretty much just as good. Besides, it wasn't like anybody ever saw it except for a few neighbors and family anyway. "It's not like I'm not gonna paint it."

Thelma snorted contemptuously. "And please not that gosh darn awful fire-engine red! It's so tacky!"

"What's wrong with fire-engine red? It's a good color!"

Both women rolled their eyes as if Calvin were the most thick-headed fool on the planet. "I swear, Mama, Cal has no sense of taste whatsoever. When Papa was alive, he kept this place neat as a pin. It was the nicest-looking farm in the county and now look at it. It's all patched up and ramshackle. You know what George says, don't ya, Mama? He says with all Calvin's ramshackle sheds lined up down there, the place is starting to look like shanty town!"

"Panties down?" Ruby looked down at her ankles just to be sure nothing was drooping.

"No! Shanty! Shanty town!"

"What in the world are you talking about, Thelma?" spewed Ruby impatiently.

"Oh, never mind, Mama," snapped Thelma. "So what are you gonna do, Calvin?"

Calvin shrugged and looked away.

"You can talk yourself blue in the face, Thelma, and Calvin is gonna do what's Calvin's gonna do," declared Ruby, turning back toward the house.

"I know, Mama, but you'd think he'd have just a little pride." With a peevish look, Thelma took her mother's arm. "And now look at that screen door! No wonder you have flies in the kitchen! For the life of me, I have never understood that man."

"He's just like your uncle Jake."

The screen door slammed and there was silence again.

Linwood, who had kept his eyes cast down during the entire scene, gave a cautious, sidelong glance.

"Count your blessings, Linwood," sighed Calvin wearily.

Both men burst into a silent contained laughter, like the pressure of pain finding an unexpected release.

The river was liquid silver streaked with pink and gold in the day's dying light. Linwood liked the river at this time of day. It was the stillness hanging in the balance between worlds that soothed him like nothing else could. He leaned on the railing of the new bridge crossing the wide flat river, turning his face into the breeze. The old bridge had been carried off by the flood of '69. This one was wide and serene with plenty of room for a man to take his leisure.

People rarely stood as he did now, overlooking the lavish beauty stretching out before him. They were too busy hurtling past in cars on their way to somewhere else. Most days it was only him and maybe old Dan, rambling about the invasion of Italy and his days in Patton's army. Smelly and covered with warts, tobacco juice leaking into the deep crevices around his mouth, Dan was too loud, too opinionated, and too northern.

Almost nobody wanted to have much to do with the old white man, but the river received him without complaint and the beauty of the sky and the gracious air—besides, Linwood didn't really mind listening so much. They were good stories, and he knew the old man was here for the same reason he was—just hoping that the wind might, for a moment, blow away the haze that hides a man from his spirit.

However, today was not to be one of those days, for he hadn't been there two minutes when a black Mercedes with tinted windows eased up alongside of where they both stood. It was JT, pretty much the last person he wanted to see. The car stopped in the middle of the bridge, and JT got out along with Philly and Red. All the doors were left standing wide open. JT approached Linwood, relaxed and grinning amiably in his expensive silk shirt, his coffee-colored skin oiled, hair meticulously braided. He was a beautiful man and he was king of this bridge. He stood on top of the railing and stretched his arms wide. He was king of this river, too, and everybody there knew it, which made him smile. However, nobody else smiled, least of all Linwood. Linwood owed JT

$6,000. It was an old debt, but JT charged interest, and the older it got, the bigger it got, and the bigger it got, the more depressed and useless and hopeless Linwood had become.

Old Dan made the mistake of looking annoyed. "You gonna get one of them car doors ripped right off, leaving 'em open like that in the middle of the damned bridge!"

"Oh yeah? So tell me—whatcho doin' on my bridge, old man?"

"This ain't your bridge. This is a public bridge and I can go on it when I please!" Dan may have been a smelly old cuss but he was bold.

"You think so?" Philly closed in on him menacingly.

"I ain't afraid of you, little man! I know what you are!" he said to Philly, who prided himself on being as tough as he was short. "You think you're all that but you wouldn't last ten seconds where I been! I'd like to see your big man act in Patton's army! He'd set you on your ass that quick!" He snapped his fingers dismissively.

Linwood stepped hurriedly into the breach between them. "Shut the hell up, you crazy old son of a bitch! I'm sick of your loud-mouth-ugly-assed face. We'd beat you to an inch of your life if you didn't smell so bad!" The chorus crowed with delight. He went on playing to his audience. "Yeah, you're just lucky we don't wanna touch your greasy-assed self 'cause we don't wanna get contagious! Now get out of here! And stand down wind, man! You stink!" Red gave him the high five. Everyone was convulsed with laughing, except for JT, all the while coolly evaluating Linwood's performance. Linwood had not proved himself yet. He was a fringe player, and JT did not give his approval for free.

Meanwhile, Old Dan trudged off, cursing and spitting brown streams of chew. Inwardly, Linwood breathed a sigh of relief. He would make peace with the old man tomorrow. In the meantime, he had JT to deal with.

CHAPTER 16

An Intruder

Around 2:00 a.m. the following night, Calvin's phone rang. It was Leslie. Being that it was her left foot that was broken, she'd decided to try driving again and had been into Richmond earlier that day. She'd come home late and after going to bed, awakened to the sound of a crash coming from the cellar. Someone was in the house. In the background, he could hear the dogs were going wild.

Adrenalin pumping, he'd jumped into the truck, arriving to find all the lights on, the dogs howling, and Leslie on the front porch in her nightgown, her broken foot propped up on a crate. She was holding a broom. Calvin started to head into the house.

"Wait a minute!" she cried. "Take this!" She gravely handed him the broom.

"What am I supposed to do with it?"

"Well, what if they're still down there?"

"Then they're not too smart," he said but took it anyway.

She followed him to the top of the stairs. He flipped on the switch, and the solitary naked bulb at the bottom of the stairs issued forth a sickly yellow glow. As Calvin started to descend the rickety steps, Hooch, according to custom, chose to barrel past, nearly knocking him off his feet. Leslie screamed. Cursing the dog, Cal continued on down and then disappeared from sight. After a long silence, he appeared again at the bottom of the steps wearing a grave expression.

"Nobody here---not now anyway." He mounted the steps slowly. "But I did find this." He held out a broken silver chain in one hand and her great-great-grandmother's cameo locket in the other.

"So that's where it's been all this time! It must have broken when I fell!" Her moment of happiness dimmed when she noticed the strange look on his face. "What is it?"

"Have you been digging holes in your cellar?" he asked.

"Holes?"

"There are three holes in the cellar about yea wide, yea deep." He rubbed his chin thoughtfully. "I'm thinking maybe that's what tripped you that night you broke your foot."

"Are you saying someone has been digging holes in my cellar?"

"That's what it looks like to me." He seemed deeply unsettled.

"But why would anyone do something like that?"

"I don't have a clue." He ran his fingers over the rough stubble growing on his chin. In a moment, the adrenalin rush was over, and he looked worn out. "They escaped through the outer door. Didn't bother with the padlock, just took off the hinges. But whoever it is, they like bologna—a lot!" He held out a handful of meat wrappers.

Leslie thought ruefully back to the first day she'd shown the place to her parents and how she had been so cavalier in dismissing her father's concerns about the security of the doors and windows. He had been especially worried about the outside entrance to the cellar. It was just secured with a wooden cross bar. She'd laughed at him when he'd insisted on installing a padlock on the inside. Who was she supposed to be afraid of, she'd asked—the raccoons?

Suddenly the full realization of what had just happened set in, and Leslie started to shake so violently that her teeth were clattering together. Cal guided her back to the couch. "Sit here while I call the sheriff." All she could do was to nod.

Not long after, the police car drove up, setting the dogs into a new frenzy of excitement. It was Sheriff Tuttle, a big beefy man with a red face and big teeth and his deputy, R. "Squirrel" Jones, an officious string bean of a fellow full of nervous energy.

The sheriff sat in the most comfortable chair and questioned Leslie about the order of events while Calvin showed the deputy down into the cellar and around back to where the cellar door had been forced open. She gave all the details she could think of—that she'd been out all day, returned after 11:00 p.m., and no, she hadn't noticed anything out of place or unusual but had gone directly to bed here in the living room on the couch, where she'd been sleeping since she had broken her foot.

She hadn't awakened again until shortly before 2:00 a.m., when she'd heard a loud crash coming from the cellar.

At this point, the deputy arrived from the basement looking disturbed. "There's a bunch of holes dug in the floor down there."

"Holes!" Sheriff Tuttle frowned. "What the hell?"

"Holes. Padlock ain't been touched. He just took the hinges off one of the doors and just put it back in place, so nothing looked like it had been disturbed."

"Huh—holes," mused the Sheriff, drumming his plump fingers on the armrest.

"Whoever it is has been doing this for a while," added Cal. "I figure that's how she must have tripped a few weeks back during the blackout when she broke her foot."

Everyone's eyes turned toward her cast. "So he's been coming in and out." Sheriff Tuttle scratched his jaw thoughtfully and then shot Leslie a piercing look. "You heard anything before this? Anything suspicious?"

"Well, sometimes, but I just thought that—well, that it was just old house noises or—you know." She didn't want to mention the ghost. "But who would have thought I'd ever have this kind of trouble out *here* of all places!" exclaimed Leslie.

Sheriff Tuttle shook his big square head and clucked his tongue. "Let me assure you, Miz Hillerman, this county may have nary a stoplight, but you'd be surprised the weird happenings taking place back on these ol' country roads."

"Family quarrels mostly, folks getting hot under the collar, shooting each other and whatnot." added Squirrel officiously. "Sometimes, it ends up real tragic."

"We had a rash of breakin' and enterin' six months ago—a ring of teenagers lookin' for electronic equipment mostly. Things they can sell on the black market," continued Sheriff Tuttle, meanwhile jotting down his notes.

"You had anything of value stolen, ma'am?" interjected Squirrel sharply.

"No, not that I noticed."

"Course, you might have interrupted them," continued the deputy. "You say you was in town this evenin'? How long were you gone?"

She was now forced to repeat all the details once more.

Calvin apparently knew Sheriff Tuttle and Squirrel from way back. The three men chewed on this information for a while, repeating the details over and over several times to each other. "So she came home at eleven . . ."

"But she didn't notice anything out of place . . ."

"Didn't hear *any* sounds at all?"

"Woke up at 2:00 a.m."

Finally, the sheriff announced that the whole thing made no sense at all. There'd been a whole string of house burglaries, but this certainly didn't fit the pattern.

"It's that business with them holes. That's what's got me going round and round," muttered the Sheriff.

"Could be another psycho on the loose," declared Squirrel gravely.

"A psycho?" Leslie turned white.

Sheriff Tate drew himself up to his full proportions. "Ma'am, now if you choose to remain here, I seriously recommend you have that cellar door permanently barricaded and your doors and windows locked at all times."

"I can take care of that," interjected Calvin.

"And a woman alone in the country needs a good guard dog, Miz Hillerman."

"Oh, but I already have one." Everyone's attention turned to Hooch splayed out on his back, snoring softly.

"I said a *good* guard dog, ma'am. Something that can do some damage?" said Squirrel with a sniff.

"Believe me, Hooch can do plenty of damage!" A mysterious surge of loyalty kept her from mentioning that it had been she who had awakened him during the crash in the cellar incident.

"I noticed your neighbor has a sign on his tree advertising pit bulls for sale," continued Squirrel.

Cal and Leslie exchanged a dubious look.

Squirrel appeared defensive. "Pit bulls make excellent guard dogs, you know!"

It was decided that there was really nothing they could do at the present time, but she was to call immediately if anything suspicious happened. After delivering another severe lecture on locking her doors, they made a motion to leave. On his way out, Squirrel gave Calvin a wink with two thumbs up and a not too subtle nod in Leslie's direction. "Way to go, bro."

As the police car disappeared up the dirt lane, Leslie sat on the porch swing and wept. For a moment Cal stood helplessly by and then, on an impulse, sat alongside and drew her soft warmth to his body, his heart pounding like a pile driver. She did not resist but turned her face into his shoulder, trembling from pent-up emotions. He tightened his embrace, and they stayed that way for what seemed a long time though it most likely lasted but a minute; still, as that minute dragged by, Cal had time to reconsider the wisdom of having made such a move, for now the logical question was: what next? However, she solved that problem by pulling away.

"I think I need something to drink," she said, hastily wiping away her tears. He asked if she was cold since she was shivering all over and her teeth were chattering, but she shook her head no, and then he offered to get her a drink of water. "No," she said, "I think it's gotta be something stronger than that."

Without a word, he went to his truck and returned with a six-pack (minus one) of a strong red lager that he liked to enjoy in the evening after a long day working in the sun. "It's warm," he said, "but if you like lager, this is the best."

"Right now anything will do! I just need something to get me—to stop—stop shaking." There was no doubt she was in bad shape, he thought. He opened a bottle for her and then one for himself. What the hell! If anybody qualified for stress relief at the moment, it was him. They drank in silence for a while, sitting side by side, gazing up into the Milky Way stretching like a carpet of stars across the moonless night.

"Don't worry," he said once the beer's comfortable warmth was coursing through his veins. "Whoever it was that broke in got scared but good tonight. They'd be stupid to come back. I don't think you need to worry." Rocking gently back and forth, the old wooden swing added its reassuring creaks to the chorus of crickets and cicadas swelling in extravagant counter rhythms from out of the darkness beyond.

"I just wish it were that simple," she said quietly, looking away with a heavy sigh, her face twisted with misery. "God, I'm so stubborn sometimes. What made me think I could do this on my own?" She dropped her head into her hands, hair falling like a dark curtain across her face.

Cal hesitated, not sure of how to respond. "Of course," he said finally, "you might keep in mind that not many women would dare to even try." He took a nervous swig of beer for fortification.

She laughed harshly. "There was nothing brave about it, believe me. I was just running away from everybody else because they knew what I didn't want to see! That's what it really was all about!" She gave him a weary smile. "You don't even know what I'm talking about—but don't worry. I'm just talking to myself again. I've been doing that a lot lately." She looked at him now more attentively, as if really seeing him for the first time. "I bet this happens to you a lot, doesn't it—people telling you their deep dark secrets! It's because you're a good listener. You're so calm. In fact, you're a really good person," she proclaimed, showing the first signs of the extravagance with which good beer invariably endowed her.

He looked at her with a sad, almost wistful smile. "Well, I'm glad you think so," he said.

A hoot owl called out from deep in the woods.

"How be-e-e-autiful," she murmured in breathless wonder.

"Yeah—" He closed his eyes and breathed in the sweet balmy air.

They continued to rock back and forth, not saying anything. "You know for a while, I'd actually convinced myself that things were going to work out between him and me. I actually really thought that—" She was sounding more detached now. "Wow! What a sap, huh? Earth to Leslie!" She heaved a huge sigh. "If only I could sleep." She downed the remains of her beer and let out an unexpected belch. "Pardon me! So"—she eyed the rest of the unopened beers—"do you think I could possibly have another one?"

His eyes opened wide. "Already?"

"I'm afraid I'm a guzzler," she confessed sheepishly.

He laughed, which made her smile and made him want to do something reckless like kiss her, and maybe he would have if she hadn't erupted into another lament. "It's this jealousy," she cried, putting her hands over her heart. "It's like an anvil right here. I swear sometimes it's trying to suck the life out of me." She exhaled forcefully as if to throw it off into the universe and then looked at him apologetically. "I'm sorry, you don't want to hear this—do ya?"

He looked at her intently. "Fire away."

Her face crumpled. "You know you shouldn't be so kind. You're gonna make me cry again!" With her clever paint-stained fingers, she tracked down an errant tear sliding down the side of her cheek and wiped it away. "You're a good person, Cal—and I'm to the point of thinking that that is very rare in the male species!" She paused, looking puzzled and slightly drunk. "Wait a minute! Is the male a species or—"

"Sex. It's a—sex."

"Whatever—sex, species—it's the same thing!" She turned on him, glowing now with a sudden revelation. "But you are different, aren't you! You're so"—she waved her hands in the air searching for the right word—"nice!"

He frowned. "First I'm good and now I'm nice. I'm not so sure I like that."

Puzzled, she peered into his face, searching for a sign of what he was feeling. "Why not?"

"Nice guys finish last."

Startled, she sat back and contemplated this for a moment, taking a few more swallows of beer. "Actually, that's probably correct, but do you think it's true for women too?"

"I wouldn't know about that. Of course, what are we talking about here? Niceness—I never liked that word. It's not goodness we're talking about. It's something superficial, just a thin cover over what's really there."

"Like all the anger—" She withdrew momentarily into a brooding silence. "You know what I hate? When you're finally living in a beautiful place like you've always dreamed of, but when you go to the river, you don't see the trees, you don't hear the birds, you don't see anything beautiful because your mind is trapped in this dark hole, spinning round and round, thinking the same stupid horrible thoughts over and over again!" She wiped her nose on the hem of her nightgown. "I'm babbling!"

"You're too hard on yourself. Don't you think this would be difficult for anybody?" he offered quietly.

She was thoughtful after that as they rocked gently back and forth; and maybe it was his solemn quiet presence or maybe just the safety of darkness; but suddenly the whole story started spilling out of her, her marriage, the separation, the conversation with Lenny at the party—everything. They kept rocking, their eyes fixed on the stars as she talked and he listened. It felt good to finally let it out with a neutral bystander or, in other words, someone who wasn't her mother.

When her feet got cold, he held the door, and she hobbled inside where she sank onto the couch, exhausted. He hesitated in the shadows beyond the doorway, as if ready to leave. "You're not going to go, are you?" she cried, unaware of how beautiful she looked to him at that moment, with her hair streaming like a dark river onto her breast.

"If you want me to stay, I'll stay," he said.

"I just don't"—her voice contracted—"I just don't want to be alone right now."

"Of course, you don't," he replied calmly, purposefully avoiding the chair with the broken springs and sitting instead on the pink high-backed Chippendale chair opposite. He propped his feet on the footstool. He was wearing flip-flops and some kind of loose shapeless pants. They were probably the ones he slept in. He must have jumped right out of bed to come over when she called. He had beautiful feet for a man, with high arches, and below the hem of his pants, she could see the soft curly golden hairs that covered his legs.

There was an awkward silence. In the naked stare of the electric light, it was easy to think that maybe she had revealed too much. It would be wise to keep the conversation more impersonal, she thought. "So what was it like for you growing up here?" she asked.

"Hmmmm . . ." His eyes diffused dreamily back to a different time. (His eyes, she wondered—were they blue or green?) "Well, if you can imagine living with about six and a half Thelmas, you'll get the jist of it."

"Your sisters?" He nodded gravely and she grinned. "Why six and half?"

He smiled. "Because Tina could be nice about half the time. She was right above me in the pecking order. I was the youngest and the only boy."

"You were spoiled is what I hear."

"Probably in some ways but not in others."

"What do you mean?"

"You'd have to know my father. He was very powerful man, who liked things done his way and his way only. Let's just say fate was unkind to him making me his son. I figure Thelma should have been the boy because I generally hated working. I was always disappearing, hiding up in a tree or out in the woods somewhere so I could read—that is if I wasn't down at the river fishing with my grandpa. Reading books was a useless occupation as far as my father was concerned, and he had no patience for fishing. Consequently, I was over here with my grandfather every chance I got."

"So what was your grandfather like?"

"If you hear my mother talk, you'd think he was the laziest man that ever lived, but that's because she has no understanding or respect for what he was. He was a fisherman and the best storyteller you'd ever want to hear. I'll never hold a candle to him. I do know that." His expression darkened.

She looked uncomfortable. "Listen, I've been meaning to tell you about your book—"

He dismissed it with a weary wave of the hand. "Forget it. I know it's no good."

"Wait, you don't understand!" Opening the drawer of the side table, she pulled the few wrinkled pages that she'd been able to save from the river and laid them on the coffee table before him.

His eyebrows drew into a knot. "What's that?"

"Your book—or what's left of it. I'm so sorry! The rest got blown down the river. I didn't even get a chance to read it, and I guess I sort of kept forgetting to say anything because I was so embarrassed!"

Oddly enough, he looked relieved. "Well, it was probably for the best. It's not ready yet anyway. I'm still making changes although I don't know why I bother."

"It takes a long time, doesn't it—writing a novel?"

He paused. "This one's going on five years, give or take a few eons."

She could tell he didn't want to talk about it. "Well, I'd like to read it when it's ready."

"Yeah, right—sure." He was guarded again all of a sudden. "I think I need some water." He disappeared into the kitchen and then returned with a glass for her as well.

Suddenly, she was swept by a feeling of déjà vu, as if this had all happened before.

The conversation flowed so easily between them after that, and it struck her as quite natural that he should be here in her front room, sleepy and barefoot in a holey T-shirt, his sand-colored hair wildly adrift.

In the midst of talking about the pros and cons of going to art school, she realized that he had fallen asleep. Soon she had drifted off as well, and suddenly it was 4:00 a.m. The lamp was still on and she was cold. She got up, covered him with a blanket, and, yawning, turned out the light. The last thing she remembered before sleep sucked her into the deep was that someone was standing in the hall—a man, spare and wiry, tipping his hat—and somehow she knew that he was pleased.

The next thing she knew, there was a loud knocking on the front door. A shaft of early morning sunlight was now illuminating Calvin's foot, poking out from beneath the blanket. Hooch let loose a bloodcurdling howl, and the two dogs skidded into the hall like cavalry to the rescue with Calvin stumbling sleepily after. He returned with Pendleton Caughey announcing in a loud voice that Calvin's *mama* wanted him to call home. She was *worried*! He gave Cal an insinuating look. Calvin scowled and went into the hall to call Ruby.

Meanwhile, Penny sat down beside Leslie and put his arm around her shoulders with the pretense of being comforting. "I heard about what happened!" he said. "A break-in, huh? So what happened, babe? Tell me all about it." However, by the suspicious way his eyes roved the room, he was looking for evidence of a different sort.

The day was already starting to heat up outside, but Leslie defensively wrapped herself in the blanket and launched into yet another rendition of the night's adventure. When it came to the part about hearing the sound of the crash coming up from the basement, Penny interrupted impatiently. "So where was Calvin?"

Leslie stopped abruptly. "Why he was in his house, of course."

"Oh." He looked momentarily disappointed. "Okay, just checking. So go on, babe."

She gritted her teeth and continued on to the part about calling Calvin, at which point Penny again interrupted a bit more sharply this time. "And he's been here ever since . . . to *protect* you, I suppose." He looked skeptical. "He didn't try nothin', did he?"

"Mr. Caughey!" she cried, indignant.

"All I'm saying is that a woman in your situation can't be too careful. Him being a bachelor so long, he's bound to be a pervert. I'd watch him if I was you. Them quiet types can be real weirdos."

Calvin came back into the room at this point.

"Hey, Cal—remember a couple years back? That retarded boy Miz Henderson found in her basement?" said Penny.

"Mason's not retarded. He's autistic," answered Calvin testily. "They ran out of money, and he stopped taking his medication is all."

"I still say they should have sent that son of a bitch to the electric chair and put him out of all of our misery," continued Penny. "Miz Henderson comes home one night, and there he is doing tae kwon do in her living room. Scared the living hell out of her, let me tell ya."

"He's back on his medicine and he's doing perfectly fine now." Cal addressed Penny as if he were someone very slow-witted.

Penny scowled. "Yeah, and what happens next time he forgets to take a pill? Somebody gets their throat cut, that's what. Like back in Jersey—I used to live a couple of miles from a mental institution and one time—"

"Would you shut up about the mental institution!" There was a stunned silence as all eyes turned to Calvin. It was unlike him to raise his voice.

A gleam of satisfaction lit the old man's eyes. "What's got you so steamed?"

"I just don't think we *need* to be talking about psychos in New Jersey right now, okay?" Cal's lip tightened with undisguised dislike.

"Well, we sure as hell can't depend on Andy of Mayberry to protect her. Those clowns in the sheriff's department don't know their ass from a hole in the ground!"

"And do you have to talk like that—in front of her?" snapped Cal.

"Like what?"

"Never mind."

Penny rolled his eyes as if to say "There goes moody Calvin again." Cal turned to Leslie as if Pendleton Caughey weren't even in the room. "Don't worry. I'll be over to, you know—stand guard tonight, if you want me to."

"That would be good, I think."

"And I'll do it *tomorrow* night!" chimed in Penny. Cal turned and gave him a black look, which Penny boldly returned. "And don't worry, babe. If the old bachelor gives you the least little trouble, I'm just a phone call away."

That night, Calvin came over at about ten o'clock. He put a sleeping bag down on the front porch, and they sat and talked for a few minutes, but both of them were far too tired to have much of anything to say. There were no signs of an intruder, and all was peaceful until dawn. She awoke with sunlight streaming through the window. Cal was already gone.

Later that morning, Frank's mail car came around the bend. He leaned out the car window, waving a white handkerchief. "Cease fire! Truce!" Grinning mischievously, he squeezed his big belly out from behind the steering wheel. "It's not every day you get door-to-door service," he said, handing her a stack of mail. It'd been piling up in her box until he couldn't fit anymore in; besides, the police dispatcher happened to be his sister-in-law, so he'd heard all about the break-in. Beneath a layer of concern, there was no mistaking his excitement.

Old Buttermilk, a nearly deaf and blind sausage-shaped dog was in the backseat. She liked to accompany him on his neighborly visits and often rode around in the car with her nose stuck out into the wind while he delivered mail. He opened the door, and she plopped out and waddled with a stiff-legged strut over to Leslie to be petted.

"Now remember, Miz Hillerman—I come under a flag of truce, so don't pull anything sneaky on me, hear?" He gave her a sly grin.

"This is not a war, Mr. Hawkins. It's just a disagreement," she said, feeling very hypocritical in light of the things they'd been saying about him of late.

His brow darkened. "When Pendleton Caughey comes down and threatens me with a .22 rifle, I'd call that a war."

"Well, maybe he wouldn't have to do that if you—"

His eyes narrowed. "If I what?"

"If you would keep your dogs in a fence, Mr. Hawkins!" She dared to look him in the eye.

"You think I'm just a dumb ol' redneck, don't ya!" He was sneering now. "I see how you do—driving by with your nose in the air—"

"I waved but you wouldn't even look my way! Look, I don't hate you. We're talking about dogs running wild in packs, and we're talking about a fence."

"Uh huh—a fence like they do in the city, and I suppose next you'll want a leash law, too, like they do in the city!" His eyes hardened. "So tell me, Miz Hillerman. If you like the city so much, why'd you bother coming out here?"

To hell with diplomacy, she thought. "This is just a about being considerate of your neighbors, Mr. Hawkins! That's what I'm talking about but you don't seem to want to understand me! You just want to twist everything around to make it seem like big government against the little guy or some ridiculous—*hogwash* like that!" She'd never used the word "hogwash" in her life, but there it was, lingering in the air between them like a loaded gun.

"Hogwash?" An unexpected ray of humor glinted in his eyes. "I dare say you don't know nothin' about hogs, Miz Hillerman, but I do. I reckon that's the difference between you and me. Now the truth is there's no fence in the world that's gonna keep those dogs in. Not unless I sink that fence in a foot of concrete, they're just gonna dig right under it. Fences cost money too. They don't just come out of thin air, and where I live, the air is mighty thin!" He put up his hand. "I swear on my redneck badge of honor!"

She shook her head. He was baiting her again. "So tell me something. How *did* you come to have all those dogs, Mr. Hawkins?"

Frank rolled his eyes and sighed. "I find myself asking the same question every night and day, believe you me. But the truth is that it's my wife, Miz Hillerman. She'll pick up every stray dog and cat that comes through town. She's the Mother Theresa of stray dogs and cats and they're all strays . . . every last one of 'em. Olympia is the mecca of stray dogs and cats."

Leslie looked confused. "I didn't know you had a wife."

"Well not anymore. She dumped me." He laughed humorlessly. "You ever been dumped, Miz Hillerman?"

She paused and then gave him a sad smile. "Actually, yes, I have." It was his turn to look surprised.

"Well, then you know." He looked her gravely in the eye, and she nodded slowly, and just like that, their war was over.

He turned to Hooch. "So what happened to *you*, Prince Charming? I thought Miz Hillerman had banished you from the castle?"

"Yes, well that's what I thought too! The only one who didn't seem to get the message was Hooch." Hooch belched from his spot under a shady tree. "I think he's unbanishable."

"You hear what the lady's saying? You've been dumped and you're so thickheaded you don't even know it."

The next moment, Penny Caughey's car pulled up. "Uh-oh! Here's trouble," muttered Frank with a dark look.

Penny got out slowly, slammed his car door shut, and strutted over on his short little legs, puffing out his chest like a banty rooster. "I come over to check on things. He ain't bothering you, is he?"

"You keep your damn distance, Caughey! I just came to bring her the mail." Frank swelled himself up to his full proportions.

"Yeah, sure—bring her the mail and nose around, no doubt. I knew you wouldn't be able to keep away, but just remember, curiosity killed the cat." Pendleton Caughey's stiff white mustache gave a twitch.

Frank's eyes narrowed. "Is that a threat?"

Leslie, who was already standing in between them, raised both arms like a referee. "Please for God's sake—stop!" she shouted. They both looked away, muttering.

"All I came for was the story about what happened here last night," said Frank. "Straight from the horse's mouth."

After a blow-by-blow account, the two men immediately had to go down into the cellar and see the holes for themselves. They came back up, arguing about what needed to be done. According to Penny, she must install a security system like the one he had. Alarms would go off anytime a door or window was opened and would immediately alert the local police. It was expensive but worth it. You put that little sign at the end of your road, and nobody in their right mind was going to take the chance. In the meantime, a good dead bolt and better locks on the windows needed to be installed.

Frank was insisting that Leslie needed a gun. In fact, he would teach her how to shoot one and had brought a pistol from his collection for just such a purpose.

Leslie looked dubiously at the gun. "I've never even touched a gun in my life, and I don't plan on it."

"There's always a first time and don't worry! I'll teach you everything you need to know."

"She ain't gonna need that!" piped up Penny. "Me and Calvin are standing watch every night."

"All the more reason for her to have one." Frank glowered meaningfully in Penny's direction.

"I'd like to know what the hell you mean by that!" From the looks of it, Penny and Frank were facing off for another showdown.

"This is ridiculous!" shouted Leslie. "Totally ridiculous! Now stop it! You're both here out of the goodness your hearts to help me, so let's just leave it at that!"

"Come on outside and I'll show you how this thing works," said Frank softly, his eyes still locked in Penny's deadly stare.

She balked. "Look, honestly, I don't believe in guns."

Both Frank and Penny had to smirk at this one.

"What's to *believe* in?" said Frank. "It's not a religion. It's just a gun."

Penny was shaking his head, chuckling. "Guns don't kill anything, babe. People do."

"Yes, but guns in the home lead to more gun deaths. Most gun deaths are between family members and friends. That is a statistic."

"Look at that, Caughey! She's wagging her finger at us!" Frank seemed to find this immensely amusing. "Okay now, so I'll wag my finger back at you! An armed populace is a free populace. Ain't no dictatorship gonna take over America so long as we have our guns. That is in the constitution. It's on paper in black and white, and ain't no liberal gonna take that away from us except over my dead body!"

"I got your back on that one, Frank." It was Penny chiming in from the choir.

"Yes, but do we want semiautomatic weapons on the open market, unregulated so any school kid can get one?"

"If you regulate it," countered Frank, "the only ones who will have it are the bad guys. You want some of the good guys to have the good guns so they can fight the bad guys, don't you?"

"Frank's right," said Pendleton Caughey.

"So you gonna learn to shoot this gun or not?" Frank said.

Leslie sighed. "All right, but I haven't changed my mind, and it doesn't mean I'll ever use it!"

"Believe me, if your life depended on it, you would."

He set up a line of cans on the fence and quickly shot every single one right in a row. Clearly, he was a crack shot. Pendleton coughed self-importantly and declared in a deep voice, "Not bad, Hawkins." Then he proceeded to demonstrate his prowess with the pistol—100 percent accuracy.

"Not bad yourself!" exclaimed Frank. The two enemies sized each other up with a newfound respect.

Then Frank set about showing her how to stand, how to hold the pistol, aim and shoot; and while she tested the weapon, he started talking about hunting and the tradition of his forebears. It wasn't long before Penny joined in with his hunting stories, about the elaborate pranks he and his brothers had played on each other and all the amazing animals they'd seen. Before the afternoon was through, they were drinking iced tea up on the porch and having a grand time. The brotherhood of the hunt had brought them together. The two men gave a sheepish good-bye to each other, and from what Ruby later reported, the PIT BULLS FOR SALE sign came down that very day.

Later that night, Penny came to stand watch. He made a valiant effort to stay awake on the front porch; however, when it was clear that he could barely keep his eyes open, Leslie urged him to go sleep in the guest bed upstairs. He meekly acquiesced but not before proposing marriage. It was a casual, offhand proposal but a proposal just the same.

"But aren't you still married?" she said, keeping the urge to smile firmly in check.

"We'll get a quickie. I've done it lots of times. It's easy. I got a cousin in Nevada."

Her head was shaking no before the words were even out of his mouth, but that did not stop him from pursuing the matter.

"Why not, babe? We're a match made in heaven! I can make you happy! I can cook, and trust me, I perform where it counts."

It didn't seem to have dented his ego too badly when she continued to refuse him, though he couldn't help himself from being a little snide. "Oh, I get it. I'm too short. You like the big dumb apes like Calvin!" He shrugged extravagantly. "Oh well, you don't know what you're missing. But if you change your mind, just let me know."

As her smile faded from her lips, she couldn't help but notice that his comment about Calvin had made her blush.

CHAPTER 17

Sonny

Calvin was sitting in the living room, reading the paper, his little black dog, Ace, curled up on the chair above his shoulder. Ruby was napping in her recliner and, out of the blue, woke up and said, "What was his last name, Calvin?"

"Who, Mama? Who you're talking about!" She had the exasperating habit of starting conversations in the middle of nowhere.

"The one with the ponytail!" She sounded impatient, as if he should have known.

"You mean Sonny Hay?"

"Yeah, that's the one—Sonny Hay. I sure hope he's not thinkin' about coming back to Olympia. We sure don't need any more of his kind around here!" She closed her eyes and drifted back to sleep.

Later that night, Calvin awoke out of a deep sleep with Sonny's name on his lips, and it struck him like a two-by-four that it could be that Sonny had gotten out of jail and was coming back to River's Bend looking for something he'd buried in the cellar—maybe money or marijuana. He decided to ask Linwood about it. Linwood used to hang out with Sonny a good bit back in the day.

The next morning, Calvin headed over to Clarence's place. Linwood was sitting on the old bus seat out under the tree. Shortie, the three-legged dog, was sleeping in the middle of the road and didn't bother to move when Calvin drove by, as if daring him to run him over.

As usual, Linwood remained impassive as Calvin came into the yard. At first glance, Cal knew he had a hangover. His eyes were clouded with pain and he stank of alcohol.

Calvin called out from the truck—had Linwood heard about the break-in over at the River's Bend?

A dim light stirring in Linwood's eyes gave the only indication that he was listening. "Naw, I ain't heard nothin' about it," he muttered faintly.

Calvin told him about the holes and then asked him if he'd heard anything about Sonny getting out of prison.

"Not really. Why?" Linwood gave him a sidelong look.

"Well, you know I got to thinking"—Cal failed to notice that Linwood had all but stopped breathing—"if anybody would be wanting to get back in the house, it'd be him. Maybe he's looking for something. Ya think?"

Linwood shrugged as if he couldn't be more disinterested. "I don't know."

Calvin stared thoughtfully into the distance. "Yeah, me neither, but it's been three years. He's probably out by now."

"Could be." Linwood failed to mention that Sonny was dead, and though his expression had not changed, inside, his heart was galloping. The situation was suddenly getting way too complicated.

CHAPTER 18

The Reunion

The night of the high school reunion was drawing near, and one day, Cal got a letter. It was from Annie Clay, except on the return address her name read Anne Baker. She was married, had three kids, and lived in California. She'd been a high school art teacher for ten years and was planning on going to the reunion. Would he be there? *"I don't even know if your family lives at this address anymore, but it would be great to see you and all the old friends again."* Anne (Annie)

Thelma had found the letter and had been trumpeting it around all week. Meanwhile, Ruby had remained strangely silent on the matter. Cal, too, was silent. He had two choices—dread the whole thing or refuse to go. So he said he wasn't going, but he didn't answer Annie's letter one way or the other. It sat on his desk, tormenting him, and periodically, he would get it out and read it again. He'd never escaped Olympia, whereas she had gone out and made a life in a beautiful and interesting place. No, the humiliation of a life that had been wasted would be too much to bear at such a public event. Better to stay away.

However, all that went straight out the window when, on the night of the reunion, he came downstairs to find Bob Wright, an old high school friend, sitting in the kitchen, chatting amiably with Thelma. Bob was on his way to the reunion. "Come on, buddy. It'll be like old times!"

"Go on, Calvin! Enjoy yourself for once." Thelma stood in the door beaming. Ruby had gone to bed early. She wasn't feeling well.

Even Calvin was surprised that he could be so easily persuaded, though it probably had a lot to do with the fact that it would have been humiliating to chicken out in front of Bob. On his way upstairs to change his clothes, Ruby called to him from her bedroom.

"Cal! Cal!" Her ragged crow's voice sounded weak, and she looked small and shrunken in the large white bed.

"What is it, Mama?"

"You going to the reunion, ain't ya!"

"I guess I am." Suddenly he realized she was crying. "I love you, Cal. I just want you to know that."

"Mama, are you all right? You've been taking your blood pressure pills, haven't you?"

"Yes, yes—I'm just a little peaked but you go—go—don't stay for me." She grabbed his hand with both of hers and squeezed it hard.

A dark feeling stole over him, a memory of how he'd felt that summer he was supposed to have gone to college when her first heart attack hit. It was a feeling of defeat. That's what it was then, and he felt it all over again now; only this time, he would gladly have stayed. It was his backbone making him go and he knew that. No, this time he had to leave or it would feel like death.

"I'll see you when I get back," he said.

She nodded wordlessly and turned her face into the pillow.

Thelma waved cheerfully from the back door. "You look handsome as ever, Cal! It's amazing what getting rid of that hideous beard has done for your appearance."

"Come on, bro." said Bob, tongue in cheek. "Let's go chill." He had teenagers at home and knew the lingo.

The reunion was taking place in the high school gym since there was no restaurant in the area large enough to hold everybody. The senior class president, Margery Shaw, who'd also been captain of the cheerleading team, had gotten together with all the old cheerleaders and the class secretary, and they'd organized a big decorating committee. It resembled a school prom, with tables covered in red-and-blue tablecloths (the school colors) and colored lights and bunches of balloons hanging from the rafters. There was even a mirror ball and a DJ, with a dance floor marked out by a little white picket fence decorated in paper flowers. There was an arbor festooned with flowers set up in one corner, where a professional photographer was taking photos. Mostly, it was married couples getting their photos taken for a "memory book" of the reunion, but clusters of old friends, most of them women and heavier now, were posing with arms wound around each other, cheek to cheek. At one point, a bunch of the old football players crowded together in a brawl of shoulders and arms and legs and grinning drunken faces.

Cal stood at the entrance, surveying the sea of balding and gray-headed men. Many had already grown paunchy, and it gave him a peculiar jolt, seeing so many people his age showing signs of growing old. He had never thought of himself as being any particular age but certainly not what he associated with middle age. In some ways, he still felt like a child or, at least, as insecure as one.

Some of them had never left the county, but so many had gone beyond. From the periphery, he studied the different ways people handled themselves. There were the businessmen in their suits, looking confident and in charge. They were the ones who belonged in suits. He, on the other hand, had always felt like an imposter in a suit. He could see a few other imposters, sweating in the ill-fitting cheap ones their wives expected them to wear to church on Sundays. His, navy blue, had been bought out of necessity for his uncle Seth's funeral a few years back. Thelma had taken him to Sears and commandeered the whole unpleasant business. He hated shopping and going into dressing rooms, where strange men huddled in their undershorts in front of evil mirrors that were bound to make a person look ridiculous in some way.

Bob gave him an elbow. "Is that Kimmie Sutton?"

"Where?"

"There! In the yellow."

"Naw, couldn't be—could it?" They both squinted.

"Good God!"

A small balding guy in glasses came up beside Bob, flapped his arms, and oinked. Calvin stared at the man uncomprehendingly as recognition slowly dawned on Bob's face. "Piggie!" He clapped the guy in a bear hug. They jumped up and down gleefully, oinking and flapping their arms.

"Hey, Bobby—guess what my new business logo is? Flying Pigs!" exclaimed the little man in a piercing nasal voice.

"Flying Pigs! Wow! That's perfect!" Bob turned to Cal excitedly. "Remember Matt Toonie, the Intolerable Pig?" He and Bob had been thick as thieves back in school.

Cal smiled. Yes, Matt had been intolerable all right. Matt punched the same small hard fist into Calvin's midsection. Calvin remembered that small hard fist well.

"Hey, it's the Jolly Green Giant! How's the weather up there?" Matt was laughing merrily as a machine gun—eh-eh-eh-eh—the same annoying way he'd always done.

"Still keeping up the Intolerable Tradition, I see," said Calvin with a pale smile.

This inspired Matt to deliver one more well-placed punch while laughing all the harder. Apparently, he was still as hyper as he'd always been. Bob and Matt disappeared to scavenge for beer. Cal scanned the crowd. Was she here? Would he recognize her? Would she recognize him? On the way to the punch bowl, he ran into Marjory Shaw surveying her kingdom.

"So what do you think?" she asked.

"Looks good."

"We really could have used your height when it came to hanging the mirror ball, Cal. I called. Did you get the message?"

There'd been a time when everyone had thought she and Cal would end up an item. They'd gone out on half-hearted dates for about a year, but then she claimed she got tired of him and went onto greener pastures, but the truth was the relationship had ended due to a fatal lack of interest on his part. He was still pining for Annie, and someone as superficial as Marjory just didn't appeal, and besides, her pushiness reminded him of Thelma. She'd eventually married a chicken farmer from Cloverdale and now lived just over the border with four kids. She'd long since given up all claim on Calvin, and they had become good friends.

"You'll never guess who's here," she proclaimed with a secretive smile.

Cal's blood ran cold. "Who?" He pretended not to know who she was talking about.

Marjory's eyes trailed to a spot just behind him. He turned and there she was—Annie Clay.

"Hi, Cal." Annie smiled, but she kept her eyes even with his shirt collar, reminding him that she wasn't Annie Clay anymore. She was Anne Baker. For a moment, he wondered if she was more flustered than he was. "Margie, Cal ... um ... I wanted you to meet my husband—Ben!" She plunged into a group of women chatting by the cookie table and pulled out a good-looking man of medium height with sleek graying hair. He had a cookie in his mouth but handled the awkward situation with aplomb, smiling and bowing and sticking out his hand while chewing.

"He's a shameless cookie monster," explained Annie with benevolent disapproval.

"Sorry, it's just that I can't resist free cookies!" He was pure charm through and through, and he knew it. This was obviously their standard introduction routine. Annie and Marjorie laughed heartily, but to his shame, Cal could only manage a wan smile. For his own self-respect, he had to at least appear self-confident and on top of his world enough to smile at his old girlfriend's husband for god's sake! However, the most he could manage was something closer to a grimace, which would have to do.

Fortunately, Marjorie handled all the conversation. Ben was a pilot for a West Coast airline. He talked about himself easily with unaffected confidence. There was a lot to talk about—his hobbies, the windsurfing, the golf, the travel. One had to like the guy though it hurt to like him in a dark secret way. Cal kept smiling now for all he was worth, just thankful nobody had asked him the first question about himself. From here, Annie and her husband were heading to Italy for a two-week getaway.

"Really! Wow!" Marjorie wasn't looking at him, but he could feel her watching him telepathically.

The kids were staying with her parents, continued Annie. "This is the longest we've been away from them, but they're ready for it. I think they're going to be glad to have me out of their hair for a while. Grandma is so much more lenient than I am."

"We'll come back and they'll be totally corrupted," joked Ben, stuffing another crumbling cookie into his mouth.

"You can still eat all those cookies and not be fat?" marveled Marjorie. She herself had put on about thirty pounds.

"He works out like a mad man. He's in the Polar Bear Club. Swims in the bay every morning. Don't you, sweetie? Fifty-degree water. Last Christmas day, he swam all the way to Alcatraz! He's a madman."

While Marjorie fell all over herself oohing and awing over Ben, Annie and Cal exchanged covert glances. She had not changed. He would have recognized her anywhere—the same smooth round cheeks, the same peachy glow, the same calm gray eyes. Her hair was cut short in a sophisticated style, which gave her a professional look. She'd always worn her clothes well, and her figure did not hint at having had three children. Cal wished he hadn't come.

"Good to see you, Cal," she said. Polite. She was only being polite.

"Good to see you," he mumbled. He was having trouble controlling his voice. He had to get out of here. "You . . . want some punch? I'm getting some—"

"Sure." She gave him a frozen smile. Fake. It was all fake. She was bored and having to put on a show of interest. Why was he here?

Leaving the drink table, he stumbled into Bob, stepping on his toe and spilling red punch on his shirt.

"Hey! Watch it!" He could be so loud sometimes. Several people turned to look.

"Sorry."

"God, what a klutz! Geesh! My wife is going to kill me. This is a new shirt too!"

"I'll buy you a new one."

"So did you see Annie?"

"Yeah, I saw her."

"Wow! She looks great, doesn't she? Hasn't aged a bit."

Cal pushed past groups of people in a fog, being extra careful not to spill. He didn't want to make a worse fool of himself than he already had.

When he got to them, Annie, Ben and Marjorie were chattering merrily away, completely unaware of his standing there with the drinks. He tried to insinuate himself into their little triangle, but Marjorie was unconsciously blocking him out. Finally, he just stood there and sipped from the clear plastic cup. Even after the punch, his mouth felt like a desert. Finally, he was able to catch Annie's eye. She was about to take a sip from a beer. Cal raised the cup of punch.

"Here, Ben! You can have it back! Cal has brought me something to drink."

For the first time, Ben seemed to notice Calvin's presence. He gave him a friendly wink. "Thanks, pal. I'm lucky to get a taste before she's guzzled the whole thing." Everyone laughed.

At the first opportunity, Cal drifted away and headed straight for the restroom, where he hoped he might get a moment to think. Maybe he could just hide in there until it was a respectable hour and tell Bob he had a headache so they could leave, but when he came out again, she was standing there.

"Hey, Cal." Her voice had always been so musical, a low rich fruity voice, a relaxing, calming voice. This time she smiled but with real warmth. No one else was in the hall. They were all alone. "I'm glad you showed up," she said. There was an alcoholic glow around her. "Thelma said you might not make it."

"Thelma?" Suddenly he realized that Bob's coming over had been no coincidence.

"Sorry—I hope it wasn't out of line. I was just afraid you wouldn't come."

The tone of her voice, the look on her face—it was the old Annie, the one he'd dreamed of so long ago, but this was all wrong. He was confused.

"Look, at first, I thought—no way was I coming," she continued. "But I just knew that this was probably my only chance to clear something up. I mean, I just needed to know. You know?" A thin layer of tears sprang to her eyes, and suddenly he realized that beneath her calm, she was nervous too. Clearly, this was the confession wrought by one too many beers.

"You mean was I coming to the reunion?" He was genuinely confused now.

"No! I mean what happened—back then!" Was that pain flaring in her eyes? He was stunned. What was happening here? He felt like they weren't even in the same conversation at this point. "I guess I just feel that I deserve to know," she said. "Not that it matters anymore, but you never wrote—"

"What are you talking about? I wrote to you! I wrote every day for a year!"

"No! You never wrote. I wrote to you, and you never wrote me back. I finally gave up. I even called."

"You called?"

"Your mother never told you?"

"No." That's when it hit him like a ton of bricks.

"I guess your mother never did like me, did she!" Annie was saying.

So Annie hadn't rejected him after all. He couldn't speak. A cascade of conflicting emotions swept over him.

"I loved you," she said, tears standing in her eyes, "and you heartlessly cut me off—"

At first, he was too stunned to say anything but then he stepped over the barrier. "I don't know what happened, but I wrote you, and I never stopped loving you, Annie."

She looked at him for one breathtaking moment and then grabbed him into a hug and squeezed as tight as she could. It was the impetuous hug of a young passionate girl, who felt emotions deeply, as deeply as he. "Thank you for that," she murmured. He looked down into the heaven of her hair, into the same sweet fragrance of her being.

"Thank *you*," he whispered. She pulled away and looked him in the eyes, unashamed. "I just want you to know that I am happily married, and I've had a good life, but there's always been that pain, and now it's healed." She smiled and put her hands together and did a little oriental bow and then laughing at his expression, turned and walked away, albeit a bit wobbly.

That moment, something healed inside of him too.

CHAPTER 19

Ruby's Lie

When Cal returned from the reunion, Thelma met him at the door. "Did ya have a good time?" she asked, barely containing her eagerness to find out.

He brushed past her. "Where's Mama?" His expression was grim.

"In bed. She's got a fever and thinks she's gonna die." She followed him with a puzzled eye.

Cal was already halfway up the stairs. "Again?" When had they heard that one before?

"If it doesn't come down by morning, I guess I'm taking her to the hospital—so what about the reunion?"

Cal stopped dead in his tracks and turned to face his sister, his eyes like cold steel. "I saw Annie, if that's what you want to know." He disappeared around the corner. His anger was at its peak.

Upstairs, Ruby looked waxen and lay so still that she could have already been dead.

He sat in the chair that had been pulled up alongside the bed. "Mama!" His voice was sharp.

For a moment, she didn't answer, and he wondered if she was already gone, but then her eyes slowly opened, as if with great effort. "Calvin, did you see . . . anybody?" She spoke so softly, he could barely hear her.

"No, Mama, I went to a high school reunion and didn't see a soul." At the moment, he was feeling no mercy.

Thelma, who had followed him up, now gave him a severe look. "We don't need any of your smart mouth right now. Mama is very, very ill!"

"Thelma!" commanded Ruby, her voice back to full strength. "Go on out in the hall."

"But Mama—"

"Go on—and shut the door!"

Thelma slinked in her flatfooted sulky way out into the hall. She was desperately curious to hear all the details about the reunion, but only when the door was shut did Ruby speak again. "I mean, did you see *her*?" Her shrunken eyes anxiously searched his stony face for a sign, but there was none.

"Yes. I saw her."

"Did you talk to her?"

"Yes, I talked to her, Mama."

"And—and what did she say?"

"What exactly do you want to know?" There was an edge to his voice and it cut her to the quick. Like a knife, it cut her straight through to her heart. She shut her eyes and clasped her bird hands over her bony chest.

"Oh, Calvin. I didn't know what I was doing. I didn't know and I'm so sorry. So, so sorry. Can you forgive me? Can you ever, ever forgive me?" Tears streamed out from the corners of her closed eyes, and she sobbed like a child. Never, not even when his father had died, had he seen her sob like that before, but he stood like a stone, not saying a word. He wasn't sure yet whether he could ever forgive her. At the moment, he wasn't sure of anything, so he let her go on crying pitiably for a while longer until presently she got a tad put out with him.

"You ain't gonna let me keep on crying like this—without a touch of comfort, are you?"

"I don't know. Maybe."

"Calvin! I *said* I was sorry, didn't I?"

"Yeah, well maybe you need to keep on being sorry for a little while longer!"

He knew this would make her mad and it did. She rose up, all afire with indignation. "Here I am, on my death bed, and you're gonna sit there and do me like this?"

"Mama? You all right?" It was Thelma horning in again. She had ears like a hawk. She swept in like a mother hen, rescuing a baby chick in distress. She blasted Calvin with a look. "What did you say to get her all upset like this! Go on, get out of here! Git!"

"No, Calvin! Don't go!" wailed Ruby. "Not like this." But Calvin walked out anyway. In the background, he heard his mother woefully crying out his name. "I'm *sorry*, Cal! I *told* you I was sorry!"

Without telling anyone where he was going, Calvin went out and bought a six-pack and sat in his truck down by the river until about 2:00 a.m. He was angry but seeing Annie again had done two things. It had forever sealed the past. He would never go back to that young broken life again. She was a different person, living a life he could not imagine and, surprisingly, one that he would not want. More than that, it had given him a sense of reassurance. She had not rejected him after all. She'd loved him. It had all just been a mistake.

The next morning, a ringing telephone interrupted Leslie's sleep. It was Thelma. "Mama's real sick," she said. "This might be the end. She wants to see you."

As she drove up, she caught sight of Calvin slinking out of sight behind the barn. Thelma met her at the door and immediately led her up the broad staircase. Leslie had never seen her so diminished, reciting a hushed litany of symptoms and calls to the doctor and prescriptions and pills and food offered and pushed away. "I made her soup. She didn't want soup. I got her some apple sauce. She didn't want the apple sauce. I got her hot cocoa, and Mama never says no to hot cocoa. In all my life, I can't remember a time when she turned down hot cocoa but—" Here, she stopped dramatically in the middle of the stairs and gave Leslie a significant look. "She doesn't want that either." This seemed to be the sign of all signs that indeed the end was near.

Ruby was all but swallowed up in a huge Victorian-looking bed with a massive and ornately carved headboard. The windows were hung with dark heavy drapes, and yellowed window shades that had been pulled in spite of the heat, casting the room in a stale, sickly light. Her face was impassive, like wax, the wrinkles had all sagged away from the bones, her delicate blue-veined eyelids shut tight, her small knotted hands folded on the coverlet across her chest like an obedient school girl with her long gray hair snaking across the pillow in a long wayward braid. The only sign of life was the slightest billowing of her thin lips with each breath. Thelma touched her hand reverently. "Mama—she's here."

After a few seconds, Ruby's eyes opened slowly, unfocused, as if peering into darkness.

"Mrs. Creed? Did you want to see me?"

"Leslie? Is that you?" She reached blindly for Leslie's hand and squeezed until it hurt. "It's a good thing you come, as I don't reckon I'll be here too much longer now."

"Oh, now don't say that, Mama!" exclaimed Thelma with dismay. "You're gonna be fine in no time."

"Thelma, how about you go on now and shut the door behind you."

"But, Mama—" It was the unmistakable whine of a ten-year-old.

"Go on now!" Even in her weakened state, Ruby's tone made it clear she was in no mood for nonsense.

Thelma looked put out but left the room as she'd been told.

"Now I have to talk to you about something, Leslie. It's about Cal." And Ruby proceeded to tell Leslie the whole story about how she'd hidden all the letters between the two young lovers so many years before, how during all the time since, Calvin had never known why his Annie had abandoned him.

"But back then I thought he'd just forget about her and get another girl from town, somebody on his level. I thought he would move on—but how was I to know? He was tryin' to do the right thing, taking care of me and the farm and all—" Her face puckered up like she was going to cry. "Right then I should've gone to Florida like my sister. I should have let go."

Leslie patted the old woman's hand. There was nothing she could say. "So he knows now." Ruby's voice grew stronger. "He saw that girl at the reunion and I had to tell him everything I did. You don't know the terrible look he gave me." She gave out a long ragged sigh and puckered up again to cry. "He hates me now, for sure." Her whole body quaked.

Leslie gave her hand a squeeze.

"I ruined his life," she wailed. "Oh, if I could take it back! If I only I could!"

"People heal, Mrs. Creed. Life goes on. If I know anything about Cal, he'll come around."

The old woman's eyes lit up with hope. "You really think so?"

"He's a very special kind of person, Mrs. Creed."

Ruby smiled. "He likes you, you know. Maybe if *you* talk to him. Tell him what you just said. He'll listen to you." She looked away sadly. "He won't listen to me. He stopped doin' that a long time ago."

Sitting in the broken recliner in the workshop, Cal took a moment to actually look at the hat he'd worn so many years—his grandfather's hat. Cal was used to throwing it down just anywhere whenever he came into the workshop, but today, it occurred to him that it was time to start hanging it up. After all, it wasn't going to last forever.

He was searching for a nail from which to hang it when he realized that the perfect spot already existed—the hook where his father's hat had hung like a sacred icon ever since the day he died. Why, after all these years, had he never thought to question it? That struck Calvin as infinitely sad, and suddenly, a tidal wave of emotion caught him in the throat like something jagged and sharp; and for the first time, he wanted to weep for all that he had lost, all that he had sacrificed. This wasn't just about Annie anymore but a dominating father, a possessive mother, and a son who never took hold of his life.

For too long, he had put his dreams on hold, as if he hadn't a right to hope for more. He'd turned himself off and slunk off like a wounded animal into his cave, and now he was waking up thirty-eight years old, half buried in himself and alone. Maybe the grimmest thing of all was that if he'd learned anything, it was how to camouflage himself—how to be completely invisible in plain sight.

Now he was at a turning point. It was now or never. Was he going to allow himself to rot in the past or was he going to take a stand and move into the future? This feeling he had for Leslie represented the last call for a normal life, but the thought of doing anything about it completely paralyzed him. After all, what had he to offer a woman like her, and why would she ever be interested in a man like him?

He looked again at the hat he held in his hands; such a small thing to be the subject of so many arguments, the object of so much adoration and scorn. In his mother's eyes, it was a travesty and a symbol of her son's stubborn refusal to comply. But for him, it represented nothing less than the bitter struggle for selfhood, something to define him. Even if it was just a part of the past he carried around in his head, it was the only part he cared to keep, those precious hours spent listening to his grandfather telling stories on a riverbank.

With tears streaming down his face, Calvin took down his father's hat and put his own in its place. This was *his* workshop now, his "*word shop.*"

Today, the season had taken its first turn toward fall. The light had changed and the oppressive humidity had quite suddenly lifted. The entire dome of the sky seemed immeasurably higher, promising the pleasures of an Indian summer lying ahead. As a child, this had signaled the dread of going back to school, but over the years, it had come to be his favorite time of year. There was a stately sense of completion in autumn that made it a perfect time to begin again. Of course, now that he had died, his needs would be very few.

A soft meow drew his attention to the door. It was the yellow cat. She observed him with her great green eyes, talking to him while she rubbed herself against the doorframe. It seemed she had a lot to say. He lowered his hand ever so slowly and just waited, barely breathing lest he startle her. He would let her come to him or not at all. Slowly, she came and brushed her head up against his hand, purring and kneading the floor with her paws. She circled around behind his leg and brushed against his hand again. Stroking her slowly, a tiny ray of gratitude lit up the darkness inside him. "There you are, pretty lady. This isn't so hard now, is it?" His vision blurred again with tears.

"Hello."

He knew without looking that the voice behind him belonged to Leslie. He quickly brushed his hand across his eyes and then straightened up slowly, acting as if he didn't care to know what she had come to say.

"Your mother sent me," she said, standing uncertainly in the doorway in a loose-flowing blue cotton dress, her face a shadow against the bright sunlight pouring in from behind her.

"So I take it she's not dead yet!" he replied brusquely, turning away to get a box containing a jumble of screws down from the shelf.

He looked rumpled, like he hadn't slept, his sand-colored curls sticking up in unruly drifts. Suddenly, she longed to reach up and stroke them into place. "She feels terrible about what she did, Cal."

"So she told you, huh!"

"The whole story—and she wants you to know how truly sorry she is."

He kept his head down, sorting the screws. "She's sorry she got caught. That's what she's sorry about," he retorted bitterly, thinking that he didn't dare look into those dark eyes radiating such pity and concern. It would only remind him of yet another thing that did not belong to him.

"She figured you wouldn't believe it," murmured Leslie, cautiously extending her hand toward the yellow cat, who stared suspiciously.

"So why should I believe anything she has to say?"

Leslie hesitated. "Thelma thinks this could really be the end."

Calvin's mouth twisted into a sardonic smile. "Do you know how many times she's pulled this on me?"

She watched as he scraped through the pile with his rough calloused fingers, methodically picking out the smaller screws. "You can't let her die thinking that you haven't forgiven her, Cal!" She tried to make eye contact, but he had withdrawn into an indifferent silence that left her feeling oddly rejected. "Well," she said rather crisply, "I promised your mother I'd say something to you, but I guess you'd rather be alone." She walked out into the sunshine.

"And that's the only reason you came?" His voice rang out sharply, and when she looked back, he was standing in the door, his eyes blazing a hard sapphire blue.

Her heart unexpectedly skipped a beat, and she had to look away, feeling oddly exposed.

In response, his face clouded over with a patient sort of defeat. "Don't worry about it. Tell Ruby I got the message." He went back inside and shut the door, amidst waves of humiliation.

Leslie stood outside for a moment, feeling as though he might as well have slapped her in the face, and then without thinking opened the door and angrily charged back in. She had no idea what she was going to say, but the sight of him and the box of screws were suddenly unbearably annoying. "*Why* are you acting like you don't care when you know you do?" she demanded, grabbing the box away from him. She had gotten overly excited and very pink in the cheeks, her eyes flashing.

"Look, I don't need to explain myself to you or my mother or anybody else, all right?" His eyes were dead but his voice was heated. "All I ask is that you leave me *alone!*"

Though stung by his sharp reproof, she suddenly felt more determined than ever to stay and drag him out of hiding. "Why? So you can just turn into an old hermit, hiding away in his cave?" she cried and then softened. "Of course you're angry and upset about everything! Anybody would be, but it's not going to do you any good keeping it all inside!"

He turned on her with barely concealed fury. "Okay, so what do you want me to say? That my whole life has been a mistake, a tragic comedy?"

The only sound was the frantic insistent buzz of a fly trapped on the inside of the windowpane. This wasn't the answer she'd expected, but now she knew she had to say something, and it had to be true, and it had to be real. He wouldn't accept happy talk or sympathy. "That's what *you* think—but it's not what *I* think."

The dead look in his eyes had not changed. "So what do you think?"

She took a breath and plunged. "I think . . . that you're . . . a writer who . . ." She felt him watching her now with mild skepticism. "Who lives on a farm. Lots of writers live on—farms!"

"Writer!" His face twisted into a mocking grimace. "If that's what you want to call it."

"What do you call it?"

"Paper and words and time down the rat hole!"

"How can you say that?"

He erupted. "Because nobody's ever going to read it!" he erupted. "People don't read anymore! And when you think about how many writers there are writing more stuff that nobody will ever read—well, it all just seems kind of pointless, doesn't it!" He snatched the box of screws and slammed it down on the workbench.

"Stop with the screws, will you?" She grabbed the box back once more. "You're completely overreacting! I mean, you have so much talent!"

He looked down into her earnest passionate face with a cynical smile. "Tell me how much did you actually read before my book floated off down the river?"

Against her will, she found herself blushing. "Well—almost a page—"

"Ah hah!" he cried, bitterly triumphant.

"But that's enough to tell if someone is good or not."

"No, no—" He shook his head with a harsh laugh. "Last night, I got a really good look at my life and realized that I can't live on dreams anymore. It's time to try a little reality for a change."

"Sounds dreary." She perched on an old wooden stool in the corner.

"No." He looked grave. "Being stuck in a gray limbo is dreary."

"So what do you intend to do?"

"Well, I've got this farm. I never wanted it but now it's the only thing I've got so—"

"So?"

"So I'm thinking I'll sell off a piece of woodland, maybe invest in that restaurant my brother-in-law keeps telling me about." He took a deep breath and continued in a matter-of-fact way. "Then I suppose I should settle down and get married."

"Married?" This pronouncement elicited an unexpected pang of alarm. She looked away shyly. "I—I didn't know you had a girlfriend."

He cleared his throat. "Actually, I don't so, of course, I'll have to get one first. That's sort of how it's done, right?" He smiled ruefully. "But the main thing is that I've decided. It's time to stop being so particular." The fly resumed its battle with the glass again. Cal reached out and slid open the window, and it escaped into the sunlight. "Hell, I'll take the soprano in the church choir even if she does talk too much. I'm just damned sick of—being alone." There. He'd said it. His heart was beating like crazy but he was still intact and at least she wasn't laughing. In fact, she looked like she was taking it all in quite seriously.

She cleared her throat. "Cal—you know, I—" She stopped. He was standing so close, and all she could think about was how he'd held her on the porch swing that night.

"What?" His voice was husky and low.

"You know," she said, her voice barely above a whisper, "you could probably have any woman you wanted." Suddenly they were both staring at the box of screws, the air between them thickening with electricity.

"Cal!" It was Thelma screaming from the house. "Cal! God help us, Mama's having a heart attack!"

CHAPTER 20

The Screwdriver

    As it turned out, this time, Ruby really was having a heart attack. Thelma wanted to call the ambulance, but her mother had insisted on rising up out of the bed and walking down the stairs to Calvin's truck. "Give me a damn aspirin, Thelma, and stop fluttering around like a chicken with its head cut off! I don't plan on dying anytime soon!" She'd been through this drill before with the tightening arm and the pressure in the chest, and she knew Calvin could get her there faster than waiting on "that damn rescue squad." Ruby let the cuss words fly. It seemed to lend her strength, and despite the pale pinched face, her eyes glittered like blue fire. Thelma and Cal argued about which truck to take but Ruby settled it quick. She wasn't about to climb no damn ladder to get up into Thelma and George's monster truck, sitting up on its giant macho wheels. She would ride in Cal's truck. She squeezed Leslie's hand real tight. "Don't forget me!" she said, and Cal helped her into the truck, followed by Thelma, who as she hoisted herself in alongside, made the sulky observation that they were not to blame her when they'd broken down on the side of the road.

    "Thelma," Leslie heard Ruby say as they pulled out of the yard, "you're about to worry me to death!"

    "Mama! Would you stop saying that word!"

    It was almost eleven o'clock later that same night, when Cal returned from the hospital. His mother was going to be fine. They'd swept her into surgery and found a blocked artery, but the surgeon had solved that problem with a stent.

All through the long hours in the waiting room at the hospital, Cal had been high as a kite, and now he knew exactly what he was going to do. He'd go to Leslie and he'd bring her another copy of his book, and this time he'd really talk to her and tell her how he felt—about everything. It was now or never. "I love you," he would say. "I hope that's okay." And she would smile unexpectedly. "It's more than okay," she'd reply. "I'm glad. I'm—" And he would stop her mouth with a kiss. He knew it was late, and she may have already gone to bed, but he was on a wave of action that would not be denied, so he headed over to River's Bend.

The house was lit up when he got there and his heart rejoiced. It was a sign. This was meant to be. The dogs came barreling noisily from out of the giant boxwoods, and he could hear Leslie's voice calling to them from behind the house. He found her sitting on the back porch, wrapped in a shawl, looking into the full moon. A single candle burned on the railing. Her dark hair was loose and tumbling around her shoulders, her broken foot resting on a crate.

"Cal?" There was a note of uncertainty in her voice, but maybe it was just surprise. After all, it was late for a visitor to be showing up at someone's door.

"Hey," he said, hesitating before boldly coming into the pool of candlelight to perch on the edge of the porch.

"I was so glad to hear your mother's doing all right." Thelma had called her the instant they'd gotten the good news.

"Yeah, she'll be raising hell again before too long. Course the truth is she's never stopped." And he told about the intern on intake at the emergency room that had made the mistake of addressing her as a "young lady." "Don't you talk down to me, young man," she'd snapped indignantly. "I am old enough to be your grandmother."

Leslie threw back her head and laughed her wonderful earthy laugh. "I know you don't think so but your mother is a charm."

"When she's not being a complete and utter annoyance," he said with a pained look.

"So I take it you've forgiven her."

"Truthfully"—he couldn't stop himself from grinning—"she may have done me a favor. Who knows?" He was so jubilant that he failed to notice that her smile had faded. "I brought you another copy of my book," he continued, laying the envelope at her feet.

She made a little sound of pleasure as she picked it up.

"This time I promise I won't let it get blown away by the wind," she said and he laughed. Elliot jumped into his lap, circling a few times until he'd found the perfect position and settled in with his tail curled over his nose. Cal concentrated on stroking his white fur, his mind blazing with the words he'd practiced in his head. *I love you . . . I hope that's okay . . .* Meanwhile, Hooch positioned himself strategically at Calvin's feet and rolled onto his back for a belly rub. Cal slipped off his flip-flop and stroked the dog's belly with his foot. The hound gave a blissful grunt of contentment.

Cal shook his head. "O thou glutton!" This made her laugh and again his confidence soared. The conversation lapsed comfortably and they were looking at the moon. It was the perfect moment staring him in the face, the moment he'd been imagining all the way back from the hospital, the pent-up words ready to spill out like water over a dam. "You know there's something I've been meaning to tell you . . ."

In retrospect, it was fortunate that the cicadas chose this precise moment to break into their equivalent of the "Hallelujah" chorus loud enough to drown out what could have become a very impulsive declaration because a stranger suddenly stepped out of the house. He was mid to late thirties, good-looking and trim, a country club golfer type in a crew neck shirt and khaki shorts, and he was carrying a bottle of wine and two glasses. He looked just as surprised as Calvin did.

Calvin stood up, stammering apologies. Elliot slid from his lap in a sleepy tumble and then, after an elaborate stretch and a big yawn, ambled over to sniff at the man's white deck shoes. The man promptly shoved the puppy away with his foot with a disapproving sound.

Leslie cleared her throat. Suddenly everything had become intensely awkward. "Cal, this is Stuart." Cal shot her a questioning look but she avoided his eyes.

With an easy smile, Stuart hastened to put down the goblets to extend his hand. "Stuart *Hillerman*."

The deliberate way he emphasized the name Hillerman was not lost on Cal. This was Leslie's estranged husband. He had the well-practiced ease of a people person—like Annie's husband. The irony of that was another thing that was not lost on Calvin. He stretched out his hand with a polite smile.

"Stu, this is my neighbor, Calvin Creed. His mother was actually born in this house."

Stuart grinned with false interest. "Really. Wow. So, Corvin! How about a glass of Cabernet?"

Cal felt every inch the country hick. "Actually, I've got to get going. It's really—late." He turned and headed blindly into the shadows at the side of the house.

"But wasn't there something you wanted to tell me?" called Leslie from her circle of light.

"It can wait," he said. He was just a voice now, hidden by darkness. His heart was heavy as he waded back toward the truck through the mint patch, berating himself for even thinking whatever it was he'd been hoping might happen here tonight. That's when his toe struck painfully on something hard and unforgiving hidden in the mint. Cursing, he felt around in the greenery. It turned out to be a screw driver.

At the same precise moment, there was a puppy's yelp from the back porch and an eruption of curses. "Damn it! Get away from me, dog!" It was Stuart's voice sounding petulant.

"Elliot! Bad dog!"

"That hurt, damn it!"

"Sorry, Stu!"

"Stupid dog!"

Once back in his truck, Cal instantly recognized his father's old long-handled screw driver with the initials SHC emblazoned on the side. Stephen Harriman Creed. Everything his father owned had born his mark—a territorial man, his father. Cal leaned his head back against the rear window and shut his eyes. "Linwood—you idiot!"

Though still reeling with the shock of Stuart's sudden appearance, his anger was now squarely aimed at Linwood. He set out in the direction of the sheriff's department, and for all of ten minutes, he was determined to be heartless. But driving past Linwood's place, he saw that the dim yellow porch light was on, and he impulsively turned into the yard.

Linwood was sitting under the tree on the old bus seat, smoking a cigarette and listening to the radio. In one hand was an open can of beer and five of the empty ones that had preceded it on the ground at his feet. Cal glanced at his watch. It was near midnight.

Linwood barely stirred at his approach, his voice languid and thick. "What's happenin', man?"

Cal thrust the screwdriver into his face. "My grandfather's old screwdriver. Remember? The one I loaned to you last fall? It's got his initials burned into the handle right here."

Linwood took his time, lighting another cigarette off the one already burning. "So?"

"So! Tonight, I almost broke my damned toe on it coming through the mint patch outside River's Bend." Linwood was stone silent. "What *exactly* have you been doing over there, Linwood?"

Linwood cursed under his breath.

The door of the house suddenly opened, and Linwood's grandfather peered suspiciously out into the dark. "Who is that there with you, Linwood?"

"Hey, Clarence. It's just me, Cal!"

"Oh, Calvin!" The old man sounded relieved. "What you doin' out here so late?"

"Just stopped to talk to Linwood for a minute or two."

"Well while you're at it, talk some sense into that knucklehead, why don't you!"

"I don't know about that."

"You and me both. Mission Impossible!" Clarence still laughed with his whole body the way he always had, but it made him wheeze and cough like an old car that hadn't been started for a long time. "You come around and see me before I shrivel up and blow away, hear?"

"You'll outlive us all, Clarence! You know that!"

"Sweet Jesus, don't put that curse on me!" He limped back into the house, chuckling.

The sound of cicadas swelled all around them. "You gonna turn me in?" The mask of indifference had lifted, and for a few moments, Calvin caught a glimpse of the original sweet-faced Linwood.

"First, you might try telling me what the hell you've been doin' down in the cellar at River's Bend!"

There was a long tortured silence while Linwood paced back and forth a few times like a nervous cat. Finally he turned to face his accuser. "Why should I? I know you're not gonna believe me!"

"Try me."

Linwood took another nervous pull from his cigarette. "Okay then—so remember how Sonny used to always talk about how society was gonna crash, how he was getting *prepared*?"

"What," demanded Cal tersely, "does this have to do with you breaking and entering someone else's house?" Linwood was a practiced liar. Calvin had no illusions about that and he wasn't in the mood to be taken in.

"I'm gettin' to it!"

The insolent tone to Linwood's voice made Calvin's temper flare. "Look, I'm already this close to going straight to the sheriff, Linwood! Don't push it!"

"Hey! I said I was gettin' to it, but if you want to go to the sheriff then go to the sheriff, man!"

"To hell with you," muttered Calvin, getting into his truck and slamming the door behind him.

"Why you gotta cop an attitude with me, man?" sneered Linwood, his face a contorted mask of hatred. "You ain't gonna believe me anyhow! Nobody will—so why bother?" Suddenly his head dropped like it was too heavy to hold up anymore, and his shoulders started to quake. He was crying. "No matter what I do, man . . . I'm goin' back to jail!" He rubbed the spot in the middle of his forehead. "Maybe that's all I'm good for anyway!"

Calvin slowly got out of the truck and closed the door, his angry zeal only somewhat dampened. "Okay, I'm listening."

Linwood struggled to gain control of his voice. "Well, Sonny had bank accounts and all kinds of stocks and dividends and shit. Everybody thought he was a drug dealer, but hell, he didn't need to deal drugs. He was already rich."

"How do you know this?"

"One night we were drinkin' and he told me all about it. He was like going off on like—how we were the Roman Empire all over again, you know—falling apart. The same way he always talked. Well, he told me that he'd turned a lot of money into gold coins and buried it in the cellar at River's Bend. He called it his secret stash."

"Great! He confides in you, and now you're going in there to steal it when he can't do anything about it? Has it ever occurred to you that Sonny is gonna need that money when he gets out of jail?"

Linwood sighed and then looked away guiltily. "He's never getting out of jail, Cal. He's dead."

Calvin's face fell.

"He had a heart attack back in May," continued Linwood softly. "Died in the recreation hall playing ping-pong. I found out from a woman, whose brother's a prison guard over there."

"And you didn't tell me?" yelled Calvin. "I came over here and I asked you about him and you didn't tell me?"

Linwood looked down, ashamed. "I'm sorry. I figured, well, maybe it was better if you thought he was the one going over in there. It might, you know—take the heat off me."

"You know I really just can't believe you'd—do something like this, Linwood!"

"I know."

"Of course, maybe I do believe it!" Calvin glared at his companion for a moment. "So what would happen to your grandfather if you go back to jail? Did you think about that?"

"I don't know."

"I mean, god—do you ever *think*?"

The two men leaned against the truck side by side and gazed solemnly at the moon. A gentle wind rustled through the trees. Calvin's eyes blurred with tears. Sonny was probably the only person who'd ever really understood him. "I can't believe he's dead."

"Good ol' Sonny," murmured Linwood, casting a sidelong glance at Cal. "Now I know you may not want to believe this," he said, "but he did tell me that if anything ever happened to him, I should come get the coins. I swear to God on a stack of Bibles that's what he said."

Calvin scowled. "And I'm supposed to believe *you*? You're a liar, Linwood. I'd be a fool to believe anything you have to say!"

"Hey, you don't have to believe me but I'm telling the truth," he mumbled. "He said he wanted me to-to make something of myself. I swear to God that's what he said." His voice tightened as he fought back his emotions.

He'd heard about Sonny's death back in early May, but it took a while before he even thought about the coins, and by that time, Leslie Hillerman had already moved into River's Bend. At first, this made him want to give up completely, but then he remembered the old hunting cabin up on what had come to be known as Bone Hill.

Long before the Great War, his great-great-grandparents had lived there, working as day laborers for the neighboring white farmers. There had never been a paved road of any kind, and now just an overgrown footpath was all that marked the way, leading to a crumbling old cottage falling slowly into the earth. Years later, it would be used as a hunting shack. Their graves still rested in a dense thicket of boxwoods, lilacs, and bridal wreath; daffodils and daylilies blooming every spring; the worn gravestones sagging beneath a tangle of trumpet and honeysuckle vines.

From the shack, it was just a short walk to the edge of the bluff and a clear view of River's Bend. From there, it had been easy to track the woman coming and going. She was predictable in her habits, always walking with the dogs down to the river for two or three hours every afternoon, and since she never locked her doors, it had been simple enough to get inside. He'd just walk in through the front door.

However, one day she'd come back unexpectedly while he was still digging down in the cellar, and he'd been forced to unscrew the hinges on the old plywood door in order to slip out of the back and vanish through the boxwood hedge.

Sometimes she'd leave with an overnight bag, and then he knew he'd have full run of the place. So long as he brought bologna, the dogs were not a problem. In fact, they were soon welcoming him like a long-lost friend, and as long as he had his treats, the brown one willingly left him alone. It was the puppy who got in his way the most, chewing on his shoe strings and getting under foot.

Aside from the fact that the ground had been hard, which made digging difficult, it had never been easy for Linwood to go down into that dark cellar alone. He was always thinking about the man who'd died there at the foot of the steps. He'd grown up hearing all the old stories about the haunted house at River's Bend. At times, he could feel the disapproving presence of the ghost watching his every move, and with every creak and thump in the distant recesses of the house, Linwood was ready to bolt.

The only thing that had kept him going was the promise of getting out from under JT's control. For an unemployed man living in the country with a prison record, no driver's license, and no car, gambling had seemed like the best and only option for survival; but true to form, Linwood tended to lose more than he won. JT, as a wealthy drug dealer, acted as the local underground banker, and Linwood had borrowed heavily from him to cover his debts. There'd been times when Linwood and his grandfather would have starved were it not for JT. Consequently, JT felt that Linwood owed him not only money but also loyalty; and in a sense, as long as he continued to owe JT money, JT owned Linwood.

But there had been problems lately. On the one hand, it was just a matter of simple male dominance. Linwood was independent by nature and never one to play into JT's self-delusions. And then there was Devon, a delicious curvy little sprite with huge gray eyes and an infectious beaming spirit. JT was obsessed with her, but though he did nothing to encourage her, she only had eyes for Linwood. He knew better than to be so foolish as to challenge JT on anything, much less a woman. Still, it had sown bitter seeds between them.

Linwood knew he needed to do something to gain his favor. At first, he'd figured all he'd have to do was find something at River's Bend that he could fence to JT. But it was Leslie's self-portrait, the painting of the sad woman that had stopped him. He recognized the look in her eyes. She was lost and that was a feeling he knew all too well. He didn't take anything that day. After that, when he had a chance, he'd just walk around inside the house, not with any intention of stealing but just to look at things. He'd become curious about this artist woman living alone in the country.

The night when she fell in the basement, he'd happened to be hiding behind a shelf the whole time. She'd left earlier in the afternoon with a suitcase, and he wasn't expecting her back that night, so he was digging in the basement when she'd suddenly shown up. Then the storm hit, and the damned dog had come howling down into the cellar, and in his panic, Linwood had inadvertently knocked one of the shelves over. He was hiding, sweating in terror, when she called down and the lights went out. It was pitch dark when she fell and he knew she was hurt. He was struggling with himself over whether he should try to help her and risk getting caught, when he felt a cold hand on his shoulder. No doubt it was Henry's. Linwood had jerked away, knocking a jar off the shelf, his startled cry hidden in the thunder.

"I swore I was gonna quit after that," continued Linwood, shivering at the memory, "but I have debts—big debts—and JT waits for no man."

JT. Calvin knew a little about JT. He'd seen him and his entourage up in the parking lot at the grocery store or lounging in their cars at the corner market by the railroad tracks, doing their best to look dangerous. The word was that gangs had started to infiltrate these rural communities, and JT was their leader. He'd spent time in the urban ghettos and in the post-graduate training in the prison system. He had personal magnetism. Anyone could see that and he walked among his people like a young prince.

Cal frowned. "JT doesn't know about Sonny's stash, does he?"

There was just a heartbeat's hesitation and a sidelong glance, but in the dark, it didn't register that Linwood was lying. "No, man! I didn't tell him!" He took a quick drag off his cigarette and then crushed it on the ground under his heel. "You still going to the sheriff?"

"I'll have to think about it because truthfully, I don't know whether to believe you or not, Linwood." Suddenly Cal realized how tired he really was. As usual, his anger had been short-lived, and though it sounded farfetched, he could easily imagine Sonny making such a reckless and magnanimous promise in the small hours of the night. Even so, it wouldn't hurt to let Linwood twist in the wind a little bit. Maybe then he'd start to show some sense. Cal wearily got back into his truck and shut the door.

Though Cal had tried to sound stern, Linwood took his indecision as a cause for hope nonetheless, and his face relaxed. "You know, Cal—I swear to God he knew something bad was going to happen. He told me about this dream he'd had. You know how he was about his dreams." They were both quiet, digesting the sad wonder of this. Linwood wiped his eyes on his shirt, and for the second time, Cal's eyes filled with tears. Sonny always had been something of a mystical quirk, believing in dreams and signs and the movements of planetary influences. He would miss that.

Calvin turned the ignition and slowly backed out of the yard. In the rear view, he could see Linwood standing in the middle of the road, a lonely figure etched in moonlight.

Cal headed back home, where he went straight into his workshop and wrote in a fever until dawn. As the gray light leaked into the eastern sky, he collapsed into the old brown recliner and fell into a dreamless sleep. Waking after nine, feeling irritable and thick, he went into the kitchen to discover Thelma—her head poked inside a lower cabinet, clattering through the pots and pans and complaining loudly about the disorganization of the kitchen. Before she had a chance to notice him, he'd grabbed an apple from the fruit bowl and headed out to his truck.

He was going back to River's Bend, but there was no emotion about it this time. It was as if some part of him had died the night before, and in place of anguish was an odd sense of triumph. He would never be a fool over a woman again. Maybe he wouldn't have to feel anything again, and that was an immensely satisfying thought.

As if to test him, there at the end of Leslie's driveway stood Frank Hawkins, waving him down with a mischievous grin. He wanted to show Calvin his new pistol, but when he made a sly comment about Cal getting "romantic" with Miz Hillerman, Calvin exploded and told him to go to hell with such ferocity that Frank immediately shut his mouth and stepped back as Cal roared past in an angry cloud of dust. There were certain advantages to being dead. Thus, a few moments later, without a trace of hesitation, Calvin boldly walked up to Leslie's front door and knocked. Let her husband open the door. It didn't matter to him now one way or the other.

However, it wasn't Stuart Hillerman who appeared but Leslie, looking disheveled and subdued. He didn't bother to ask how she was but went straight to the point. She need not worry anymore about the intruder. The problem had been worked out, and before she could even ask him what he meant, he'd turned and left.

Cal's mysterious pronouncement left Leslie feeling more confused than she already was. In the past twenty-four hours, everything had been turned upside down twice over. Like a dream, Stuart had walked up onto her porch. "I got your letter," he said. He wanted to get back together. He was tired of his escapade, and he wanted his old life back—he wanted Leslie. She'd watched in amazement as the very thing she'd envisioned all these long lonely months was now coming to pass. Of course, there were tears, but he seemed in a hurry to get through that part and on to normalcy, as if it were a foregone conclusion that she should be deliriously happy to have him back. He'd brought wine and flowers and an elegant picnic supper. They ate together just like old times, except that it wasn't just the way it had been. He'd changed and, as she came to realize, so had she.

It wasn't long before the conversation faltered. After all, what had they to say to one another? He'd been traveling through Europe having a romance while she'd been wallowing in a black hole of depression. Bitterness was hard to give up. In a far corner of her mind, she found herself noticing his clean, manicured hands and couldn't help but to compare them to Calvin's rough honest hands, oil stained and calloused with the blackened thumbnail from a hammer's blow.

Later on in the evening, Stuart started laying out his grand plan. He was looking at a job with a firm down in Fort Lauderdale, where he would buy a condo on the beach. He'd already seen the apartment—fifteen stories up, big sliding glass windows overlooking the water. With lots of rich old people, Florida was a great place to sell art. He talked very fast, like a salesman trying to close a deal. She'd never thought of him that way before, but now that was just exactly what he seemed like—a salesman, like Lenny.

She didn't ask if he'd seen Lenny or what it had meant to have betrayed his old mentor. Surely he felt some guilt or remorse, but if he did, he never let it show. He acted supremely self-confident. He was moving out of Richmond. Richmond was a one-horse town. It didn't have the opportunities that someone with his talent required.

And then the truth slipped out. Stuart had gotten well into the second bottle of wine by then, Calvin had come and gone, the candle had sputtered out, and the moon had slipped behind the trees, leaving them only starlight above. Under the cover of darkness, things got confessional. With quiet tears trailing down her cheeks, Leslie told him how she'd dreamed this exact moment so many times over the past eleven months, how part of her had never given up hope. Meanwhile, he stared out into the night, silent and brooding, and then poured himself the last dregs of wine and started to talk about Sherry—how self-centered she was, how she used people, and that he wasn't about to be used. That's when it dawned on Leslie. Stuart had gotten dumped.

He failed to notice the flat tone of her voice when he asked her if she wanted to go inside. If he had, he would never have been so foolish as to try to pull her into an embrace.

"No!" she said, firmly pushing him away.

"Les—come on now." He sounded mildly disapproving, his face a white blur in the darkness, his breath sour with an alcoholic stench. He leaned in for the kiss.

"I don't *think* so!" Suddenly it was like a clumsy high school date, with her fending off an octopus.

"You know I never stopped loving you, babe," he crooned. Suddenly, there it was—that *word*! The one she detested. He'd never, in all the time they were married, ever once called her "babe." It was Sherry who used that word.

"I said stop!" She shoved him again, this time rather violently. He lost his footing and crashed into a chair. The dogs started to howl.

"What the—What'd you do that for?" he gaped at her, incredulous.

"You'd better go." She brushed past him as she limped into the house. When he tried to follow, he was met with a door slamming in his face. She went to sit like a statue in the dark living room, burning with fury and silent as a tomb.

Meanwhile, the dogs went into a frenzy. Partly so he could talk to her through the window and partly to get away from the dogs, Stuart was now perched on the porch railing, his knees pulled up around his ears. "Leslie! What are you doing? What did I do? Talk to me, babe!"

There was only stony silence from within.

Pleading now turned to indignation. "At least call your dogs so they don't maul me, for god's sake?"

She called the dogs in and then slammed the door.

"So I made a mistake." He was whining now. "I know that now, and I'm sorry for all the pain I've caused you, but don't throw away all that we've had!"

After a few minutes, she opened the door again and threw his jacket and the flowers he'd brought out onto the porch.

"You know this is typical of you, Les! Never say what you're feeling!" He was very drunk right now. She could always tell by the slurring of certain words and the subtlest shift in his personality. "In fact, your communication skills pretty much stink!" He belched loudly.

Presently, she opened the door. He was now sitting on the top step, his head in his hands.

"You want to know what I'm feeling?" Her tone was dangerous. He stood up warily. "Okay, I'll spell it out for you. You're a complete self-centered, self-absorbed, self-deluded jackass, which makes you and Sherry the perfect couple!"

His face twisted into a smirk. "You've always been jealous of her, haven't you?" he said and then stood up unsteadily, closing his eyes to keep the world from spinning. Suddenly the anger left her. She only felt sad. This was the alcohol talking. This sneering braggart wasn't Stuart at all.

"You know something, Stuart? You can't hurt me anymore." She closed the door softly this time, her face wet with tears and her heart free like a wide-open sky.

"You better come to your senses before it's too late," she heard him grumbling. "I won't wait around forever, you know!" He stumbled on the last step and rolled out onto the grass like a man stuffed with straw, only slowly picking himself up. Leaving a trail of muttered curses in his wake, he staggered back to his car.

Love is a spell, she thought, watching him drive away. Now that it was broken, she could hardly remember what it was that had made him so necessary.

CHAPTER 21

The Orange Glove

The next day following Calvin's cryptic declaration that he'd taken care of the intruder, Linwood showed up at her door with a face full of woe.

"Hey, Linwood! I'm sorry if you came for your art lesson, but it's not a good time for me right now." She stood propped up on crutches, looking like she was dressed to go out, purse in one hand and an overnight bag slung on one shoulder. Her face was worn and her usual sunny disposition was under a cloud.

"That's okay," he said. He stood there, shifting from one foot to the other, acting like he wanted to say something. He was there to confess and to warn her that there could be trouble, but the words were stuck in his throat. The truth was he wanted her to think well of him, though deep down he already knew it was too late for that. When she seemed impatient to go, he quickly mumbled something about maybe mowing her grass again, and that's when he spotted the tattered orange glove. It was the same orange glove Leslie had found on her living room floor back in June. Thinking that it had been Calvin's, she'd left it beside the rocking chair on the porch, hoping that he would see it next time he came over.

"Oh, I've been looking for this." Linwood picked it up, forgetting that he'd dropped it on the day he'd broken in, the day he'd been sitting in her living room reading her diary, which was why he didn't understand the stunned look that now came into her eyes nor the feeling that she was pulling away from him in fear.

If he could have read her mind, he would have known that she was, at this moment, calculating exactly how many times he'd been inside her house. To her knowledge, it had been only once—that first day he'd introduced himself when he'd stood in the front hall, looking at the Medusa painting. Then how had his glove come to be lying on her coffee table if he had not been inside her house when she wasn't there?

"I need to get going," she said, her voice suddenly cold. She gave a big show of locking the door but then made no move to go, as if waiting for him to leave first.

"Sure," he said. *She knows*, he thought. *Calvin told her the truth.* He kept his head down as he walked out the long lane, despair and self-hatred coursing through him. Why did he always have to ruin every good thing?

The moment Linwood was out of sight, Leslie went back into the house in a cold sweat and telephoned Calvin to demand an explanation. What exactly had he meant when he said not to worry about the intruder? Did he already know it was Linwood? And if so, why was he keeping this from her? But there was no answer at his house, and when she called the hospital, Thelma said he wasn't there either and that she hadn't heard from him since late the night before.

Leslie hung up the phone, seized with anxiety about Calvin. After what had almost happened in his workshop the day before and then seeing her with Stuart later that night—God only knew what he must be thinking or what rash thing he might do! No wonder he'd acted so abrupt and strained at the door earlier that morning. Suddenly she felt almost crazy to see him, just to know he was all right.

"Knock, knock! Anybody home?" She was startled from her thoughts by the sound of Penny's voice at the door. The door opened. He had gotten into the annoying habit of walking in without an invitation, but at the moment, she was too emotionally and physically overwrought to do anything about it. As usual, he stood in the door of the living room, scrutinizing her and everything in the room.

"Brought you your mail. Hey! You look worn out, lady!" In contrast, he was brimming with energy, for nothing made him happier than coming to see Leslie.

"I didn't sleep well," she said rather curtly, pretending to look through the advertisements. She dreaded the inevitable prying questions. "So are you ready to go?"

"What's wrong, babe? Somethin' on your mind?" He was making himself comfortable beside her on the couch when she abruptly got up to leave. "I told them I'd have the car there at eleven. I'd guess we'd better hurry."

He looked disappointed. "It won't kill 'em to wait."

"Oh, and will you put this bag in the trunk of my car?" she added, deftly ignoring his suggestion.

"Going somewhere?" he asked, turning the name tag on the strap and reading the name "*Stuart Hillerman.*"

"No, actually," she said. "It's just something I have to return."

"Right!" He gave her a knowing wink. "No wonder you didn't sleep last night."

Leslie held her breath and counted to ten. In an ideal world, she would have slapped him silly, but she needed him to take her to the auto mechanic. The car was making weird noises.

As for the bag, she had found it that morning sitting in the front hall, where Stuart had apparently left it the night before while still under the impression that he would be staying the night. At the moment, the mere sight of it was odious to her, and she wanted it out of the house.

It was about a twenty-minute drive to the mechanics, and it gave her a chance to think about what to do about Linwood. Nothing drastic like calling the police, she decided, until she could discuss things with Calvin. She certainly didn't want to jump to conclusions. After all, there could be a simple explanation for all this. Still, she was absolutely positive that she did not want to be alone in the house right now.

Unfortunately, earlier that week, she'd called off the whole guard duty thing, saying she didn't want to impose on anybody anymore, but the truth was she'd been tired of having to entertain them and wanted her privacy back. Since Cal could not be found and Frank was at work, the only one left to call upon was Pendleton Caughey, who, she had no doubt, would be overjoyed to stay over. She wouldn't tell him about Linwood though. He'd jump the gun, and who knew what he was capable of doing. All she would have to do is to suggest that she was a little nervous being alone at night, and he would volunteer to stay in a heartbeat. All she needed to worry about was how to keep his hands off of her, and they'd be fine.

Not knowing where else to go, Linwood ended up at his great-grandparents' cabin, where he spent a few hours brooding about his future. He couldn't really believe that Calvin would turn him in, though he had never seen him look so angry. But it wasn't just that. It was the fact that she knew now. That bothered him deeply. From up here on Bone Hill, he'd watched her come and go these past few months, playing with the dogs or working in her gardens, sitting, and painting; and he'd come to feel a certain affinity for her. She wasn't like the bossy, possessive, empty-headed gossips he'd known at school or the hard-edged sluts and druggies, who clung to the fringes of the male gangs. She was intelligent and curious, but even more importantly, she was an open door into a world he wanted to be in—the world of the artist.

He'd never felt a part of any group. He'd never felt he belonged anywhere. He was a loner. He was the antihero. Sonny Hay had taught him about antiheroes. He'd showed him movies and given him books. Sonny was no artist, but he'd seen Linwood's abilities and had praised him for it, but Linwood had never been so foolish as to believe it. The possibility of going for something better, something beyond, was not in his genetic code. He had learned only resignation to fate, like that Greek god he'd read about in English class, forever pushing that stone up the mountain, only to see it roll back down again. No, his life had already been decided before he was ever born. He was destined to suffer and lose. In his world, the young males with drive aspired to be drug dealers, not college graduates. The girls who did well became secretaries or nurses, more often than not ending up as single mothers, bitter and hard, carrying the entire load on their backs and raising yet another brood of angry, disaffected kids.

He sat in the chair at the edge of Bone Hill, watching River's Bend with the hope of catching a glimpse of Leslie, but her car never returned, and the place remained empty and silent all afternoon.

An ad in an old newspaper lying on the table suddenly caught his eye. It showed a clean cut and exceptionally alert-looking young black man in a lab coat above the caption reading *"Earn Good Money as a Trained Medical Technician."* With a wave of sadness, he realized that he could have been that person, but now that chance was gone. A painful longing gripped his chest as he imagined himself with a job, a clean decent place to live with money in his pocket, a car, and even a wife. He could have had this if he'd only tried, but instead he was going back to jail, and that made him deeply sad.

Late in the day, an attack of hunger drove him out to the road. He didn't look forward to going home, where his grandfather was liable to give him grief, but he had no money and no place else to go to fill his stomach. A police car suddenly materialized, coming over the hill. Linwood ducked his head, hoping to go unnoticed, but it slowed down. The window slowly lowered, and a gush of air-conditioning billowed out into the muggy heat. It was the rather pudgy deputy, who had arrested him a few years back.

"Watcha doin' in the middle of the day, Linwood?" inquired the officer in a sly tone. Potato chip crumbs clung to the pale bristly mustache that adorned his rosebud mouth.

"Walkin'."

"Walkin', huh. I thought you was supposed to be getting a job."

"I'm goin' for an application to McDonald's tomorrow."

The deputy looked dubious. This was what Linwood always said. "Uh huh. How you gonna get there?"

"My uncle's got a car. He'll take me."

"Uh huh." He didn't believe that either. Then he got to the real question. "So you seen JT around?"

"No, I ain't seen him."

The deputy gave him a cool penetrating look aimed at the root of Linwood's lying soul. "You stay out of trouble now," he finished off in an authoritative tone. Linwood set his jaw to force back the contempt that longed to spew forth. This cocky little sucker with the imperious attitude was most likely younger than he was. "Hear me?"

"I hear you." The words were like ashes in his mouth. Burning with humiliation and anger, he headed across the field, the hunger gnawing at his stomach full-blown now. It would take longer but he would follow the back road home. It was worth it not to have to see anybody; however, that was not to be, for in a matter of seconds, a dented red Chevy pulled up alongside him. It was JT's girl, Devon, the gray-eyed sprite. The driver was her older sister, Teesha, who worked as an aide in the hospital an hour away. She was just coming off a double shift, and he could see by her expression that she just wanted to go home. She was only nineteen but already had a two-year-old child and another one on the way. She was as beautiful as Devon except for the hard shell that covered her light.

Devon jumped out of the car. Her radiant coffee-colored skin slightly overcast from worry. "JT is looking for you," she said in a low voice, as if the trees might be listening.

"Why?"

"I don't know. He said something about taking over the project."

What ordinary thugs would call a "job," JT called "projects." He liked to think he had class, modeling himself after the players he'd brushed elbows with during his time in the big house. For this reason, he liked to say he was from Philadelphia, like his cousin whom they called Philly, but he'd only been born there and had mostly grown up outside of Olympia. At the tender age of thirteen, he'd had the distinction of being shipped off to juvenile detention, eventually to drift among the criminal elements in two major cities before landing in a real prison. After jail, he was back in his "countryside," getting some recuperation and assembling himself for his next major move back onto the scene.

In the meantime, he'd been solidifying his base and doing good business here in the county, where he didn't have to worry about the competition. He was playing the outsider, forging alliances with the Mob syndicate in Philly and the Jamaicans, who were fast coming up from Florida and sweeping Atlanta. The word was they were soon to take over Richmond, where the murder rate was climbing daily. Richmond was soon to become the murder capital of the nation. But playing both sides against each other had finally taken its inevitable toll and put JT into a tough spot, and to get himself out, he needed cash and lots of it. It was a game that required buying allegiance and paying for favors, and he'd had a bad streak of luck playing the numbers.

"They're going over there tonight," she added immediately, setting off tremors of cold fear deep in his core. She continued in low urgent tones. "Don't you go with them, Lin." She always called him Lin. "You need to stay away from that shit." She was so soft, so beautiful, even ugly words sounded sweet on her lips. Her big luminous eyes clouded with tears.

In the background, Teesha yawned and lit a cigarette. "Whatever you do, it's gotta happen now 'cause I'm crashin'!"

He looked beyond Devon to Teesha. "Take me over there first," he said. He didn't know how but he would try to talk JT out of it. He jerked on the rear-door handle, but it was dented from a collision with a deer and wouldn't budge.

"Are you crazy?" Devon tried desperately to push him away, but she was too small to have any effect. "You could end up in jail!" She threw her arms around his neck. "I'd die if I lost you! Please, Lin—I'm begging you!"

He remembered that two of her brothers were in jail and a cousin and her father too—though he hardly counted since she'd never even known him. He gazed down at the fear mirrored in her great gray eyes. If she only knew how afraid he really was, but he couldn't show it, not to her, not to anyone. He peeled her arms from around his neck and set her firmly aside. She had to be ten years younger than he was, and he'd always thought of her as just a kid until this past year, when she'd sort of bloomed like a woman flower, and suddenly there were feelings mixed up inside of him that he couldn't afford. She was JT's girl.

Teesha yawned again and turned her hard dull eyes on him. "Well, make up your mind, baby, because I'm ready to crash. I gotta be back to work at eleven."

Most of the time, JT stayed at Mary Harding's place. She was an older heavyset black woman, who laughed all the time, regardless of whether things were funny or not. It was her defense against the world. She'd worked as a maid and a cook until her kids were raised and her back gave out, so now she lived off social security and the favor of well-placed friends like JT, who didn't mind kicking in to cover expenses. She liked to drink and smoke weed and cook, though she was strict about cleanliness and didn't abide any disruptive behavior in her house. This made for a good combination as far as JT was concerned. He was a clean person and very particular about his personal space.

When Linwood arrived, Mary was cleaning up from supper. She must have read the hungry look he gave the leftover pork chop because she offered it to him, and he gratefully accepted it. JT was out back, where she kept a glider and plastic chairs and a picnic table set under a tree. This was where JT usually held court, if he wasn't hanging out at the parking lot by the grocery store. This evening, Red and Philly, his chief lieutenants, were there with him. Red was huge, about six feet six inches, and dressed like a biker in a black leather vest with tattoos on both arms. He was white with freckles and a long flame-colored beard and hair he wore in a braid down his back. Today he wore a bandana around his forehead like a pirate. He'd been with JT "since before time," as he put it, and bore a mindless loyalty to him. He swore often that there wasn't anything JT wouldn't do for him. Regardless of whether this was actually true, he fervently believed it, and his entire sense of honor was bound up in the notion that there was nothing he wouldn't do for JT. He was also not the sharpest tool in the shed and knew it with an endearing humility.

Philly was small and wiry with skin like black coal so that when he smiled, his teeth flashed like a neon sign. Unlike Red, who was a man of few words, Philly tended to talk a lot. Philly was JT's first cousin and pretty much did as he felt, regardless of what JT said. That was his way, and everyone understood that, regardless of how it strained JT's patience; he was the only one who could get away with it.

Normally, Linwood was not afraid of JT. That didn't mean he wasn't cautious. He knew that thugs like JT get their energy from playing off other people's fear. It worked well in lieu of legitimate respect and got JT what he wanted—the power to control others. But Linwood had learned a mental trick in prison when faced with a threatening situation, and it all had to do with remembering that he had nothing left to lose and was, for all practical purposes, already dead.

This mind-set allowed Linwood a certain inner freedom when facing thugs like JT, and JT sensed it; and this was one reason that, with regard to Linwood, JT still retained a faint distrust verging on dislike. He was too independent. But today, Linwood was afraid because it was Leslie who was in danger, and it was his fault.

JT was sitting on the glider, arms outstretched, legs spread wide, a man enjoying the evening air. "Where you been all day, man? We've been looking all over for you." JT acted put out, as if he expected his people were supposed to be accessible to him day or night.

Linwood scratched his head. "Fishing." He kept his eyes dead on, his voice casual. He knew how to lie.

"Fishing?" JT rolled his eyes. "So where's my fish?" Red and Philly snickered from the picnic table, where they perched side by side, the audience in the bleachers.

"I ain't catch nothin'."

JT narrowed his eyes in a calculating look. "Seems like you never do. So you got my money?"

"No, but soon as I take care of a few things I'll—"

"Soon as you take care of a few things? Isn't that what you always say? You gotta take care of a few things? What you got to take care of, Linwood?"

"My grandfather's been sick and—stuff."

"And I suppose your dog ate your homework too." JT threw up his hands in mock horror amidst loud guffaws from the picnic bench. "I'm talkin' business here, Linwood. You have any idea what kind of pressures there are on me right now? Now I need my money, and I don't understand why it is you ain't gonna give it to me when you said you had it."

Be easy now, Linwood told himself. He thrust his hands in his pockets and shrugged. "I don't have it *yet*—but I promise I'll get it." Linwood forced himself to look JT in the eye. "I'll get it as soon as I can."

"Tonight?" JT's voice cut through the air like a knife. There wasn't a sound from the peanut gallery now, just silent anticipation for the ax to fall. Meanwhile, JT played his part with cool aplomb. "How about tonight?"

"Tonight's not a good night, man—but maybe tomorrow."

"That's what you keep saying, but I'm to the point that I don't believe you anymore. I don't trust you either. How do I know you ain't already found the gold? How do I know you ain't just leading us on?"

Linwood smirked. "You really think I'd still be hanging around if I had?"

JT took his time assessing this answer. "Then you'll be coming with us—and its tonight. Not tomorrow, not two weeks from now. Tonight." The audience looked on, little smiles playing about their lips. They'd never cared for Linwood's arrogant attitude either.

"Us?"

"We gotta move on this project, bro." JT's brown eyes glittered with triumph.

"Now or never, bro," echoed Philly.

"But this is a one-man operation, JT. You know that. You get too many people involved, man—it gets out of control. No, let me do it. I already know my way in, and besides, I'm tight with the lady."

The peanut gallery erupted into mockery. "Oooh! He's tight with the la-a-a-dy!" Philly stuck his puckered-up lips into Red's face and promptly got knocked off the picnic table.

"Get away from me, fag!" erupted Red, scowling mightily.

Meanwhile Linwood slouched down in his plastic chair like he didn't care one way or another—real casual. "Yeah, well have it your way, man. I mean, I was willing to, you know, take all the chances while you stayed high and dry, but if this is how you wanna play it—"

If there was one thing JT could not abide, it was someone who was smarter than he was. Deep down, everybody knew that somebody was Linwood, though he normally chose to underplay it. Now his only chance to turn things his way was to make JT doubt the intelligence of his plan.

Acting nonchalant, JT reached for his can of diet soda and drained it, but Linwood knew he was thinking hard. The truth was that the pressures from higher ups to come through with the money far outweighed the common sense of Linwood's argument. "No. I've made up my mind. It's time, whether you are ready or not. Philly, you got the poison?"

"What you need poison for?" Linwood asked sharply.

"The dogs, Linwood. You said she had dogs, right?"

"Hey, the dogs know me. They trust me. You don't need to poison them!"

"Okay, then you take care of the dogs. Philly, give my man Linwood the poison—just in case. I don't like no out-of-control dogs."

Philly handed it over with an evil grin. "This smack will do some damage, man. One bite—out like a light!"

Red took up the rhyme and together they started the chant. "One bite—out like a light!"

"Shuttup and get serious!" JT glared them into silence.

Red looked penitent. "I'm serious, JT. I don't know about this fag here." Philly landed a murderous knuckle punch on Red's shoulder, but Red only sneered. "You don't wanna fight me, man. I'll clean your clock."

"Well, I ain't queer. Tell him, JT. I ain't queer."

"Well, stop acting like it then!" snapped JT. Philly stuck out his lip and withdrew into a sulk. As JT started a long lecture on seriousness, Linwood eased up out of the chair and started for the back door, his blood racing.

"Hey!" It was JT. "Where you think you're going?"

"I got to use the facilities, man."

"She don't like my people going in and out her bathroom, man. Go out behind the bushes."

"No, I mean I got serious business, if you know what I mean."

Philly giggled. "He got serious business, JT! He's serious, all right! Serious business!"

Red smacked the back of his head. "You laugh like a little girl, man!"

"Would you please shut the fuck up! You both gettin' on my nerves." JT's patience had worn thin.

"Yeah, get off his nerves, Red!"

As Linwood went inside, someone made a comment he couldn't make out, and JT laughed.

Inside, it was dim and quiet. She kept the blinds shut on the street side day and night, and it was frigidly cold from the air-conditioner that hummed loudly on the kitchen window. Right now she was nowhere in sight. For such a small house, that hardly seemed possible. The door to her bedroom was closed. He looked around for the phone. It took him a few moments to locate it. It was one of those new kinds that were cordless so you could walk around anywhere and talk on it. JT had bought it for her, though more for his own purposes so he could use it in his "office" out on the patio. He'd seen JT parading around with it out in the backyard, waving his hands and talking like the big man. Linwood had never used one before and was a little unsure of how it worked. He put it to his ear, but there was no sound whatsoever. He pushed the biggest button and jumped when it emitted a loud beep and then the dial tone came on. His eyes darted to her bedroom but it remained closed and the house quiet. He pulled out his wallet and found a small slip of paper with Devon's number neatly printed in a flowery feminine hand. It rang five or six times, and then suddenly someone picked up, and in the background, he heard a child crying. "Get off the freakin' couch! I said get off it before I knock you blind!" It was Teesha and now she directed her ferocity into the phone. "What you want?"

"I need to talk to Devon."

Without a word, Teesha dropped the phone and bellowed, "De-von! Phone!" Against a backdrop of screams and shouted curses, Devon's soft voice came on the line.

"Hello?"

"You gotta do something for me."

"Who is this?"

"It's Linwood."

"How'd you know my number?"

"You gave it to me, remember?"

"I did?" She giggled. She sounded high.

"Devon, I can't talk long. Just listen. You gotta go see Calvin Creed and tell him what you told me. You know, in the car. It's real important."

"I don't know Calvin Creed."

"Yes, you do. Everybody knows Calvin. Now you go. It's life or death."

"They ain't gonna hurt you, are they?"

"Just go." He hung up. He'd broken out into a cold sweat and was shaking all over. Mary came out of the bedroom. She slipped into the bathroom, but if she saw him, she made no sign of it. It was like he wasn't there. The house was so cold.

He slipped the phone back onto its holder and headed back outside. It was going to be a long night.

CHAPTER 22

In the Dark of Night

The whole day, Cal had been fishing down at the river, which was where he usually went to make peace with himself. He couldn't bring himself to go to the hospital, where the ever-present Thelma would be in her glory, hovering over Ruby, micromanaging every move the nurses and doctors made. Besides, she blamed him for sending their mother into the hospital in the first place. No, it was best to avoid her right now as much as possible. Soon enough, his other sisters would be traipsing into town, filling the house with endless chatter, grilling him about his love life and (thanks to Thelma's big mouth) the reunion and generally picking him apart for their own amusement. No, there would be no peace after that, not a moment to set his mind straight or get his bearings.

Thinking he'd take just a short nap before going to the hospital that evening, however, he'd fallen into a dead sleep in his recliner and had only just now awakened. It was nearly midnight before he made his way across the yard in the silvery darkness of a waning half-moon, and the phone was ringing as he walked in the front door. His heart stopped for a moment, fearing it could only be Thelma with bad news, but it wasn't. It was a soft childlike voice on the other end, talking very fast. She'd been calling and calling for hours, trying to reach him, she said. He was on the verge of telling her she had the wrong number, but when she added that Linwood had asked her to call, she suddenly had Calvin's full attention.

"He's in trouble, Mr. Creed. Bad trouble. JT is gonna break in over at River's Bend tonight. I been trying to reach you for three hours and I'm so scared. Please don't call the cops! I'm begging you, please—"

"They're going to do what?" It was as if a three-hundred-pound weight suddenly landed on his chest.

"JT is tired of waiting, and he says he's going in after the money tonight. Linwood told me to tell you! They could already be there!"

"And Linwood is with them?"

"That's why you can't call the cops, Mr. Creed. I'm begging you. He don't need this. He's already been in jail once, and they'll send him down and throw away the key forever if they catch him again."

"Well, I just can't promise that right now."

"But—"

He hung up on her, cursing Linwood for lying to him, all sympathy for the young man's fate utterly vanished. Now he would throw Linwood to the wolves. He dialed the operator, who connected him to the police dispatcher. A woman, whose voice he didn't recognize, answered.

"I've been informed of a planned break-in tonight," he said.

"And where would that location be?"

"River's Bend—at the end of Route 653. You turn right and—"

"I know the place. But it's a *planned* break-in, you say?" she said, the tone of her voice insinuating that this wasn't a serious concern. "Who told you this?"

"Does it matter? I mean, somebody—I don't know who. The point is—"

"The point is we'll get to it when we can but I can't promise anything right now. We have a fire over on Route 3 and a bunch of drunks brawling over at the VFW hall. All the police personnel are otherwise occupied."

The VFW hall was a lonely-looking brick building set in a field way on the opposite end of the county and was famous for having dances that got out of control. "But this is an ongoing case. There have been other break-ins before!"

"I'll radio over and see if somebody can come but it may not be for a while."

Calvin hung up and then quickly dialed Leslie's number, anger and fear thrumming through his body. There was only a busy signal—but at midnight?

Frank was deep in a dream, wherein the cats had finally taken over. He was knee-deep in cats. They were literally hanging from the chandelier (even though he didn't have a chandelier), coming out of dresser drawers; and when he opened his closet, there was his wife,

Clarice, dressing them in little hats and coats. Why, he'd asked, was she sitting in his closet? She'd told him to go away and then he'd woken up. Thanking God that it had only been a bad dream, he turned over to go back to sleep, when he heard a strange noise and went out to find a six-foot cat kicking a tambourine around the living room. That's when the telephone rang and he woke up yet again. He expected to hear a meow on the other end when he picked up the telephone, but it was Calvin saying, "Get your gun. They're breakin' in over at River's Bend. I'll be right over."

Frank laid there for a minute, trying to decipher whether this was reasonable. Was he really awake this time or was this just another layer of the dream? However, as he rose up out of bed, the screech of sciatica was all it took for him to know that he was definitely back in the world of pain.

He was fully armed but still dressed in his pj's when Cal appeared at his door, dogs swirling around him in a howling frenzy. A terse argument quickly broke out as to whether to go for a full-frontal assault versus a sneak attack. Frank was all for the full frontal, but not surprisingly, Cal saw it differently.

"I think we're better off with stealth as our main weapon," he said in his slow reasonable way, "and hopefully the sheriff's department will get there before anything bad happens."

Frank's eyebrows lowered in a snarl. "Yeah, right! We'll be waiting all night for that bunch. No, it's up to us, Cal. I say we go in there and show 'em who's boss!"

Cal frowned. "First off, there are only two of us and who knows how many of them." He didn't mention that the villains were young and in shape.

"Yeah, well, if anything, we can shoot the guns in the air! Scare 'em off the old-fashioned way!" Frank broke out into a grin. He was primed to enjoy this.

"Or start a gunfight," broke in Cal savagely, "and Leslie could wind up getting hurt!" Suddenly, he realized what the adrenaline had so far disguised, and that was a cold fist in the gut—the horror that something could happen to Leslie. "Which means you gotta get those dogs up under the house."

Frank scowled. He could depend on Cal to take the fun out of everything. "Well, that's easy for you to say!" He went grudgingly to the refrigerator and pulled out the roast beef he had squirreled away from Sunday dinner at his sister's house. Once outside, he threw it through a gap in the foundation cover to lure the dogs under the house, where they were used to sleeping on cold nights. He covered the hole with the loose piece of metal sheeting and stacked a couple cinder blocks against it to keep them in. Inside, it sounded like World War III going off.

"It'll be a miracle if a one of them is left alive," muttered Frank accusingly.

"Well, that's less dog food you'll have to buy," said Cal, sliding into the front seat of his truck.

"Wow! Now that sounds like a real humanitarian talkin'! Whatever happened to 'what's good for the owls is good for humans'?"

"Maybe you finally talked me over to your side, Frank. I'm turning into one of you!"

Frank snorted. "Then here." He held out a 9-mm pistol.

Cal hesitated and then took hold of it, examining it under the light. "Damn, Frank!"

Frank grinned. "Don't worry. It's loaded but the safety's on."

Cal pushed the air out of his lungs. "I just hope I won't have to use this." He started up the truck and headed slowly up the dirt lane toward River's Bend, headlights out and only a pale half-moon lighting their way. A quarter of the way there, Cal pulled off behind a tangle of briars and proceeded to walk the rest of the way through the woods. Though the moonlight was bright enough to allow for some visibility, it passed behind a bank of clouds, and suddenly it was harder to see. That and the fact that the ground was uneven and unpredictable, slowed them down even more, as Frank was in no mood to break an ankle stepping in a hole. It was a good three quarters of a mile in, and soon Frank Hawkins was out of breath and holding his chest.

Cal, who had already pulled ahead, came back to check up on him. "You're not gonna have a heart attack on me now, are ya?"

"Don't worry. I'm fine," hissed Frank. He was feeling a tad resentful about Cal's plan, which he thought was overly tepid. If he'd had his way, they'd have pulled in, guns blazing. He went another twenty yards but had to stop again and bent over double. "I told you we should have taken the damned truck!"

"Shh! Look!" Ahead, Cal had spotted a car parked on the far side of his grandfather's old tobacco barn.

"You stay here. I'll check it out." Cal went swiftly on ahead while Frank could only stand there, struggling to calm his breath. Within moments, Cal was sprinting back toward him.

"It's empty."

Meanwhile, Frank had already decided what he was going to do. "You go on. I'll catch up."

"You sure?"

"Don't worry about it."

Cal put a hand on Frank's shoulder. "Take care of yourself," he said sternly and then quickly melted into the shadows.

Back at the house, as per usual, after talking Leslie's ear off for several hours, Penny had started nodding off at his post on the front porch. Though he had fully intended to stand watch all night, by 10:00 p.m. he was, as usual, already thinking wistfully about that soft guest-room bed upstairs.

By this point in the evening, she was usually more desperate to be rid of him than she was afraid of anything bad happening, and suddenly the whole glove incident seemed farfetched. "Why don't you go on up?" she said finally when he was on her last nerve. "I'll let you know the instant I hear anything."

After making the customary show of resistance, he succumbed to pressure and went upstairs. Yes, she was definitely overreacting about the whole glove thing, she told herself as Penny headed upstairs. "Good night!" she called but he made no answer. *He probably didn't hear me*, she thought. She turned out the light and settled down to sleep in the living room, but no sooner had she closed her eyes than they were open again. The reason he hadn't heard her was because he was practically stone deaf! If anything *did* happen, she was on her own!

She continued to lie in bed, thinking obsessively about the front door. At first, after her interview with Sheriff Tuttle the night of the break in, she'd been diligent about locking it at night even though it made the house unbearably hot. It also created the added inconvenience of having to get up to let the dogs in and out a dozen times a night.

She knew she shouldn't spoil them so but didn't know how else to manage it. If she tried to lock them out, they would just howl and cause such a ruckus that she'd have to give in anyway. The beauty of keeping the front door open and the screen door unlocked was that the dogs could come and go on their own and not bother her. Besides, the cool night air cleared out the stagnant heat that had collected inside the house during the day. Consequently, every night, she was in a bind as to whether to follow the sheriff's advice or take the path of least resistance; and as time went on, she'd been, more often than not, letting it slide and leaving the door open. Now she forced herself to get up and lock the door.

No sooner had she settled back into bed and closed her eyes than the phone rang. She didn't have to guess who it was because he'd been calling all night. It was Stuart. She'd made the mistake of talking to him the first time 'round but had been hanging up on him ever since. One thing she could depend on was that he was probably drunker now than he had been the first time he'd called and five times more stubborn to deal with. It seemed he was having a hard time accepting the fact that she had dared to reject him. After the tenth ring, she finally hauled herself up out of bed and hobbled to the phone. It was Stuart, all right, begging her not to hang up as the dial tone erased the sound of his voice. This time, Leslie laid the receiver on the table. It would wail like an air-raid siren for a little while but only to remind her that she'd finally done something she should have done long ago.

Again she returned to bed and closed her eyes with a sigh, relieved that she wouldn't have to talk to him anymore. However, now, worries about Calvin started to seep in. It wasn't like him not to have shown up at the hospital to see his mother. And if he wasn't at home then where had he gone? And what must he be feeling? She cringed, thinking about the reckless thing she had said to him that day in his workshop. "You could have almost any woman you wanted," she'd told him. She blushed even now just to think about the way he'd looked at her in that moment and, worse, how her traitorous body had reacted to what had almost happened between them.

Now that she thought about it, it had been irresponsible of her, reckless and cruel even, knowing how vulnerable he was. Still, she'd only wanted to reassure him, not lead him on or at least that's what she'd told herself at the time.

Okay, so maybe it was true that she cared about Cal—but as a person. After all, he was nice and kind, and he'd been a really good neighbor—so why shouldn't she care about him? And yes, maybe it could be said she was even slightly attracted to him—and okay, maybe she had been all along, in a subtle sort of way. Even so, she was way too mature to get swept away by something that was so impractical, really. After all, they were from such different worlds.

She was just a little unhinged right now, she reasoned to herself. Obsessing about getting back together with Stuart was what had kept her afloat all these many months, and now that was gone. It was only natural to feel a little confused. She turned over and pulled up the sheet. That's all that was happening. She was just a little confused and that was very natural.

But even when she closed her eyes, she couldn't stop thinking about how devastated Calvin must be. She should never have been so open with him. Men just didn't understand that kind of emotional openness. So often, they took it the wrong way when a woman just wanted to be friends. She would have to apologize and try to explain that she was just a little confused at that moment. That was all.

She threw off the sheet and flipped over on her other side. It really was too hot with the door shut. She listened to the sounds of the cicadas outside the window.

He was such a quiet person and not one to easily show his feelings. She only hoped he hadn't gone off and done something desperate. That's what she worried about the most because how could she ever live with herself if he did?

Both dogs were now sleeping in the studio. Since her fall, neither dog had had a bath, and now Elliot stank as much as Hooch did, which had finally given Leslie all the spine necessary to boot him out of her bed. Suddenly they exploded in howls loud enough to wake the dead (though seemingly not Pendleton Caughey). However, a whiff of skunk floating in on the night air gave her all the reassurance she needed. Of course! That was what they were all worked up about! She limped to the door to let them out and then left the front door open and the screen door unlocked so they could get back in by themselves.

Linwood had approached the house alone ahead of the others, praying that no one would be there, but his heart sank when he saw a car parked out in front. All he could do now was hope that it wasn't her but someone else inside. The house was dark. At least whoever was there was likely to be asleep. The question was where were the dogs? He moved up to the edge of the woods, pulled out some packages of bologna, and waited. He still had the poison that JT had given him in his pocket, but he wasn't about to use it. The lawn was washed in a silvery glow under the half-moon—the surrounding trees, ghoulish silhouettes against the starry sky. The question was where were the dogs?

In a matter of moments, he had his answer when they came barreling out of the house, barking so fiercely that he feared they might attack. It wasn't until he waved the bologna around in the air that they calmed down enough to remember their old routine, and soon, he was giving Hooch his belly rub and scratching Elliot behind the ears in his favorite spot. Meanwhile, he quietly slipped ropes around their necks and then settled down at the foot of the tree to pet and ply them with treats. He needed to keep them quiet and happy so they wouldn't figure out that they were tied up. Now that he was in this mess, he was determined to make the job go as smoothly as possible so nobody got caught and nobody got hurt.

However, just then, the skunk decided to double back through the vicinity. Hooch promptly sounded the alarm as if someone had stepped on his tail, with Elliot quickly joining in sharp staccato. Linwood desperately pulled out more meat, but this time the dogs only ignored it. Cursing mightily, Linwood yanked hard on the ropes. If the dogs worked themselves loose, there would be hell to pay from JT, who would no doubt shoot them in a heartbeat.

Meanwhile, as they were attempting to sneak through the woods, JT, Red, and Philly had already had a fateful encounter with the skunk, Philly having gotten the worst of it. Being from Philadelphia, he wasn't used to the woods in daylight, much less at night, and had already been obsessing about bears when he and the skunk had had their unfortunate rendezvous. After that, no amount of threats could keep him from walking out onto the dirt lane, no matter what anybody had said about staying out of sight.

"I keep telling you there's no bears around here, man!" coaxed Red softly from the edge of the trees. "Besides, bears hibernate at night. Now come on back in the woods so nobody sees you!"

"Bear's hibernate in the winter, dumbass! I'm from Philly and even I know that!"

"Would you two shut up?" snapped JT. "Now get in the fuckin' woods!"

"Yeah, well don't blame me when this whole thing turns into a disaster!" Philly grudgingly returned to the eerie moonlit forest.

A few moments later, there came the sound of dogs barking from up ahead. They froze, listening.

"I told you Linwood would screw it up!" muttered Philly. He had always been resentful of the interest JT had showed in Linwood.

JT impatiently waved him into silence but Philly wasn't about to cooperate. "Well how long will that poison take to work anyway? I thought them dogs was already supposed to be dead? I ain't goin' up in there if there's dogs around. I ain't getting bit by no dog!"

JT turned on his cousin with a vicious punch to the shoulder. "You know what? I hope a bear *and* a dog comes and rips off your arms *and* your legs! How do you like that? Now shut the fuck up!"

"Hey!" It was Red. "I don't hear the dogs no more!"

Everyone listened intently. The only sounds now came from the crickets and cicadas.

"Okay then, let's go. And you"—JT turned fiercely on Philly—"keep the hell away from me! You stink!"

With Philly tagging sulkily behind, they struggled on through the scratchy underbrush, stumbling in dips and holes until they got in sight of the house, only to discover another unexpected problem—a car parked in front of the house.

"I thought *you* said *Linwood* said nobody would be here," sneered Philly triumphantly. He was already fed up with this whole adventure and ready to call it quits.

JT stared coolly at the darkened house. More than anything, JT disliked having his judgment called into question, for like any politician, he could never afford to be wrong. "Well, I guess Linwood was wrong."

"I say we don't do it then," went on Philly excitedly. "This whole thing is cursed, man. It ain't worth it!"

Red added in a quiet respectful tone that maybe Philly was right, but JT only lashed out viciously at them both.

"She's a fuckin' woman and she's on crutches, people! What the hell you afraid of? The door to the cellar is already loose, Linwood's got the dogs. Now if we can be *quiet*"—he glared roundly at the others—"then there shouldn't be a problem!"

"But what about the"—Red lowered his voice—"you know . . . ghost?"

"Ghost!" exclaimed Philly. "You didn't tell me about no ghost!"

"If you believe in ghosts then *you* are the dumbass! Now let's go!" JT started to move out onto the lawn, but Philly remained stubbornly behind.

"I still don't see what's the rush, JT!" He was pleading now.

Red looked at JT, who said nothing. There was nothing to be said. Everyone knew that Linwood wasn't the only one with debts. "Don't worry about it," said JT darkly. "Now stop being a wuss and get moving."

Even so, Philly was determined to give it one more shot. "I'll stay here and stand guard."

JT gave him a disgusted look. "You're going to stay here in the woods *alone* and stand guard? Fine. Knock yourself out," JT and Red slunk off toward the boxwood hedge, leaving Philly behind, where he lasted all of thirty seconds before he thought he heard a sound and came running after them.

Linwood had promised it would be easy to get into the house. He'd already taken the screws out of the hinges of the cellar door, and all they would have to do was to lift it off the opening and climb down into the cellar, but he didn't know that Calvin had reinforced the door on the inside with a steel bar. When the door didn't budge, JT was cursing Linwood's birthright. On top of everything else, the skunk chose to make a surprise appearance, causing Philly to let out a muffled shriek.

"That damn skunk is here spraying on me again!" he cried, waving his pistol in the air. "I swear I'm gonna kill that mother—"

JT turned on him in a hissing fury. "Oh no, you ain't!" He delivered a blow up the back of his cousin's head just as the woods erupted with howls. They froze again and waited but no dogs appeared.

"I told you not to trust that son of a bitch!" grumbled Philly.

From her bed, Leslie lay listening to the voices, waves of fear washing over her. There was no longer any doubt in her mind that something very bad was happening. She hobbled to the stairs and called up to Penny in a loud whisper, but all she got were snores. Meanwhile, she quietly closed the front door, sliding the deadbolt into place, marveling at her presence of mind. This was no time for emotions. She needed to call the police; however, the moment she picked up the phone there came the sound of stealthy footsteps on the porch. In cold terror, she watched as someone quietly tried the door handle. Flinching at every squeak of her crutch, she headed back into the living room and managed to slip behind the heavy drapes at the back window just as a silhouette appeared at the front. She heard the screen being popped out and the sound of someone sliding through the opening.

Whoever it was went out into the hall; and she heard the deadbolt sliding back and the front door opening, and then more footsteps and tense whispers, the rustling movement of bodies, and the creak of the stairs, followed by voices.

"Nobody up there except an old man but I took care of him."

"Why can't we turn on the lights? This place give me the creeps."

"Forget it."

"JT! I found the door to the basement! Come on."

"JT, how about I stand guard outside?"

"No way! You're digging. Now get movin'."

The voices retreated into the cellar.

Leslie's mind was reeling with horrible visions of what they might have done to poor Penny. She'd been so brusque with him earlier, when all he wanted to do was help. Where were the dogs anyway? Should she go out into the hall and try to call the police or just stay put behind the curtain? She could try to get out of the house, but with the cast, she'd be too slow going down the steps. She'd never make it. Oh, where were the dogs?

Then suddenly she remembered the pistol Frank Hawkins had left for her. It was in the drawer of the side table just a few yards from where she was hiding. If she was very careful and very, very quiet, she thought as she stepped out from behind the curtain. The gun felt cool to the touch, and at first, just holding it sent a thrill of power through her body, which quickly turned to terror. Who was she kidding? She wasn't going to shoot anybody. It was more likely that they would grab the gun and shoot her. She had no sooner put the gun back in the drawer than she heard the long muted screech of the front screen door opening ever so slowly. Somebody else was coming into the house. With no place to hide, she flattened herself against the wall just inside the doorway, grabbing the nearest thing she could find, which ironically happened to be an oversized book of Monet prints. Monet had been a great influence on her career as an artist, so why shouldn't he be her weapon of choice?

When a shadowy figure stuck his head in through the living room door; she let him have it as hard as she could flat in the face. "Jesus!" she heard him exclaim as he bent over double, writhing in pain. Then she realized who it was.

"Oh, my god—Calvin?"

He instantly pinned her against the wall, clapping a hand over her mouth. "Shh . . ." They remained like that in the darkness for what seemed like a long time, the only sound being the thud of her heart and Calvin's quick shallow breathing in her ear, when suddenly they heard the sound of whistling and the creaking of footsteps coming down the staircase from above. It was the slow halting rhythm of an old man, slowly descending, pausing to catch his breath. Frozen with fascination, they watched as the ghostly apparition of Calvin's grandfather made his way slowly down the hall. He did not appear to see them but proceeded with the same faltering steps down into the cellar, leaving the distinct aroma of cigar smoke in his wake. Immediately, there were shouts from below, and in a matter of moments, the three intruders came trampling up the stairs and out the front door, shouting and shoving at each other in confusion. Stunned, Cal and Leslie watched from the porch as they sprinted down the lane and out of sight.

"If I hadn't seen it, I'd never have believed it!" murmured Calvin with an air of satisfaction, but Leslie only turned on him in a renewed panic. Penny was upstairs! Cursing under his breath, Cal vaulted up the steps two at a time and then, in a matter of moments, returned but more slowly this time.

Seeing that he came alone, Leslie's hands flew up to cover her eyes, as if to blot out the horrible vision in her mind. "What happened? Is he—"

Cal shook his head, chuckling. "Out like a light." From above, a loud blissful snore punctuated the stillness. Cal grinned with a flash of white teeth in the moonlight. "They tied his hands to the bedpost, and from the looks of it, he slept peacefully through the whole thing."

Leslie broke down in a flood of tears as Cal stood uncertainly by. "It's okay," he said, patting her shoulder. "Everything's okay."

To his surprise, she wrapped her arms around him and clutched him tight. "I was so worried about you! I thought maybe—" Then she realized he was not hugging her back but standing like a fencepost, so she collected herself and pulled away.

And that's when, off in the distance, the guns went off.

"What the hell was that?" It was Penny's voice from upstairs.

Cal instantly took off running.

"Are you crazy?" shrieked Leslie. "What are you doing?"

"I gotta help Frank!" He disappeared around the bend with the dogs suddenly close on his heels. For a moment, she caught a glimpse of a man standing at the edge of the woods before he, too, disappeared but in the other direction.

Running at full tilt reminded Cal of his days on the high school track team. It had been years since he'd run like this, and it would have been exhilarating had it not been such a desperate situation. Soon the dogs were running right alongside of him, but when a voice called out from the trees, they suddenly veered off into the woods. Cal stopped and looked cautiously left and right. No one was on the road. He peered into the trees.

"Psst! Cal! Hey, Cal!" It was Frank, a shapeless mass huddled on the ground.

"Is that you, Frank?"

"It sure as hell ain't Santy Claus."

Cal made his way to where Frank sat propped against the smooth silvery trunk of a beech tree. "What happened?" he asked in a low voice. "We heard shots!"

"I stepped in a hole and my gun went off," muttered Frank gloomily. "I think I sprained my ankle."

"Did they shoot back?"

"Hell yeah!" Frank broke out in a grin. "They got all freaked out and fired off a few wild shots, but when I shot back, they just took off runnin'!"

Cal smiled to himself. This would be the highlight of Frank's existence for years to come. "Well, they're probably long gone by now."

"I wouldn't be so sure about that!" Frank was in good spirits now. "I disconnected the battery on their car!"

"Way to go, Frank!" They made a high-five with their hands before Cal helped Frank to his feet.

Suddenly an unearthly howling mayhem broke out in the direction of the dead end.

"What in the hell is that?" exclaimed Frank, taking an exploratory step down on his bad foot.

"Sounds like the Mongrel Horde got out of jail, Frank."

and when his pick hit on a giant stone, Pendleton Caughey literally sat down on the ground and cried.

Everything that had gone wrong with his life came pouring out of him in a moment of desolation and despair. He looked back on his life and saw nothing but struggle and failure, humiliation and loss. Every good thing he'd ever had, he'd destroyed, and that included at least four of his wives (one of them had been nothing but trash and a case of good riddance). His kids, if they did not actively hate him, certainly didn't give a rat's ass about him. He'd never lived up to his potential, and though he'd papered over the disappointment with a fatalistic philosophy that the world was a crap hole, in the end that did nothing to save him from a feeling of desperation and tragedy. Without Peanut, there would be absolutely no one who loved him—no one who cared whether he lived or died.

Somewhere, a finch started to sing. Where was it coming from? His eyes searched until he found it, perched on the topmost branch of a poplar tree. What a glorious life to sit on the top of a tree and sing your heart out without sorrow or care. What he wouldn't give to be such a creature, he thought.

Only a few times in his life had he ever really prayed. In the navy during the war, there had been those times, but those had been scattered and desperate prayers. Today's prayer called for a long accounting of his sins. He knew he was dirt and soon to be laid in the ground like this dog, now wrapped in one of Libby's best tablecloths (one last act of revenge which he'd reserved the right to keep). The laundry list of his mistakes started out like daggers and knives piercing him in vital organs—the pain of the past, his obstinacy, his relentless, stupid acts of violence against every good thing, hatred that had percolated in his veins like a sickness. After a while, he got into the swing of it though and started digging even deeper into the minor offenses (with the exception of the tablecloth and wife number 3 who deserved everything she'd gotten), and when he was feeling just about as flat and low as he could go, the minister from the Episcopal church came sauntering around the corner of the house, followed by Brownie, his bald Down-syndrome son.

With lightning speed, Penny's mind raced through a series of mental calculations, but nowhere could he recall having put his name in the church registry book in the narthex. In fact, he was for damned sure that he had made a conscious effort to avoid any such blunder because the last thing he ever wanted was some oily eyed minister backing him into a corner to come to church and fork over his last dime. He'd never cared for priests or pastors, never mind the religious name tag. Either simpering do-gooders or self-righteous windbags, they were all panhandlers living off the sweat of another man's brow. And now here he was, trapped—Pendleton Caughey, sitting on the ground and bawling like a baby for all the world to see. There really was no mercy in this world.

Oddly enough, the minister didn't seem to notice right away but, without introduction, started discoursing on the subject of weather conditions in California, where wildfires plundered whole neighborhoods. He was especially fascinated by the fact that people had been taking refuge in their swimming pools. "A symbol of our times, y'see?" he said, smiling through crooked teeth.

Meanwhile, his bald-headed son, looking less monkish now in a T-shirt and a Redskins baseball cap, gazed out of his round little eyes with adoration at the man on the ground, his lips moving continually as if on the verge of saying something but thinking better of it.

The minister gestured grandly to the chestnut trees and went on at length about how it took him back to his grandfather's farm, where they had such trees in his yard during his growing-up years. Meanwhile, the soft-headed innocent, with eyes as gentle as a newborn pup, watched Penny's every move so intently that when Penny wiped his nose, he would wipe his nose, and when Penny cleared his throat, he would clear his. A silence ensued, and everyone found themselves gazing at the mound under Libby's white tablecloth beside the hole in the ground—Peanut's grave.

"That your dog, Caughey?" ventured the minister matter-of-factly.

"Yep."

"A sad task, burying a dog. Best friend a man will ever have in this world." A soft kiss like butterfly wings landed on top of Penny's head. He looked up into Brownie's face beaming like the moon. "Sweet," he said, his moist lips quivering into a smile. "Sweet."

The minister laughed. "That's Brownie's way of saying God is with you, Caughey!" He pulled a folded piece of paper out of his back pocket. "Oh, here—before I forget, we're having our annual homecoming next Sunday. The ladies put up a real good lunch for everybody. Why don't ya come on over? We'd love to have you."

Meanwhile, Frank Hawkins was struggling with a fence post—a metal fence post for a chain-link fence—and cussing up a storm. First of all, it hurt his pride to be doing this at all mainly because everybody would think he'd been cowed into it by the city woman and that intolerable blowhard Pendleton Caughey. Oh, they'd get a good laugh for sure, seeing him fall so far from his principles. Putting up a fence was against everything he stood for, against everything he was made of, which was "country" through and through—rebel wild and free—without rules and regulations to suffocate his light.

He heard a car approaching from a distance and gritted his teeth, deciding right then and there that if it was Penny Caughey stopping by to rub it in, he'd go straight into the house and slam the door, but it wasn't him; it was Clarice. She drove into the yard and, without a word of explanation, started to hold up the post on one end while he struggled with the other.

"What are you doing here?" he asked, suspiciously eyeing her car for the stray dog or cat she was most likely aiming to dump on him, but her car was empty.

"Putting up a fence is a two-person job, I reckon," was all she said.

They worked all afternoon, and afterward, she went to the car and started to pull her suitcase out of the trunk. It was heavy and she was struggling with it so he went over and took it from her hands. He stood, towering over her, with tears in his eyes.

"I've missed you, kitty cat," was all he could get out before a big lump closed off his throat.

"And I missed you, teddy bear." She calmly wrapped her slender arms around him, and they'd held each other tight.

"You know I love you," he croaked in a voice hoarse as an old rusty washboard.

"And I love you, Frank," she answered simply. "Now come on! Let's go in the house and show me the damage."

"Woman," he roared joyously, "you are welcome to it!"

The day after all the excitement, Leslie had roamed the house, pursued by restless demons, unable to focus on anything but the remote expression on Calvin's face when she'd thanked him for coming to her rescue. The message coming through couldn't be any clearer—it was no more than what any stranger would do for a lady in distress.

Most of the morning, she'd drifted from room to room, hating herself for her inconstancy because now that he'd shut the door in her face, she suddenly wanted him with a desperate longing.

Over and over she replayed the scene that day in his workshop, and suddenly it could no longer be denied. She'd been lying to herself. How casual and reckless she'd been, pretending not to notice that he had feelings for her, allowing him to love her from a distance, pretending that she only wanted to reassure him as a friend would do. "You could have any woman you wanted," she'd said and then promptly thrown him overboard the moment Stuart had showed up. Just exactly what kind of person would do such a thing, when he was so vulnerable?

Punishing thoughts finally drove her from the house to seek the solace of the river. Cushioned by the soft humid air, she trudged with a heavy heart down through the hushed stillness of the forest, emotionally ripped open and bleeding.

But the mercy of the river could do little to wash away the pain of love that was ruthlessly revealing itself to her, opening inside like a wound. Suddenly, all Calvin's goodness, his infinite patience, his kindness and self-restraint, the quiet thoughtfulness of his ways so undramatic that it went almost unnoticed now pierced her heart like a revelation; and she wept tears of remorse into the river, bearing her body ever patiently downstream. All she wanted now was to give herself entirely to the current, not caring how far it had to carry her before it returned her to herself. Dimly she heard the dogs barking from the bank and momentarily opened her eyes and then, without the least bit of curiosity, dropped back into the water and continued to float.

For his part, Calvin had slept like a stone in his workshop recliner, awaking in a stream of sunlight streaming through his dusty window. It wasn't exactly peace but something close enough that inhabited his soul. He had resolved to return to his old perch, distant and safe, like an eagle out of reach. He had strayed too close to the world and gotten his feathers singed in a game he had no business to play. Though it could be said it was numbness that prevented him from feeling any pain, it enabled him to step out into the sunshine with a calm sense of direction, fishing pole in hand. He was headed for his refuge—the river.

As he waded into the humid leafy presence of the forest, a subtle life force quickened inside him, and he felt the thrill of affirmation. In the end, this would be all the joy he required, lifting him above the masquerade of human entanglements pretending to be life. Suddenly he knew that he had turned a corner in the midst of seemingly tragic complications. The private bitterness that had defined him these many long years was gone. He no longer needed to hide from anything but merely turn away with freedom in his heart. He knew where he wanted to be, and it was here, at peace with the forest and with the river. Here is where he had always found himself.

He settled onto a great boulder in the shade of an ancient ironwood tree, whose gnarly roots erupted out of the soft riverbank like enormous claws. This had been his grandfather's favorite spot, and now it was his, and though the bank had changed many times over the years, the tree and the rock had stood fast. It gave him a calm sense of the endurance and enormity of time and how small his life was by comparison, a puff of wind here for a moment and gone the next.

He had learned the philosophy of fishing, sitting long hours beside his grandfather in just the way he was sitting now, keeping very still. For a small boy, this had been close to agony, but it was devotion to the man that had formed the boy. Here was where he had learned that in stillness lay a power to summon those silent shadowy forms gliding through the mysterious water. A true fisherman, his grandfather had always said, knows how to call the fish.

He'd learned patience this way and lessons of compassion—to throw back the fish that are too small and relieve the suffering of the injured quickly. And here he'd learned to savor the thrill of that insistent tug on the line and the silver flash and glittery explosion as the water spewed forth its prize. "Hold her steady now, easy, easy—stay with it! Don't pull too hard," his grandfather would be saying as he and the fish played out their tug of war. "Whaddya got here, boy! Let's take a look at her!"

Memories of those times washed over him now like a soothing balm as Calvin baited his hook and cast it in. In the leafy shade of the great tree, the speckled sunlight danced before him in hypnotic patterns, and soon a wave of fatigue swept over him, reminding him that he'd been through a lot in the past forty-eight hours. He propped the pole against his knee and, with a deep sigh, lay back against the warmth of the rock and closed his eyes.

Within moments, beneath the caress of a gentle breeze, he had floated into a dream; and suddenly there was a hand resting lightly on his shoulder. Looking up, he saw that it was his grandfather sitting beside him, youthful and smiling, radiating utter peace and calm. "Don't worry, boy," he said. "Love always finds its way."

And in that instant, like a fish on the line, Calvin was jerked out of the dream by the shock of a muffled animal cry as the fishing pole went flying. Grabbing for the pole, he looked up to see a dark-haired woman struggling to stand in the middle of the river. It was Leslie, dressed in her pink two-piece bathing suit, covered in fish wearing sunglasses, and unknowingly tangled in an invisible fishing line. She didn't seem to know that he was there, for she was flailing her arms and screeching loud curses in a panic. He realized before she did what had happened.

"Leslie!" he called. "You're caught in the fishing line! Try not to—"

She looked at him in mute puzzlement and then let out a piercing scream.

"Leslie! Stop moving!" He sloshed into the water, clothes and all.

"Oh my god! What is that? It hurts!"

"I'm trying to—"

"It's the hook! Oh, my god! It's in my—it's in me!" She was bending over backward, trying to see it.

"Just don't try to pull it out! I'm coming!" he yelled, lurching through the water. "Now where is it?"

"It's back there, what do ya think!" she cried indignantly.

"Oh," he said, seeing now that it was buried in her backside.

"This is basically freaking me out here!" she cried ominously from under a curtain of wet hair.

"Don't worry," he said, trying to sound as calm as he could. "We just have to get to my tackle box—"

"What do you mean 'don't worry'? I have a fish hook stuck in me!"

Miserable and feeling quite sorry for herself, she waded behind him back to shore, but the bank was steep and slippery, and it was impossible to get onto dry land without a few undignified shoves from behind. Adding insult to injury, she now found herself in the position of having to lie facedown on the rock with her butt up in the air as he inspected the damage.

"Is this humiliating or what!" she wailed, craning her neck to see and feeling a bit irritated that he seemed to be taking his sweet time studying the situation. "Well, aren't you going to pull it out?"

"Oh, you can't pull it back out." He observed calmly. "That'll *really* tear you up!" He gingerly touched the flesh surrounding the buried hook.

other senior citizens down in Key Largo just so they could save on social security benefits.

The fact that they weren't married made it a perfect scandal as far as Thelma was concerned, who, as daughter-in-law to the local Baptist preacher, was worried about her reputation. But more than that, it was an insult to the memory of her father, to whom Thelma was still devoutly loyal. Dave was not one-tenth the man her father had been. In fact, she was quite certain her father wouldn't have even liked the man, and that was saying something, as her father had generally liked everyone he met.

To make matters worse, Thelma had been unceremoniously demoted from being her mother's number one confidant and advisor. Even Cal seemed to have more say over her mother's decisions because Dave thought he was "an okay guy." In Thelma's view, she was downright getting ignored, and it made her hopping mad, but she didn't dare say a harsh word, or her mother would breathe fire.

So here she had gone and practically killed herself to get this party ready just to have her mother go on treating her like yesterday's leftovers. Thelma had sulked all through the party and fussed and fumed over the food and every little thing until she'd just about worn out everybody's patience. The other sisters had wasted no time putting Thelma in her place, and since she was the only one who'd listen, Leslie wound up the sole audience to Thelma's endless litany of complaints.

Meanwhile, outside, everyone else was having a wonderful time. The weather was perfect and the lilacs were in bloom—a glorious day in May. Leslie gazed out at the small gathering of people chatting amiably in folding chairs on the lawn. One year ago, she'd come here an utter stranger, feeling as though her life had come to an end, not knowing that it was really just a new beginning creeping up on her in disguise.

She passed Pendleton Caughey at the buffet table. He was standing with Reverend Weston, the Episcopal minister; his son, Brownie, wearing his Redskins cap; and Leslie's dad, wearing some cheese dip on his chin. They were discussing the finer points of the new church building project—the installation of a bathroom in the back of the sanctuary. Since last fall and his first Sunday luncheon at the Episcopal church, Penny had found a place, where he was wanted and needed. Now as senior warden, he was in charge of what he had dubbed "Operation Toilet."

"It's almost time for the cake," said Leslie in a low voice.

"Good," they answered cheerfully in unison.

"I'm ready!" Her dad held up his fork.

"Daddy," she said, fondly removing the dip from his chin, "you're always ready!"

"Did I hear someone say something about cake?" Frank broke off from his conversation with Linwood's grandfather, Clarence, about the bobcat creating havoc in chicken yards around the area.

"Hush, Frank! Ruby will hear you!" chided his wife, Clarice, dressed in periwinkle blue to match her eyes.

"Hear me?" boomed Frank. "She can't hear me unless I'm standing two inches from her ear! How's she gonna hear me way over here?"

"I got a hearing aid now, Frank—twenty-twenty hearing! So watch yourself!" shot back Ruby from across the grass.

Clarice gave a Frank a small shove. "I told you!"

"Okay, Ruby—so what'd you hear?" retorted Frank. "This is a test now!"

"I heard somethin' somethin' lake somethin' somethin'!" she declared with hands on hips.

"Oh, you got twenty-twenty hearing all right!" scoffed Frank amid the laughter.

"That's what I got, Ruby!" called out Clarence. "Twenty-twenty *creative* hearing!"

Everyone laughed even louder. It was a great party hitting its stride.

Frank summoned Leslie over with a secretive little smile. "Clarence, tell her what you just told me."

Clarence was looking "slicked down," as Frank had put it, in a shirt and tie. His eyes shone with happiness as he took her hand in both of his and pressed it warmly. "Don't you look pretty today!" Leslie immediately blushed, which only made Clarence crow with delight. "Looky that—she's shy, Frank!"

"Oh, she's shy all right!" snorted Frank. "She wasn't here a month before she was running the neighborhood right alongside the queen of cats, Clarice here!"

"Frank!" Clarice gave him a harder shove but she was smiling nonetheless.

"Love taps, that's all they are! Love taps!" announced Frank proudly.

Clarice rolled her eyes in her calm way. "Leslie, don't let these two knuckleheads get to you!" Now it was Clarence's turn to get a gentle shove. "Now go on and tell her about Linwood, Clarence!"

"Linwood?" Leslie's eyes lit up. "You've finally heard from him?"

After the break-in, Linwood had vanished without a trace, and for the past nine months, no one had known whether he was alive or dead. Clarence had been worried sick about him. Leslie and Cal had spent many long hours trying to comfort him, but it was almost unbearable not being able to let Linwood know that he was in the clear. As it had turned out, JT was not about ratting out his people, and Linwood's name had never come up in the proceedings. He had also been vindicated on the matter of the coins. To everyone's surprise, Sonny Hay's will had clearly named him as beneficiary of his buried coin collection, which, however, had to this day not been found. But as Clarence would always say, none of this mattered if the boy was still running scared, getting into who knew what trouble!

Now Clarence had a letter, which he waved in the air. It was from Linwood, saying that he was safe and living with an older female cousin, who'd always looked out for him. She worked in the registrar's office of a community college up in Boston and had gotten him a job working on the maintenance crew and helped him get his G.E.D. Part of his compensation was the option of taking one free college class each semester, and he had signed up for an art class. He decided he was going to get a degree and become an art teacher. Clarence was so proud that he was fairly busting at the seams with joy.

"Oh, I'm so glad! So glad!" She and Clarence hugged each other.

"I have you to thank, Leslie!" Clarence was convinced that what little encouragement she had given Linwood about his art had been enough to make him change. "You helped him to believe in his talent!"

He'd said this before, but as always, she earnestly protested. "I didn't do anything, really!" she murmured, thinking about what Cal had often said on the matter—that if Linwood ever did make it, it would be that brush with disaster that would make him turn around. That's when something small and hard struck her in the back of the head. She looked up to see what it was that could have fallen out of the tree.

"What you looking at?" asked Clarence.

"I thought something—never mind. Well, that is great news, Clarence. I'll talk to you later. Excuse me. I'm supposed to tell everybody about the cake." She turned to walk over to the group, where her mother sat with some of Calvin's sisters, when she felt the stinging bite of another strike, this time on her arm. "What the—" This was no accident! She looked up just in time to see Calvin disappearing around the back of the house.

"Thelma's about to bring out the cake, ladies!" she announced in a low voice. They nodded pleasantly. Her mother had really clicked with Cal's middle sister, Stephanie, who was an interior decorator living in Atlanta.

Leslie made her way casually around to the back of the house, only to find the cellar doors opened wide and Calvin sitting arms akimbo at the top of the shallow broken steps leading down into the musty depths. He looked at her and grinned, his face relaxed and tanned, his eyes clear and direct. She thought about her first impression of him—a furious tangle of hair, eyes wooden with avoidance and suspicion. How little it had to do with the person that he really was.

"Was that you throwing things at me?" She sounded exasperated but pleased.

He grinned sheepishly. "There's something I want you to see, and I didn't want to rouse the sisterhood." That's how Calvin talked about his sisters when they were en masse.

"And you couldn't just come out and—" She stopped short when she saw the shiny gold coin in his hand. "You found it—Sonny's stash!"

"Actually, Elliot found it. I went down to get the hedge clippers to trim that branch for Thelma, and Elliot was down there digging away in the corner, and suddenly he was tugging at something and I looked and—there they were." He held up a gray sack of coins. She sat beside him on the step and they looked at the bag of coins. "There've got to be at least ten more just like it."

"Oh, my god—Linwood is rich."

"And—I wanted to show you something else." He reached into the back pocket of his jeans and pulled out a piece of paper elaborately folded into a tight little rectangle.

"What is it?" she asked, unfolding the paper.

"Read it. You'll see," was all he would tell her.

"Oh my god, Cal! It's from a publisher!" Her face took on a childlike glow of excitement as she continued to read. She was more beautiful to him now than ever, he thought, leaning in to breathe the sweet-scented aroma of her hair falling loose about her shoulders.

"'*After having looked over this quite notable piece of fiction—*' Wow!" She looked up excitedly to see his eyes shining with quiet happiness. "We *are pleased to inform you that we have accepted* The Rains Come to Thorn Mountain *for publication and feel it will greatly enhance our collection!*" She beamed at him. "Cal! You did it!"

"Yeah." Though he tried not to, he couldn't keep from grinning like a fool.

Suddenly Leslie was bubbling over with exultation. "What an incredible surprise! I mean, it's not a surprise! I knew somebody would take it! I just knew it! So how do you feel? I mean, this is a really big deal, right?"

"I guess," he said, subtly retreating behind an inscrutable mask.

She stopped herself, noticing his sudden change of mood and peered at him intently. "So are you gonna tell everybody?"

He exhaled. "Nope." He said this firmly and cuttingly, as if this had been an inappropriate thing to ask.

A flash of surprise and then disapproval shot across her face. "What?"

"No!" he repeated sharply. "And you're not going to tell them either!"

"Cal! Why not?"

"Just because . . . it's private. Besides, half of them are in the book, and I don't suppose they're gonna be too happy about it." He instantly regretted lashing out at her but it was too late to change that. Elliot came over with a curious look and then nimbly jumped into his lap. Cal numbly started to stroke his white fur, not daring to look at Leslie.

She watched and waited, and finally, when he didn't say anything more, she said, "You're doing it again."

"What?" His voice was gruff.

"That old thing you do—and you're being ridiculous and stubborn, and I won't let you!" Though at the moment she felt a bit irritated with him, she caressed the side of his face, her voice softening. "It's just an old habit."

He was silent. "I guess," he muttered softly.

"Things *can* go right sometimes, you know," she said gently. "I think it's allowed."

He sighed, a fleeting look of pain twisting through a brief grudging smile. "Yeah, you're right. I guess it's just a habit to think that something will always go wrong when I want so badly for it go right." He grew silent and brooding. "It's almost like a superstitious kind of thing—like if I roll over and pretend not to care then the monsters of destruction won't find me."

"Like playing possum?"

He laughed humorlessly. "Yeah—like playing possum. Wow!" The inexplicable wave of darkness that had washed over him was gone.

Leslie remained silent for a while, watching as Cal allowed Elliot to nudge his hand to the places he wanted scratched.

"Your mother is leaving tomorrow. You're going to tell her before she goes, aren't you?"

"Of course, I will." Then his brow darkened again. "But I still don't want to say anything now. I couldn't stand all the hoopla. So don't give me a hard time."

"I promise." She turned her face towards him and their lips met in a light melting kiss. "She's going to be so proud."

"Hopefully. Of course, she's gotten so used to thinking of me as a complete loser, the shock might be too much for her."

"Oh, come on! You've got to give her more credit than that! She's your mother! Of course she believes in you!"

Cal gave her a blank stare that made Leslie giggle. "You say that you won't, but you're going to miss her when she's gone, and she's going to miss you!"

"Naw, she's gonna be too happy to miss me," he said with a mighty yawn, stretching his long limbs and dumping Elliot unceremoniously to the floor, "—and I figure I'll be the same."

She threw her arms around his neck and hugged him tight. "I love you, Cal."

"I love you," he murmured softly, resting his forehead against hers. They remained like this, the moment filling them with a quiet joy. From the front of the house, everyone started singing a chorus of "Happy Birthday" to Ruby.

Leslie jumped up. "Uh-oh! We'd better go! Thelma will kill us if we miss the cake!"

Cal rose and slung his arm across her shoulders as they slowly walked to join the celebration.

THE END

*The verse written on the cellar door plaque is a portion taken from "The Shadow of the Rock" by Frederick William Faber. From Library of Sunday Poetry, copyright 1880/1889, Dodd, Mead & Co.

Edwards Brothers,Inc!
Thorofare, NJ 08086
22 March, 2011
BA2011081